Witch Way to Vegas

by

Mark Rosendorf

The Witches of Vegas

Witch Way to Vegas

Cover Art by *Jennifer Greeff*

The Wild Rose Press, Inc.
PO Box 708
Adams Basin, NY 14410-0708
Visit us at www.thewildrosepress.com

Publishing History
First Edition, 2023
Trade Paperback ISBN 978-1-5092-4679-3
Digital ISBN 978-1-5092-4680-9

The Witches of Vegas
Published in the United States of America

Isis' throat closed up on her. Breathing suddenly became a chore. She remembered the pressure in the pit of her stomach caused by the sense of fear that came from every single village resident including herself. In that reality, she—no, the other Isis, vampire Isis—turned the energy around the village into a clear but solid dome. As the blasts throughout the sky grew louder and brighter, the dome shook. It was night, yet the blasts lit up the sky like a blinding inferno. But two centuries of experience helped Isis hold it together. She had to, because every man, woman, and child in New Salem would die if she didn't. She held on for three straight days, refusing to let all their deaths be on her conscience. They had to survive. They did survive—

"*Isis, stop!*"

Zack's panicked voice woke Isis from her thoughts.

Energy crackled around her hands like bacon on a skillet. Each of her fingers emanated a white glow. Glass covered her feet and the floor around her. The fireworks had stopped. The farmers, children, and adults all along the grounds were looking to the school with eyes pointed her way. Isis placed her hand against what used to be the window. A clear shield sparked and vibrated at her touch.

Praise for Mark Rosendorf

The Witches of Vegas

Winner of the 2021 R.O.N.E. Award in the Young Adult category

Second Place in the 2020 International Digital Awards in the Young Adult category

Listed on Shelf Unbound's 2020 Notable Indy books

~*~

Journey to New Salem

Finalist in the 2022 R.O.N.E. Award in the Young Adult category

Second Place in the 2022 National Excellence in Storytelling competition in the Young Adult category

Winner of the monthly InD'tale Magazine's "Crème De La Cover" contest

Listed on Shelf Unbound's 2021 Notable Indy books.

~*~

Witch's Gamble

Winner of the monthly InD'tale Magazine's "Crème De La Cover" contest

~*~

"*The Witches of Vegas* is a dandy read. Happily recommended especially for the young adult audience. Five stars."

~ The Compulsive Reader

~*~

"My teen, Moxie, really digs The Witches of Vegas series and is looking forward to the next book."

~ Penn Jillette, Penn & Teller: Fool Us!

Dedication

To my wife, Sue, my greatest inspiration and biggest supporter.
To my family, my friends, and all my readers, who also inspire me on a daily basis.
I thank you all.

Prologue

Amelia's eyes opened from what felt like a deep slumber. Her head pounded like a conga drum after it was banged on for a long performance. She could barely remember last night. What happened that led her to waking up in a strange place on a wooden bench with bars instead of a wall about eight feet away? If this was a jail cell, she had no idea how she ended up in here.

Amelia clutched her forehead. Jeeze, no fifteen-year-old should ever wake up with this much of a hangover. Of course, the pain in her head was nothing compared to what she'd go through if Mother found her like this. Her body wobbled as she sat up. Her feet dropped onto the floor. A puddle of what looked like greenish-brown mud lay in front of her. At first, it spun in circles, but she realized it only looked that way due to dizziness. "Where the hell did that come from?" Amelia groaned, staring down at the thick goop.

"That came out of you!" a gruff voice replied.

Two women in tank tops and ripped jeans sat on the bench against the opposite wall of the wide cell. They had to be around their late twenties or early thirties although Amelia's vision still hadn't cleared up enough to make a perfect description. She blinked her eyes until the two women came into focus. One of them was white skinned with dreadlocks. The other was black and baldheaded with hooped earrings. Both were huge in every direction. Amelia took them both for the lower end of the species.

"How'd I get here?" Amelia rubbed her eyes and shook her head.

"Damn, you talk like a mouse," the woman with the dreadlocks laughed. "This is where the police bring us to dry out. And, girl, you needed it. They brought you in around three this morning. You was wobbling and slurring your words all over the place."

Amelia took a hold of her yellow blouse. It was stained with the same goop all over the floor. None of what the woman said rang a bell, although the ache in her stomach along with a sore throat did substantiate the story.

"Are you a rock star?" the bald lady asked.

"A rock star?"

She pointed at Amelia's head. "That hot-pink mop on your head. You a singer or something?"

Amelia ran a hand through her hair. It was sticky, and not from the pink dye. "Definitely not a rock star. I don't even play an instrument."

"Then what are you?" Dreadlocks asked.

"I'm a witch, and I'm also a performer on stage. Our show is brand new, we haven't even debuted yet, but we're going to be real popular. I expect I'll be a big deal in this town."

"That right?" Dreadlocks scoffed. Both women laughed. "Yo, you may be a big deal out there, but right now, you in the tank with us staring at your insides from last night all over the floor."

Amelia took another look at the puddle by her feet. It smelled like fried mozzarella and alcohol. She must have been more trashed than she realized. Oh boy, she wasn't looking forward to having to explain this once she got back. But for now, no way was she taking a verbal lashing here by two women who must have done something just as stupid to get locked up along with her.

"That may be the case for the moment." Amelia threw out her arms and stretched. "But unlike you two simpletons, I can leave this cell anytime I want."

Bald Lady peeked over at her friend. "Yo, did she just call us simple?"

"You'd better watch your mouth, little girl." Dreadlocks stood with both fists clenched. "You may be a kid, but it's never too early to learn a lesson, even from someone simple like me."

"She got kids," Bald Lady said, pointing a thumb at her friend. "You should listen when she speaks."

"Is that right?"

Amelia peeked at the hallway outside the bars. If there was supposed to be a police officer out there keeping an eye on these two brutes, he must be on break or something. The woman with the dreadlocks glared across the cell with a look on her face that reminded Amelia of a pissed-off Rottweiler. Amelia stood, looking the woman over. The woman had at least fifteen years and about a hundred pounds on her. Amelia could only think of one way to react to this impending threat. She cackled like a hyena.

"Damn, this little girl is cray-cray," Bald Lady said from the bench.

"You really think I won't pound your face in just because you a kid?" Dreadlocks marched forward and stopped in front of Amelia whose face came up to her chest. "I think I'd be doing you a huge favor. You need to learn real fast that people who have big mouths in here, when they come back, they get their teeth knocked out."

"What makes you so sure I'll be back?"

"Oh, you'll be back." Dreadlocks rolled her eyes. "Spoiled brats like you always come back. You don't learn until it's too late to do anything about it."

"That right?" Amelia stepped back and grinned. "Tell you what, if you really want to teach me a lesson, how about I give you the first punch? Hit me as hard as you can. Don't hold back."

"Careful, kid." Dreadlocks pulled her clenched fist back. "That's the best offer I got all night."

"Then what are you waiting for?" Amelia threw her hands behind her back. "Or are you just all talk and fat?"

Dreadlocks charged forward. Amelia prepared herself, calling upon the energy to take care of her. Timing and accuracy were everything, but unlike Dreadlocks, she knew the game they were about to play. The big lady's fist flew straight at Amelia, who focused on the energy in front of her. A clear circle of blur—a portal—opened in front of her face. It was just big enough for the woman's arm to fit through. Once it did, Amelia shrank it around Dreadlocks' elbow. The fierceness in the woman's face disappeared in a heartbeat, replaced with eyes so wide her pupils looked about to fall out of her head.

Bald Lady jumped off the bench and onto her feet. "What the hell?"

"What...what is this?" Dreadlocks' voice barely registered. She tried to yank her entire body back, but her arm wouldn't budge.

"As I said, I'm a witch, and this is my Wiccan talent." Amelia's smile grew. "I make holes in space."

"A-Annie…" Bald Lady gasped. "You-your fist is in the air." She pointed over their heads where another small portal had formed. Annie's wrist stuck out the portal. Her hand was still balled up in a fist.

"Annie, huh?" Amelia stepped around the portal so she could come nose to nose with her much larger opponent who was now hunched over. "Listen up, Annie, if I close that hole, we will get to see your hand fall to the floor. After that, your new nickname will be 'Stubby.' Would you like to see that?"

Annie shook her head back and forth. She tried to speak, but she could muster nothing past deep breaths.

"Then how about you and your friend stay far away from me while we're in this cell together, okay? Don't worry. It won't be long. I expect I'll be leaving real soon."

A door outside the cell creaked open. Amelia expanded the portal. Annie's arm flew out, which caused the big woman to fall onto her back. She looked like a turtle who had been flipped over, a sight that made Amelia giggle. She willed the portals to disappear just in time for the officer, an older man with a gray goatee, to stick his key in the cell's door and turn the lock.

"Amelia Cross," he announced. Amelia raised her hand. The officer pulled the door open. "Come with me."

"Watch yourself, Officer!" the baldheaded lady shouted. "That girl, she got some kind of magic powers or something!"

The guard threw her a sideways glance. Amelia

waltzed over to the man, shrugged her shoulders, and then pranced out of the cell. The door slammed shut. The officer led Amelia across the dingy hallway and through an open doorway. They entered the police station with two desks, one on each side of the room, and a counter. All were covered with papers and file folders.

Amelia stopped in her tracks and gasped. The cold chill down her chest wasn't due to the second officer sitting at a desk and eating an egg sandwich. It was because of the tall woman standing between the desks with too much makeup on her face and straight salt-and-pepper hair, which hung down to her waist. Her long stare came without a single blink of the eyes.

"Hello, Mother." Amelia braced herself. She knew what was about to come her way.

As if on cue, the woman swung her open hand and struck Amelia across the face. Instinct tried to force Amelia to stumble back, scream out, and clutch her face, but she fought the sting along her cheek and stood in place. A finger shot up between her eyes.

"I know you and I have had this conversation before. What have I made clear when you go out and act like a fool as you do?" Mom's voice was hoarse, a permanent condition caused by a lifetime of smokes.

"I know. Don't get caught," Amelia answered in a whisper.

She eyed both officers, who were seated at their desks, oblivious to the assault that just took place in their station. Mom's doing, no doubt.

"By right, I should have let you rot in here for a few days before coming for you." The woman shook her head in disgust. "Or perhaps I could simply let these police officers remember you. They could charge you for your public indecency and let you go through the legal process. Perhaps then you'd understand."

Amelia straightened her back and picked up her head so she could look directly into her mother's dark eyes. "You know I can leave that cell anytime I want."

"Yes, I am well aware of what you can do with your Wiccan gifts." Her mom spun around and strolled to the double glass door that led to the Las Vegas Strip. "But had you escaped on your own, you would become a fugitive, and we cannot afford that. We must prepare ourselves for the inevitable confrontation."

"I thought they left." Amelia threw up her arms in confusion. "No one's heard from them in weeks. Maybe longer. What we're setting up, it could all be for nothing."

"No, they will return. I have seen it." The older witch leaned in and looked into Amelia's eyes. "That is why we must use the time to establish ourselves and prepare. We must be ready when our moment arrives. Do you understand?"

"I do."

"Good." Mother peeked over her shoulder. "Now take us back and leave the nonsense behind. We must focus on our mission. The moment will come without warning."

"Yes, Mother."

Amelia focused on the space in front of them. A large circular blur formed. Mother stepped through and disappeared. Amelia took one last look behind her. Neither officer reacted or seemed to even notice. Their focus stayed on the messy desks.

Chapter One

Four months later…

Isis stared at the oak door in front of her for what felt like an eternity. At fifteen—a few weeks away from sixteen—she had experienced more stressful moments than most anyone has in a lifetime. That included nearly getting set on fire twice, and one of those times was by a psychotic immortal witch who tried to destroy the world. This moment should have paled in comparison. Then why was she sweating more heavily than any of those times?

A concerned voice whispered in her ear, "Hey, are you sure you're ready to do this?"

"I don't know."

Isis looked deep into Zack's green eyes. His blond hair was short, but curled and messy due to the humidity which was so prevalent here. All things considered, he was more excited about starting a new school in a hidden village filled primarily with witches. Isis should have been all about this opportunity and not so reluctant.

"You don't have to do this if you're not ready," Zack said. His tone shared his deep concerns.

"I am ready, and I want to do this." Isis straightened her back. She once again faced the door. "I'm just a little nervous, that's all."

In truth, she was a lot nervous, but none of the reasons in her head made sense. She imagined the other students staring at her, but even if they did, so what? Isis performed on the Vegas stage where thousands of people all stared at her at once. Walking into this classroom would bring far less attention her way. This village only had around seventy residents total. That was a fraction of the amount of people their theater held during even one performance.

"Isis?"

She tapped her fingers along the notebook pressed against her stomach. It didn't make much sound since she had next to no fingernails. Biting them was always a problem, but that was especially the case over the last few days.

"It's just…" Isis focused on Zack's hand against her back. His touch always had a way of making her feel better. "I've never been in an actual classroom before, not since the third grade. After that, I was always homeschooled, but Mom, Dad, and even Doctor Mac think I'm ready for this. I think I am, too."

"I get it." Zack's hand left Isis' back and ran through her brown hair. "For what it's worth, I also think you're ready. If ever there was a school you should be able to fit right in, it's this one, right?"

Isis replied with a nod. Since they moved to New Salem, Zack was far more at ease than she was at adjusting to their new life. That was especially surprising since he wasn't a witch at all. Although he knew more about them than any other non-Wiccan human being on Earth, but Isis didn't want to think about that, at least not at the moment, or ever.

"Live in the now," Doctor Mac preached to her

during their therapy sessions.

"All right," Isis said. "Let's do it."

"So, how do you think this works?" Zack asked. "Do we open the door, or should you teleport us in? Maybe fly through the window?"

"I think we open the door." Isis' lips stretched into a slight grin. Zack always knew how to bring that out of her. Isis looked his way and puckered. "For luck?"

"Sure."

Their lips touched for several seconds. Zack turned the handle and pushed open the door. The teacher, a noticeably tall woman with short, dark-brown hair, was speaking to the seven teens seated at desks in front of her. All eyes flashed their way. The teacher's lecture came to a halt. After several awkward moments, the teacher strolled over.

"You must be Zack and Isis." Her voice was soft and friendly, but Isis picked up on the slight reluctance in her tone. "President Tia told me to expect you today. I'm Teacher Penelope, but you may already know me, correct?"

"Um, yes," Isis lied.

It was a good assumption on the teacher's part based on what she must have been told, but if Isis ever did know her, it was lost in two hundred years of memories. For some reason, Isis had an irrational expectation that Teacher Penelope would be dressed like a prairie woman from the eighteen hundreds. But she wasn't even close to that wearing a modern red blouse that barely covered her belly button. Her top was complemented by skintight beige pants. Definitely not a prairie woman.

"It's nice to meet you," Zack said. "Again." The

confused look on his face told Isis that they were on the same page as far as not remembering Teacher Penelope.

"Please come in. Choose any of the empty seats you'd like."

"Thank you," Isis said, in what was barely a murmur.

Isis followed Zack into the classroom. Her heart nearly jumped into her throat when the door slammed behind her. The room had twelve chairs with attached desks, all facing the old-fashioned chalkboard. There were four girls and three boys, all around Isis' age. She sensed the Wiccan connection in four of the students and the teacher. She couldn't be sure how strong those connections were, only that they were witches.

Zack waved his hand at all the eyes staring their way. "Hi, everyone," he said, then strolled to a chair and desk in the middle of the room. Once seated, he threw Isis a glance meant to tell her it was okay. Isis took a deep breath, placed one foot in front of the other, and entered. The eyes of each student never left her as she waltzed to the empty seat closest to the window, then sat. Wow, even in a classroom that was mostly witches, Isis felt like a sore thumb. Both Zack and her family came to New Salem with a unique history, and it was obvious that word had spread fast.

The tallest of the girls stood from her seat in the front row. Her golden-blonde hair swung with each step she took across the room. Her green shirt looked like it was made out of silk. She stopped in front of Isis' desk, then leaned forward. "I'm Maya," she said with a huge grin. "I'm—"

"Vice President Paul's daughter. I know." Isis' eyes stayed on her desk. She wanted to look up, be

11

friendly to this nice girl saying hello, but it all felt weird. Isis knew every intimate detail about Maya, even ones Maya had yet to discover for herself, and they were complete strangers.

"Ooh, you heard of me?" Maya asked. "Someone filled you in, or did we know each other where you came from?"

"We…knew each other." It sounded crazy when said out loud.

"Wow!" Maya's face lit up. "That is *so* cool. Were we friends? I can't wait to hear all about that."

Isis glanced over at Zack. The boy sitting behind him, who looked like he could have played for the school football team if they had one, tapped him on the shoulder. "Hey, I'm Jeb. Low-level witch. What about you?"

Jeb had enough chemical in his jet-black hair that Isis could see the overhead lights beaming off it from across the room.

Zack spun around in his seat. "Zack. Um, I'm a magician."

"Magician?" Jeb's head tipped back. "You mean like a wizard, or like the ones that pull rabbits out of hats, then say abracadabra and stuff like that?"

"The second one. Abracadabra and stuff like that."

"Oh." Jeb paused. "I…guess that's cool, too."

Isis caught the slight disappointment on Zack's face. He had a lot of pride in being a trained magician, but he knew well enough that magic wasn't something that would be appreciated in New Salem.

The olive-skinned girl in the desk on Zack's right leaned forward. She looked the exact age as the boy in the back of the room with the same ethnicity and facial features. "Is all that stuff the adults say about you guys true? Are you really from the future?"

Both she and Jeb were focused on Zack, awaiting his answer. Isis felt the same stare from Maya. She almost forgot how fast gossip spread around this village. It made sense though. There were no televisions or movie theaters in New Salem. There wasn't much in the way of entertainment besides books, music, and village gossip. Isis, Zack, and her family weren't the first new residents to New Salem, but their story was far different than anyone else's. She felt like a celebrity without a stage. Zack had to feel the same way.

"We're not from the future." Zack's face turned red like a tomato. "I mean, technically we were in the future, but we didn't time travel...well, Isis did, but not exactly how you think—" Zack's head swung back and forth. He was trapped.

"Okay, class, let's refocus," Teacher Penelope interrupted, letting both Zack and Isis off the hook. "I am sure we will have plenty of time later today to learn about our newest classmates. In fact, we will make time at the end of the day just for that, if we get through today's lessons. So let's get back to it."

"Hey," Jeb whispered before Zack could turn back to the teacher. Jeb held his hand over his desk. The pen rolled from one side of the desk to the other. "Check it out. Abracadabra."

"That's nice," Zack said, before turning around. At that point, he rolled his eyes, which made Isis giggle. She couldn't tell if the big guy, Jeb, was mocking Zack or trying to relieve his tension. He could have also just been showing off. Isis remembered him as being a genuine guy, but was this the same Jeb? She had that question about everyone in New Salem.

Teacher Penelope went on. "Right now, our farmers are setting up fireworks and will soon ignite them into the sky. Would anyone like to catch our newest classmates up on why that display is significant? Maya, would you like to explain it to them while you return to your seat?"

"It's significant," Maya whispered to Isis but loud enough for everyone to hear, "because we live in New Salem, and nothing else ever happens in this village."

"I know many of you have seen this annual event numerous times in your lives, but it's still a day worthy of honor." Teacher Penelope paced in front of the class with her hands folded behind her back. "Would someone else like to share?" The teacher paused mid-step, perhaps being caught off guard from seeing Zack's hand raised. "Yes, Zack?"

Isis knew the answer, but she didn't want to raise her hand, at least not on her first day. Zack, who apparently had no qualms, straightened his back and folded his hands on his desk. "Today is Tituba, the anniversary of the day witches left their lands to find New Salem. It is believed that at nine minutes after nine a.m. all around the world, witches created fires and explosions to mask their escape. That's why fireworks are set off each year at that exact time."

A huge grin crossed Isis' face. New Salem's history was one subject where both she and Zack excelled. They certainly had enough exposure to it. Well, sort of. Teacher Penelope's dropped jaw meant she was more than a bit impressed.

"That is correct, Zack." The teacher's hands pressed against her hips as she eyed the rest of the class.

"As Zack pointed out, the fireworks display is a symbolic reenactment of our ancestors' escape from persecution in countries around the world. Eventually, they all found their way here as if they were called upon by the land." The teacher waved a hand at the line of windows. "We will discuss this in more detail, but right now, I recommend you all observe the fireworks display and think about your ancestors, many of whom were among those we celebrate on this occasion for their courage and fortitude."

"In other countries, fireworks are shot off at night, not in the morning," Maya called out. "When I'm president of New Salem, that ceremony is going to be moved to the nighttime."

"That's a bold aspiration, Maya," Teacher Penelope replied. "But there are many steps you must take throughout your life before you become president. The first is proving yourself as a student in this class."

Maya threw a glance at Isis with squinted eyes. "Yada, yada," she whispered, then strolled back to her seat.

Jeb tapped Zack on the shoulder again. "You probably know, does Maya become president?"

Zack's widened eyes shifted to Isis. There were rules placed by the administration which she and Zack had to follow if they were going to live in New Salem. Limiting who they shared their knowledge with was one of the first rules the president and vice president made them agree to before they could attend school.

Although the rest of the class remained seated, Isis stood and walked up to the window. She was familiar with the fireworks display, as she had seen it over a hundred times from every angle around New Salem.

But in this reality, it was her first time witnessing them through her own eyes. The classroom was three floors up, which gave her a great view. Down in the quad, two farmers were busy lighting the tails with matches. When the wicks caught, they raced back. The younger classes sat along the quad to see the fireworks show close-up but with enough distance to stay safe. For them, unlike the older students in Isis' class, this was still a fairly new and fresh experience.

The tail underneath the two rockets ignited and propelled them high in the air. Then a loud explosion boomed while the rockets exploded. The chemicals inside ignited, sending four colors—red, blue, yellow, and orange—in opposite directions. The children on the ground cheered. Then another rocket was shot up. It let off an eruption so loud Isis' eardrums popped. For a moment she thought the building shook. The explosion reminded her of the nuclear war two hundred years from now. It devastated the entire planet. But those bombs didn't go off in the morning. No, the war started in the middle of the night when they heard the blasts from miles away. Then directly above as the nuclear missiles flew by in all directions heading for their targets. She remembered a few exploding long before reaching their destination…directly above New Salem.

Isis' throat closed up on her. Breathing suddenly became a chore. She remembered the pressure in the pit of her stomach caused by the sense of fear that resonated from every single village resident including herself. In that reality, she—no, the other Isis, vampire Isis—turned the energy around the village into a clear but solid dome. As the blasts throughout the sky grew louder and brighter, the dome shook. It was night, yet the blasts lit up the sky like a blinding inferno. But two centuries of experience helped Isis hold it together. She had to, because every man, woman, and child in New Salem would die if she didn't. She held on for three straight days, refusing to let all their deaths be on her conscience. They had to survive. They did survive—

"*Isis, stop!*"

Zack's panicked voice woke Isis from her thoughts. Energy crackled around her hands like bacon on a skillet. Each of her fingers emanated a white glow. Glass covered her feet and the floor around her. The fireworks had stopped. The farmers, children, and adults all along the grounds were looking to the school with eyes pointed her way. Isis placed her hand against what used to be the window. A clear shield sparked and vibrated at her touch.

Zack called her name again. Isis spun from the window to the class. Zack, the other students, and the teacher were pressed against the wall. Their feet were inches from the floor. The energy had formed a solid barrier holding them in place.

"Oh, no," Isis whispered.

"Isis, you n-need to s-sever the spell!" Teacher Penelope shouted.

Isis focused on her hands. She took deep breaths, seven seconds in through the nose, seven seconds out through the mouth. "Live in the now," she chanted between breaths. After several moments, the beating in her chest slowed. Multiple thuds filled the room as her classmates and teacher dropped to the floor.

"Holy crap!" one of the boys screamed.

Maya was the first to her feet. "Whoa, you really *are* powerful!"

"I'm sorry," Isis sobbed. "I'm so sorry. I didn't mean to—"

Teacher Penelope's jaw hung to the floor. She helped the smallest girl to her feet. The others stood on their own, but the murmuring hit Isis on all sides. She couldn't tell if it was out of awe, anger, fear, or all of the above. Zack, the last one to stand, ran up to Isis and threw his hands on her shoulders.

"Isis, get us out of here," he said.

"Yeah, I…I think that's a good idea."

Isis focused on a location outside the school. "Teleport," she said. The energy reacted, causing the classroom around herself and Zack to blur as if they were surrounded by water.

Once everything came back into focus, they were at the far end of the village's circular graveyard. A bench overlooked the last of the tombstones with miles of boreal trees and long grass behind it.

"Are you okay?" Zack asked.

Isis let out a scream. "I can't believe that just happened!" Isis covered her face with both hands. They were still shaking.

All she wanted was a good first day of school, or at least a normal one. It was bad enough people in the village, young and old, stopped what they were doing and stared at her family whenever they passed through the quad, even months after their arrival. Everyone had heard the rumors, and they were fascinated. It was the reason Isis asked her adopted family to end homeschooling and let her attend an actual class. She wanted to be seen as normal. It took some convincing, but they reluctantly agreed. So much for that.

Zack wrapped his arms around Isis and gave her a

big hug. It was exactly what she needed, and if anyone understood what Isis needed at any given time, it was Zack. They spent more time together and knew each other better than any other teenaged couple on the entire planet.

"When the fireworks went off, you were thinking about the war, weren't you?"

"Yeah, but not just that." Isis walked past Zack and stared down at the bench, a bench that would someday be removed for the sake of digging even more graves. "I was also thinking about fighting Valeria over that volcano. I'm always thinking about everything all the time."

"I do too, even though I know it's not healthy."

Isis gave Zack an accusatory glance. "With all we know, how do you look around this place and not freak out all the time?"

"I do freak out, Isis. I feel a lump in my throat with each person we're introduced to that I'm sure I remember. I get a headache each time I'm asked about the future and have to dodge the question." Zack walked up behind Isis and rubbed the back of her neck. "The only difference between us is I'm not a witch with an insane connection that goes bonkers when I lose control."

"You're lucky that way." She shook her head. "Sometimes, I wish I never had my connection. I wish I was normal like you."

Zack wrapped his hand around Isis' elbow and turned her around to face him. "You don't really mean that, do you?"

Isis shrugged. She wanted to look into Zack's eyes and assure him she'd be okay. The sentiment, true or not, would wipe the concern from his face and let them go on with their day. But the man and two redheaded women walking their way told Isis that the conversation wasn't about to end. "My mom and dad are here," Isis whispered. Zack's eyes widened just before he twirled his body around.

They were dressed comfortably, Sebastian in shorts and a white T-shirt, Selena and Sacha were decked out in tank tops, tight jeans, and sandals. Sebastian's short brown hair was messed up without a single drop of the usual mousse he used on stage in Vegas.

Sacha circled Isis and Zack with a huge smirk. "So, how was school today?"

"Sis," Selena growled.

Isis could tell from the look on her family's faces that they were already informed of Isis' loss of control. She knew the first question would revolve around why she hadn't confided in them that she was having an emotional hard time. In truth, she didn't want them to worry about her while they were adjusting to this new lifestyle. New Salem was nothing like Las Vegas, and they needed time to get used to it. Isis' hesitancy to open up was especially pronounced because they agreed to relocate for her and Zack. They never said that, but she knew it was the only reason.

Sebastian placed a hand on Isis' shoulder and squeezed. His eyes locked on Zack. "Could you give us some time alone with Isis, please?"

"Hold on, Sebastian!" Sacha threw up a hand. "I thought we agreed to make Zack part of our coven. Should we be just dismissing him from an important family discussion such as this?"

Sacha paused at the firm stare from Sebastian.

Selena flashed her a similar glance. "Oh, you mean *both* of us. Gotcha." Sacha's eyes rolled. She threw an arm over Zack's shoulders and walked forward, taking him along with her. "Come on, kiddo, let's, um…pretend we have something better to do, okay?"

Once Sacha and Zack walked off, Isis looked up at the two leaders of their coven who were also her mother and father since they took her in at the age of nine. She didn't want to see them worry. But trying to shield them from her emotions was clearly not working out. "I'm ready to talk," she said.

"I'm glad to hear that." Selena sat on the bench and waved Isis over. "Come, hon, sit next to me and tell us what's going on."

Chapter Two

Zack and Sacha strolled through the miles-long cemetery and past the circular back row of cottages. It wasn't nearly as long as the Vegas Strip, which Zack used to walk from one side to the other almost every day, yet he found himself sweating a lot more in his green polo shirt and navy-blue shorts. It wasn't that much warmer in New Salem than in Vegas, but it was far muggier. It served as a constant reminder that, despite the open infrastructure, they were in the middle of a European swamp jungle.

They finally came across the two cottages occupied by their coven. Both were more than generous offerings upon their arrival by the village administration. With the brown rooftops and timber walls, they had an old-fashioned aura about them. In fact, all of New Salem gave off that feel. It was built centuries ago, and it made no excuses for its age.

What Zack really liked was how much bigger the inside of each cottage looked compared to the outside. Both had two bedrooms, two bathrooms, and an eat-in kitchen. The living rooms had more space than the Vegas suites Zack had lived in all his life. He stopped short in front of the cottage he and Sacha shared. She ran a nice household for the two of them, although some of Sacha's rules were a bit hypocritical. She wouldn't let him invite Isis to sleep over in his bedroom, yet she had plenty of overnight company in her room.

Sacha…man, she always had a skip in her step, always flashed that nonchalant smirk no matter what stared her in the face. That was even the case in that other reality moments before it happened. Talk about a horrible memory he couldn't ever escape—

Zack's feet stopped moving. He found himself frozen in place. He knew enough about witchcraft to recognize when he was put under a spell. Sacha's glowing hand and the annoyed expression on her face confirmed it.

"You need to stop," she growled. "In fact, you and Isis both need to drop this."

"Drop what?" Zack waved his hands now that he could move them again.

"Stop staring at me like you're in mourning." Sacha shook her head. "I get it. I was murdered by Valeria in this other reality of yours."

"It wasn't our reality. It was—"

"Point is, I'm alive and well in *this* reality!"

The subject of Sacha had come up many times in Zack and Isis' conversations. The memories they shared did make them feel awkward around a woman they both saw as the ultimate hero…even if that heroic sacrifice, technically, never happened. Or did it? Either way, they agreed to keep those feelings to themselves. They weren't doing a good job of it. Clearly.

"I know you're alive, Sacha," Zack said. "And I'm sorry. I don't mean to make you feel uncomfortable. I'm sure Isis doesn't either. It's just a lot for us to adjust to. We both have two sets of memories in our heads."

"Including one without me. I know." Sacha rolled

her eyes. Then she placed a hand on Zack's shoulder. "I'll say this, you're handling it way better than my poor niece. How are you not in a corner curled in the fetal position over it?"

Zack laughed. If only he had a dollar for every time he needed to explain to a member of the coven why he wasn't a complete mess. "Look at where we are." He threw his arms out to motion at everything around them. "My girlfriend and her family are witches. I'm living in a village where half the population are witches and with one vampire. I faced off against a four-hundred-year-old witch in the middle of the Vegas Strip. That I also lived as a two-hundred-year-old vampire in a reality that doesn't exist anymore. That's not too much of a stretch, right?"

"You make a good point." Sacha's smirk returned. "You've certainly seen a lot in a short time. Or, for you, it's been a long time, hasn't it?"

"That part is still weird for me." Zack skipped to the door, staggering to avoid some of the mud puddles along the grass and dirt road caused by last night's rain. "How do you think their talk is going? Do you think they're working out a way to help Isis?"

"I have no idea, Zack." Sacha threw her hands on her hips. "I was dismissed from that conversation just like you were."

"But you can find out, right?" The enthusiasm in Zack's voice rose. "You can peek in on them."

Sacha's face scrunched. "That doesn't seem right."

"Why not? We're part of the coven, too." Zack shot Sacha a huge grin. "It's our future they're deciding on, right? Maybe we should have a heads-up before Sebastian calls the next family meeting and lays their decision on us?"

"Another good point by you, but should we?" Sacha tipped her head up while tapping a manicured finger against her chin. "Yeah, all right, let's peek in." Sacha held out her palm and swung her arm in a circular motion. "Let us see and hear," she chanted. Her arm spun faster and faster until a circle of white light formed in front of her. To Zack it looked like a round movie screen before the film plays. A small hole in the sky opened and brightened a few miles away. It sat over the area of the cemetery where they had left Isis and her folks.

"Are they going to see that?" Zack asked.

"Only if they look up."

Sacha's circle of light gave way for an image. It was an overhead shot of Isis seated on the bench next to Selena who had an arm wrapped around her waist. Sebastian stood across from the bench facing the two with his arms crossed against his chest.

"I know we can be happy here," Isis explained. "We *were* happy here. But right now, when I look around at all these familiar faces, I have flashbacks about so many of them, including how they're going to die."

"Zack is experiencing the same thing?" Sebastian asked.

Sacha turned to him. "Are you?"

"I try not to think about it as much as Isis does, but yeah."

Isis nodded. "When I talk to Zack about it, he says he tries to focus on how everyone lived instead of how they died. I know I should do that too, but those lives went by for us so quick. Now, they won't, which is just as creepy for me."

"Sebastian," Selena said, looking up at her husband. "Maybe agreeing to stay was a mistake. They're not ready, not after all they've been through."

"It wasn't a mistake," Isis sobbed. "This was our home. We all belong here. I just…I need more time to get used to it. To deal with the memories."

Isis placed her head against Selena's shoulder.

A tear came to Zack's eye, which he quickly wiped with the back of his hand. He knew exactly how Isis felt. In fact, he may be the only one in the world who could. Outwardly, he was dealing with New Salem far better than she was. He had his explanation as to why, which he repeated numerous times, but it was a narrative he stuck with so he could be strong for both Isis and himself. If he truly wanted to delve into his own head, he was still in a state of semi-denial. So far, the only one who noticed this was Doctor Mac who outright said it during the one therapy session Zack attended.

"Ooh, check out Sebastian's face," Sacha said, bringing Zack back to the present. "He's working on a plan."

"You don't think he's going to relocate us, do you?"

"I have no idea, but let's see what he says—"

The sound of a throat clearing spun Sacha around. She raised her hands in the air immediately in a sign of surrender. The circular image of Isis and her folks faded into a puff of smoke. So did the light from the sky in the distance. Vice President and head of New Salem's law enforcement task force, Paul, strolled their way. His fellow task force member, Natasha, followed him, hovering an inch over the ground, as was always her way.

"So you know, we try to teach the younger witches in New Salem how it is wrong to use their gifts to spy on one another." Paul's blond ponytail swung from the slight breeze caused by wind around Natasha's levitated body. He eyed Sacha. "Perhaps we need to teach this lesson to our older witches as well." Although there was a note of levity in his Scottish tone, Zack picked up on the veiled threat.

"Older witch?" Sacha gasped. "I'm barely thirty-one."

"I am sure Paul meant that as compliment," Natasha said, through her thick Russian accent.

Assuming they were caught up on what happened in the classroom, Zack chimed in, "Isis didn't mean to lose control like that. It's just—"

"Of that I have no doubt," Paul replied. "We understand the situation, and respect all she has done for our reality. But this is not the first time Isis has lost control of the energy. That was evident when she created an illusion that put President Tia face-to-face with a descendent she will never know."

"Wait, what was that?" Sacha asked Zack.

The incident Paul spoke of occurred three months ago—just a few weeks after they settled in New Salem, but Zack remembered it well. The descendent was Domina, the great-great-great…whatever…grandchild of Tia and her future husband, Jasper. During a debriefing about the impending war, Isis became emotional over the suffering Domina had gone through in Queen Valeria's alternate timeline. She didn't realize the energy that thrust the president's office into the middle of her memory was an unintentional illusion, but Tia ended up seeing far more than Zack and Isis agreed to share.

"That was also inadvertent," Zack said.

"Of course, we understand that." Paul gave Zack a smile—his attempt to lighten the mood, perhaps? "We also sympathize with all she, and you, are going through. It must be difficult remembering a long history that never happened."

"But?" Sacha growled.

"But…" Paul raised a hand, a signal to Sacha to calm her temper. "We've never dealt with a witch as young as Isis who has this strong of a connection. With such a unique trauma comes concern over her ability to keep it under control. We have to consider stopgap measures for the safety of herself and New Salem."

"Stopgap measures?" Sacha repeated. "What, exactly, do you want to do to my niece?"

"We did discuss, perhaps sever her connection," Natasha answered, which garnered a side glance from Paul. "But that can be done only by witch with stronger connection than her own. The only one here that maybe could is Doctor Mac. He has refused."

Sacha turned her back and closed her eyes. Her lips were moving a mile a minute although no sound left her throat. Zack knew exactly who she was contacting.

"What other ideas did you discuss?" Zack asked, to keep the conversation going until help arrived. "What are you looking to do to Isis?"

"Relax, Zack, it's simply been conversation between the task force and the president. It went no farther. Tia and I want to find a way to help the both of you overcome your trauma. We also want to make sure there are no future incidents with Isis' control. If we can also keep the paranoia in the village down, particularly with our non-Wiccan community, all the better."

"Does that include you, Paul?"

The attitude in Zack's tone caused the vice president to grimace. It wasn't how Zack wanted to come off, but his instincts to protect Isis took over. Granted, Paul's concerns were legitimate. Zack remembered the reactions in the other reality when Isis' witchcraft did spiral out of control. The people were up in arms and acted like their entire lifestyle had been thrown out of whack. Right now, The Witches of Vegas were new to the village and hadn't yet earned an overall sense of trust.

A static-like blur formed on Zack's left, a sign of a witch teleporting. Once it cleared, Sebastian and Selena stood side by side with Isis in front of them.

"Oh good, the cavalry's arrived," Sacha barked.

Zack's eyes went wide. So far, Paul's inquiry was civil and mostly unconfrontational. Hopefully, the attitude he just showed wouldn't change that.

"We understand your concerns." Selena walked up to Paul and looked up into his eyes. "We have an idea, one that may help."

"I'd love to hear it," Paul replied.

"So would I," Zack added.

Isis wrapped her hands around Zack's arm. "I'll share it with you." She walked away, dragging him along with her. "I think you're really going to like it. In fact, I know you will."

"Let me make a few phone calls." Sebastian dashed for their cottage. "I'll see how fast I can get the ball rolling."

"What ball?" Natasha asked.

Selena faced Paul and Natasha. She waved Sacha to join their huddle. Zack was ready to hear this plan as well, but he already believed in it. If Isis was sure he'd like it, then he was sure, too. After all, she knew him better than anyone else in the entire world.

Chapter Three

Three Weeks Later...

Isis skipped across the quad to the medical center. She hadn't missed a weekly appointment since moving to New Salem, although this would be her final one for a while. The medical building was an inviting sight with its two glass doors, which were never locked. Isis saw it as a huge "welcome" sign that she appreciated. That's why she and Zack made sure to keep those same doors even two hundred years later when they were in charge of New Sal— *Stop! Live in the now, Isis, live in the now.*

The double doors swung open. Isis stepped aside so a huge and burly man in dirty overalls could exit the building. "Good morning, Farmer John." Isis caught the limp in the big man's step. "Are you okay?"

"I am now, Isis, mighty kind of you to ask." Farmer John stopped in front of Isis, blocking her path to the doors. "I had a slight accident with the weed whacker. Damned blade went straight through my boot and into my foot. But Doctor Mac, he saved my toes and healed me right up."

"I'm really glad to hear you're doing better." Isis tried to step around the huge man, but Farmer John slid to the side along with her.

"It's okay. I can handle the pain. In fact, I can

handle anything that won't kill me." Farmer John leaned forward. Isis caught herself taking a step back. "But it would help to know if any of these near-misses will be the end of me. You wouldn't be willin' to do this old farmer a solid, and let me know when my time came in that other place of yours, would ya?"

"Um…" Damn, to think Isis' biggest worry was that no one in New Salem would believe her amazing but outrageous story. Turned out she was living an even worse scenario; everyone believed her. For some, it didn't even require proof, just faith.

Farmer John's narrowed blue eyes dug into Isis as if she was about to reveal the scoop of the century. She was only five steps away from the medical center doors, but the obstacle between her and escape was as formidable as it was awkward. Her promise to never share details of the other timeline was challenged on a near-daily basis. Some of those challengers were friendly and subtle, others were far more aggressive.

Finally, a loud and angered voice offered salvation. "Farmer John!"

The large farmer spun around like a child who had been caught drawing on the walls with a permanent marker. The tall but slender Doctor Mac stood between the open double doors with his arms folded across his chest. "You are cleared to return to work," the doctor said in a tone that offered no room for discussion. "Would you kindly step aside so I can tend to my next patient?"

"Yessir." With slumped shoulders, Farmer John scurried past Isis and through the quad. She threw a glance at Doctor Mac who waved her over.

"You were here earlier in the week for your

physical," Doctor Mac said. "I presume this morning's visit is for one last session before your big trip tomorrow?"

"It is. I'm on your schedule."

"Ah, yes." The doctor tapped the side of his head. "Forgive me, but my secretary is out sick today. Something imported into the market has caused a rash of food poisoning. If we do not soon figure out which food item it is, I may have to shut the entire place down and purge it of everything edible. I know many residents would not be happy about that, not to mention the massive waste of perfectly good consumables."

"Do you want me to go so you can work on it?"

Doctor Mac raised a hand. "No, no, this is your scheduled time. I've been working all night on ideas, both medical and Wiccan. I should have the problem licked by the end of the day. Right now, I could use a distraction, so let's you and I speak."

The hallway had several doors, each leading to Doctor Mac's various offices and examining rooms. He liked to vary which rooms he used for his patient consultations. Normally he'd point to the door he had in mind, and Isis would walk ahead. This time, he looked around the quad and took in a deep breath of air. "It's a beautiful day. How about we hold your session outside?"

Isis nodded. The man obviously needed to work, but if he felt he had the time, she'd utilize it. Isis enjoyed her sessions with Doctor Mac. They always made her feel better about everything, and not just because she could spend thirty minutes staring at his deep brown eyes and curly black hair. Of course, she'd never look at anyone besides Zack in that way, especially someone who was old. Doctor Mac had to be at least in his mid-forties, which made him at least ten years older than her folks. But for a guy his age, he was sure easy on the eyes.

It was also a relief to have someone other than her family to talk to about the images that randomly popped into her head. Doctor Mac was great at helping Isis collect and sort out her thoughts. It was as if he understood what she had gone through even though there was no way he really could. How she wished Zack could be coaxed into taking advantage of Doctor Mac's therapeutic services.

"Okay." The doctor raised his hands in the air. "Let's take this outside and breathe in some fresh air."

"Aren't we already out—" Everything around Isis blurred, which meant Doctor Mac was teleporting them. Once her vision cleared, she suddenly felt warmer, as if the sun had moved closer to her body. She stepped back at the sight of the quad and the people walking through it. They were a great distance below her. Both Isis and the doctor were on the school's rooftop, which was the highest point in New Salem.

"Why are we all the way up here?" Isis asked.

"It's something you said in an earlier session about the other reality." Doctor Mac joined Isis at the rooftop's edge. "You mentioned standing on this rooftop to get a perspective of New Salem. I thought you could use that perspective today. Like the rest of the world, it is a small and fragile place. The day may come where it falls under your protection once again."

"Once again?" Isis bit her bottom lip. She hated how often references were made to the other her from a now defunct reality. Doctor Mac certainly meant well.

Maybe they all meant well, but damn, it came up at least three times a day. "I never asked to be a powerful witch," she growled. "Or to follow in the footsteps of another me."

"That is true, but we don't always get to choose our destiny. Sometimes, our destiny is chosen for us."

"I guess." Yet another subject Isis struggled with, destiny and free choice. The other, much older, Isis changed everything. It gave her future a clean slate, but she still felt an obligation to live up to what the other one accomplished even though that was an impossible task. There were times she wished she never "accidentally" met the other Isis or was ever gifted with all of her memories. Of course, Isis couldn't blame her. She would have done the same thing in that position...obviously. Plus, not all the memories were bad. In fact, most weren't bad at all.

"That happens a lot to you, doesn't it?" Doctor Mac pointed a thumb over his shoulder.

"What does?"

"Farmer John."

"Oh. Yeah." Isis shut her eyes. "It happens to me; it happens to Zack. People even ask my folks and Sasha about the other time, and they don't know anything about it except what we told them. Sasha started making up stories, but I don't think that's really helped the situation."

"When they ask you questions about the future, how does that make you feel?" The doctor stepped forward off the ledge. Floating in mid-air, his body turned so he could face Isis. Doctor Mac, although a focused doctor, tended to flaunt his connection in the most nonchalant of ways. Isis suspected he did it for his own entertainment, or as a subtle reminder to others of his strength as a witch.

"It makes me really uncomfortable," Isis answered, focusing on the therapy session. "I don't know what to say. Even if I could tell them, the future was changed. Things won't be the same."

"Well, actually, only *your* future was changed, correct?" Doctor Mac floated forward, causing Isis to jump back. He placed his foot onto the rooftop. "I've analyzed everything you've told me, and I believe you're slightly off on one factor."

"What do you mean?"

Doctor Mac waved an arm out to New Salem. "This is not a different reality. There's only one constant reality in which you, in the future, journeyed through the timeline and changed. We are living in the change, but it is still the same world, same actuality. I realize there's a butterfly effect going on here, but while the future will now be different for you and Zack, that's not necessarily the case for everyone else. We are still moving forward all the same. Does that make sense?"

Isis dropped her head and shrugged. "I think so. Our future and Valeria's are what she...I changed." Her head popped up. "What are you saying?

"First thing, you shouldn't think of this as a different timeline, or the other Isis as a different person. She is you, but an older you from before you moved back in time and changed the timeline."

Isis' brain was ready to shoot out of her skull and explode. Right or wrong, the fact that Doctor Mac was able to explain all this so nonchalantly made her wonder if he was more of a genius than she realized. Or maybe he was just secretly a huge sci-fi geek.

"And the second thing?" Isis asked.

"Second, based on that unique experience, and the memories of that time in your head, you have an actual knowledge of everyone else's future. I'm sure you can understand why so many of your fellow residents are curious." Doctor Mac rested his other foot on the solid rooftop, his flotation spell apparently canceled. "Regardless, that does put you in an awkward position, doesn't it?"

Isis returned to the edge. Her eyes focused on the farmers tending to the crops on the other end of the quad. "I don't blame anybody for wanting to know. But I feel like that's all anyone thinks about whenever they look at me."

"Is that why you and your family came to the decision you've made?"

Isis peeked over her shoulder at Doctor Mac. His eyes weren't as accusatory as she expected them to be. Instead, they were filled with a genuine concern. They made Isis comfortable enough to answer honestly. If she didn't know better, she'd think he was using a spell on her, except she couldn't sense the energy crackling around them, at least not at the moment. Maybe it was just his psychology degree at work.

"The first time, once we came to New Salem, we never left. This trip…it's something we never did. It feels like it's actually our choice."

"Do you expect to return?"

A smile crossed Isis' face. "For sure. This is our home. It's where we belong." Somehow Isis knew that question wasn't being asked for therapeutic reasons. It was more likely an inquiry Doctor Mac made on behalf of the village's administration.

"I understand." Doctor Mac strolled away from the ledge. He waved Isis to join him. "If I may offer some parting advice. Remember to breathe, live in the present, and feel free to contact me if you need to talk."

"Contact you how? Through witchcraft?"

"Or you could call." Doctor Mac let out a slight chuckle. "We may not have the world's latest technology like where you're about to go, but we're certainly not cavemen."

Isis let out a snicker, both in response to his joke and out of embarrassment. "I'm sorry. It's just, I sometimes think in terms of being a witch."

"I know you do," Doctor Mac responded. "It tends to be an ailment among our kind. But sometimes, whether in a situation involving your Wiccan connection or not, you need to think outside the box. There are always solutions at your disposal."

"I'll keep that in mind, thanks."

With that, the doctor teleported them both off the roof. Isis once again stood in front of the medical center by herself.

Chapter Four

The next morning…

Zack dropped his packed suede suitcase in the middle of the quad. He was several feet away from Sebastian and Selena who were double-checking the contents of one of their suitcases. The huge square grassland that made up the quad had a large building on each side. This time, there were a few dozen villagers in front of those buildings, preparing to see a grand display of the Earth's Wiccan energy. Few witches could manipulate their connections to teleport themselves, let alone with a passenger, across the entire globe. But Selena and Sacha, with their sibling connection, were ready to do just that with their entire coven.

Zack jogged to Isis who was several feet behind him. She fought to drag her suitcase. It did have two wheels, but they wouldn't roll in the mud and grass that made up the quad. After a few heavy breaths, Zack offered a hand, but she waved it off.

"I got it," Isis said. Although at barely ninety pounds, she didn't have enough upper body strength to move that overfilled suitcase without manipulating the Wiccan energy for assistance.

"You sure you don't want a hand?"

"I'm sure." Isis let go of the suitcase and exhaled.

"I want to do this on my own. No help and no witchcraft."

Maya and Jeb strolled their way. Zack nudged his chin in their direction to signal Isis to turn around, which she did. "Hey, guys," Zack said.

"Hey, hey." Maya spread her arms and threw them an expression of surprise. "So, you're really heading back to America? You sick of New Salem already?"

"No," Isis screeched. "It's not like that at all."

"It's only for ten weeks," Zack explained. "Thirty shows, which is just enough time for us to clear our heads. Then we'll come back fresh and ready for village life."

Jeb stepped forward. "Hey, when you get back, how 'bout we hang out some, okay?" With his size, he'd be an intimidating guy if not for the boyish face. Maya once described him to Zack as a big scary teddy bear. Zack thought she was being facetious. He soon realized it was an apt description—this Jeb was exactly like the one he remembered from the other reality. That's because they were the same guy.

"Yeah, we really should," Maya added. "Then we'd have a chance to get to know you as well as you know us."

"I'm sure we'd be up for that." Zack swung his head to Isis. "Don't you agree?"

He realized Isis was no longer in the conversation. Her eyes had drifted to the crowd surrounding the quad. Specifically, her attention was on a young boy in overalls. His name was Brandon, and in the other reality, he was one of the few residents who wasn't afraid of her. Isis kept an eye on him throughout his childhood until he turned seventeen and left New Salem to attend college in the UK. Brandon was working on becoming a lawyer until a tragic drinking and driving accident after a frat party took his life. They had seen a lot of death in that other reality, but Zack had to work a bit harder to get Isis past that one.

They knew the fates of everyone in this village, at least in that timeline. Did it mean their destinies were the same here? That conversation had kept both of them up throughout several nights.

"Isis?" Zack tugged her arm, trying to bring her back to the conversation.

"Um, yeah, I guess." She spun around. "We need to go. I'll tell my folks we're ready." Isis walked away, speeding up as she moved farther through the quad. It left no doubt of her intentions to escape the discussion. Her bag was left behind.

"I'm sorry about that," Zack said to Maya and Jeb, trying to break the tension that suddenly rose. "I should probably get going, too."

Zack picked up Isis' suitcase. As he turned away, Jeb grabbed him by the shoulder and spun him back. "Hold up!" he shouted. "What's the deal with us in that other world of yours? Were we assholes or something?"

"No, not even a little bit," Zack shot back. "We were actually really good friends. For a while, we were close."

"For a while," Maya repeated. "What happened?"

Zack threw up his arms and sighed. He knew the rule, don't share information about the other reality so freely, especially events that happened—or would happen—in the future. But he couldn't leave these two thinking they did something wrong, or that they were being wronged. Perhaps they did have a right to know.

41

Maybe everyone in New Salem did. After all, it wasn't like their future would mirror the other timeline, not anymore.

"There wasn't any sort of beef or anything like that," Zack answered. "It's just...the other us, we were vampires. You got older while we stayed the same age. The two of you got married and had kids."

Maya flashed a grin at Jeb.

Zack went on. "Pretty soon, Isis and I looked the same age as your children. Then your grandchildren. Then we watched the two of you die of old age." Zack paused when he caught Maya's grin disappear.

"That does sound kind of sucky." Maya shook her head. "And here I thought being an immortal vampire would be the coolest thing ever. Guess not."

"Are you saying we were friends then but we can't be now?" Jeb asked.

"No, I'm not saying that at all," Zack said, after a deep sigh. "I'd like us all to be friends, I really would. Maybe we can. But Isis is having a harder time dealing with all of this than she wants to admit. Honestly, I get why that is."

"Because you both remember how we died," Maya said.

"Well, yeah. We just need time to accept living here, again, around the people the 'us' in all these memories knew. It's not the same place, not anymore. We have to wrap our heads around that, you know what I mean?" Zack took a good look at both their faces. They seemed to understand, but not really. How could they? None of it made any sense, at least not to anyone but Isis and himself.

"You think going to Las Vegas and doing magic

again will help?" Jeb asked.

"I don't know if it will, but it's worth a shot."

At least for Zack, his mind was always clearest on stage in front of an audience. That was something he couldn't do in New Salem. Magic just wasn't impressive in a village where witchcraft was a normal and everyday thing. Any illusion Zack could create, half the village could replicate without gimmicks or sleight of hand. As much as he liked everyone here, he looked forward to reuniting with his deck of cards in front of regular people.

Maya offered an outstretched hand, which Zack shook. "I hope it works because you seem like our kind of people. You're different, and that's a good thing. I think we will end up real close—again—eventually. I can sense those kinds of things."

Zack did like that idea. He hoped Maya was right. A circle of friends wasn't something he or Isis were accustomed to having, in either reality. Maya's eyes shifted over Zack's shoulder. "But first, are you all absolutely sure about your newest recruit to your magic team?"

Zack rotated his body. His eyes widened to match that of Isis and her folks. The plump body of Simon waddled their way. He twirled his oak cane in his left hand with each step. "Make way, make way!" Simon shouted with his long white cape dragging along the grass. "Stage vampire coming through!" The long-haired black wig couldn't have been more obvious if it was a hat. It also didn't match the green camouflage pants and boots. Or the ruby-colored wide-rimmed sunglasses.

"Seriously, man." Jeb rolled his eyes. "That guy's a

little bit weird."

"Nah, he's just eccentric," Maya said, with a hand over her mouth. "Perfect for a stage in America, right?"

"I sure hope so. Um, if you'll excuse me?" Zack about-faced and ran the length of the quad to cut off Simon's path. Wow, his face had layers of makeup which made his skin far paler than usual, except for a slight red in his cheeks. "Hey, Simon, you know our first show isn't until tomorrow afternoon, right?"

"Of course I do, my boy. The schedule has been permanently implanted in here." Simon tapped the side of his noggin. His soprano tone was far louder than it needed to be. "However, it is never too early to jump into character, and I will be playing the part of The Witches of Vegas' undead vampire. It is a responsibility I take seriously, and I wish to truly immerse myself into the role." Simon stepped back and bowed. "I will do my best to be convincing."

Convincing? "But you actually *are* an undead vampire." Zack glanced over his shoulder at Isis. Her face had cringed to the point it scrunched up like a raisin. A glance behind him revealed Maya and Jeb pointing and giggling. Zack could only hope their Vegas audiences were as easily entertained.

"Indeed. I am a vampire." Simon stretched out his arms, his right hand gripped around the handle of his cane. "But now, I will be a vampire on stage."

"What's with the cape?" Zack asked.

Simon motioned to his outfit, showing it off as if he were on display. "My vampiric predecessor in The Witches of Vegas wore a cape for your performances. I shall follow in his mighty footsteps and wear one as well!"

"Great." Zack's glance swung to Sebastian and Selena. The wide-eyed looks on their faces mimicked the thoughts going through Zack's mind.

"I really hope this is a good idea," Sebastian mumbled to Selena loud enough for Zack to hear.

"He did say he has stage experience on Broadway," Selena replied. "For his role, this shouldn't be nearly as complicated."

Sebastian looked back and forth at the crowd around them. "Where's Sacha? She should be here by now."

Selena closed her eyes and concentrated. "Sach is by the cottages with Carolyn. They're saying goodbye. I'll let her know we're about ready to leave."

"If I may…" Natasha's voice spooked Zack. He didn't realize she was standing behind him. In fact, he was sure he didn't notice her anywhere around the quad. The others turned her way. "The president would like to see all of you in her office before your journey."

"We'd be happy to," Sebastian replied. "But first, we need to let Sacha know to meet us here—"

"Go ahead!" Simon announced a lot louder than necessary. "I will locate Sacha, wherever she is in New Salem, and lead her to this location."

"We already established where she is," Zack muttered under his breath.

Selena threw a hand on Isis' shoulder. "Sweetie, why don't you handle the teleportation to the president's office?" It was a fair request since she and Sacha were preparing to teleport the group of six all the way to Las Vegas. They needed to conserve their strength.

"I can do that," Isis answered, with a tone that said

she was anxious to leave New Salem.

****

The blur caused by teleportation cleared up. Isis eyed the huge office with Zack on her right and her folks on her left. They were facing an oak and marble desk. New Salem's President Tia was seated behind it with her hands folded. "Good morning." Her tone was friendly and inviting.

"Hey, Tia." Zack gulped at the slanted glance he received in response. "Um, I mean, good morning, Madam President."

The president leaned forward. Her wide brown eyes and exotic dark skin radiated behind her confident smile. Isis was impressed by Tia. The woman had just turned nineteen, yet she had the responsibility of running the entire village—a sanctuary for witches from all over the world. New Salem may have only housed around seventy people, but that was still more than anyone fresh out of their teen years should have to handle. With all the pressure that had to be on her shoulders, Tia managed it with grace and confidence. How could Isis not feel small around her? How could anyone not be impressed?

"You wanted to see us?" Sebastian asked.

"That I did."

Tia waved them to come closer to her desk. Isis stepped forward. There was reluctance in her step. She hadn't seen Tia since "the incident" a few weeks ago. Isis didn't expect to ever be welcomed into this office again, especially since Vice President Paul had taken over the inquiries with her regarding the future of the other reality. Yet, there was no hint of anger or resentment anywhere on Tia's face. Perhaps Isis had avoided her since that day for no reason. It was most likely Tia was busy with presidential duties and that was why she no longer ran the inquiries herself. Best not to ask.

"Hey," Isis said in a tone that was barely above a whisper. "I'm really sorry about what happened last time."

"Don't give it another thought." She snorted and waved a dismissive hand in the air. "At least now I have a physical description to add to that letter we are keeping locked away for the next two hundred years."

"What can we do for you, Madam President?" Selena asked.

"First, is everything set for you on the other end?"

"It is," Sebastian answered. "We couldn't get back into The Sapphire as we hoped; they have a show that's doing well, and they didn't want to bump it for us. But we found another venue to perform."

"We're going to be in my old home," Zack said with a hint of pride. "The Galloway Theater in the Felicity Hotel. It's not as big as The Sapphire but..." His eyes drifted to Sebastian and Selena.

"But that's okay. It doesn't have to be." Selena threw him a confident nod. "It will fit our needs, and those who come will be entertained."

"I'm glad to hear that." Tia stood from her seat. Her back was perfectly straight, which created an aura of being the tallest one in the room even though she only had a few inches of height over Isis.

The president made eye contact with each of the four people standing in front of her desk. "I want to make sure it's understood that you are in no way being run out of New Salem. Since your arrival, you have each proven yourselves as productive members of our village. You fit in well, and we'd hate to lose you as residents."

"Thank you for saying so, Madam President," Sebastian responded. "We feel the same way. That's why this is a limited time show, and once it's over, we plan to return and resume our duties here in New Salem."

"Yes, this is something we all need." Selena placed one hand on Isis' shoulder and the other on Zack's. "One last hurrah on the big stage, and an escape from what occupies our thoughts."

Isis dipped her head. She knew well enough that by "we" and "occupying our thoughts," Mom didn't really mean all of them. She meant Isis' and Zack's thoughts.

"Understood. I wish you all the best in finding your balance in Las Vegas." Tia folded her hands in front of her chest. "Just remember, our biggest concern is always exposure. We wouldn't want any sort of slipups leading to New Salem's discovery."

"We would never let that happen," Sebastian said in a statement that spoke for the entire family. "You can always trust us on that."

"I believe I can." Tia flashed a grin with her eyebrows raised. "Just make sure to keep an eye on Simon, okay?"

Chapter Five

With their meeting over, it was now time to say goodbye to New Salem, at least temporarily. Zack didn't expect it to be a big deal since they had only been residents for five months. But, from the number of faces around the quad, it looked like the entire village had come out to see them leave. However, the timing was terrible. Isis never outright said it, but Zack knew well enough a small part of why she wanted to go was due to the awkward animosity she expected from the village administration after that horrible incident.

As it turned out, President Tia held no grudge, a fact that just came to fruition now. Would this have changed their decision? Maybe, but perhaps this was for the best. Isis needed to get away for a bit, and if Zack was going to be honest with himself, he needed to as well. There was just one last issue delaying their trip.

"Is she here yet?" Sebastian asked. "We don't want to dawdle too long, not when we have an appointment to meet with the hotel manager in an hour."

Selena pointed past Sebastian and to the left of the school. "Yes, she's here."

Sacha had finally made her way toward them. She waved to all the villagers, then joined the others in the center of the quad. Soon, with a snap of her fingers, two huge pink suitcases on wheels appeared in front of her. This was in spite of her big sister's advice that they conserve their Wiccan energy and pack lightly.

"It's about time you made it," Sebastian barked. "Do you realize how late it is already?"

"Yeah, where were you?" she retorted through a devious smirk.

"At least we're all here now," Selena said before Sebastian could respond to Sacha's teasing. "Let's do this."

Zack and Isis stepped behind Sebastian. It was time. Anticipation shivered throughout Zack's body. He threw Isis a quick glance. From her hands clenching and unclenching, he knew she was just as anxious.

The sisters were on opposite sides of the group, as was all the luggage. They were now all within the five enchanted crystals that lay on the grass an equal distance from one another. It was through those crystals that Selena and Sacha would focus their shared connection to accomplish this long-distance teleport.

"Is he still joining you?" Paul asked, while facing the family from outside the crystal pentagon.

"As far as we know, he is," Sebastian answered.

A slight ruckus grabbed everyone's attention. Simon pushed through a section of the crowd that had surrounded the quad. He stared down at one young child with dirty-blond hair. Zack pegged him for around six years old.

"Young man, please step forward!" Simon spoke like a general commanding a soldier in his army. He waved the boy over.

Zack caught the confusion on the boy's face, but the kid complied and approached Simon from out of the crowd. The boy walked with a slight limp. His body hunched to the right.

"Never let it be said that the vampire Simon does not give back to his community." Simon held his cane straight out, placing the handle against the boy's chest. "Go ahead. Take it," Simon announced. "I shan't need it on the stage or in Las Vegas. Please take good care of this helpful walker. It is yours now."

The boy glanced at a couple in the crowd, both in chef's aprons—his parents—then again, to Simon. He took the cane and offered an awkward and reluctant "Thank you."

"Use it well, young man. Perhaps it shall be of great value to you." Simon wobbled to the center of the quad and stepped inside the crystals' pentagon, standing to Sebastian's right.

Sacha looked Simon up and down. She reached out and felt the material of his costume. "You really have a flair for the dramatic, don't you?"

"Which I will bring onto your stage," Simon replied, flashing his pearly white teeth which Zack was sure were porcelain.

"Best wishes, my friends." Paul stepped away from the pentagon. "On behalf of New Salem, it is my sincerest hope that you find what you are looking for, and we will anticipate your return."

A number in the surrounding crowd applauded. Wow, people actually had come to like them. Zack had no idea.

"We'll do our best, Boss," Sacha answered. "And we'll be back before anyone misses us." She and Selena exchanged a nod.

Zack sucked in a breath and braced himself for teleportation. Isis clutched his hand. He hoped she wouldn't notice how sweaty it was.

"Take us to Las Vegas," the sisters said in unison. Their eyes were shut tight, focused on a specific location, one that was no doubt away from the crowds on the Strip. "Take us to Las Vegas."

Selena and Sacha's chant echoed as if they were speaking in a tunnel. Isis' hand tightened around Zack's like a vise while New Salem's quad blurred. Everything around the pyramid formed by the crystals looked like they were seeing it from inside of a soap bubble. A few of the villagers, which included Maya and Jeb, waved goodbye. The rest watched with inquisitive intensity.

Within seconds, everything came back into focus, and they were in between two tall buildings with a green dumpster in front of them. Roaring engines filled the air along with beeping horns. They were sounds alien to the atmosphere of New Salem.

"We're here," Sebastian said, as one of the many suitcases lined up fell on its side.

"Let's check it out!" Isis tapped Zack on the arm and then ran out of the alleyway to the busy Vegas strip. Zack sprinted to join her.

They stopped short on the sidewalk where hordes of people scurried in all directions. Isis leaned the side of her head against Zack's shoulder. "I don't recognize any of them," she said with glee.

"I know. Me either." Zack wrapped his arm around Isis and gave her a squeeze. He felt the same sense of relief she did. These were all strangers that they never saw grow old, die, and then get replaced by their descendants.

Cars passed on the two-way street, which included one public bus that stopped at the corner to let people on and off. Across the asphalt road was the Strip's larger-than-life Ferris wheel, which took up the entire block. The top cabin was higher than even the tallest building, which gave its occupants, at least for the moment, an amazing view.

Although Zack had never ridden on the Ferris wheel, it had been in the heart of Vegas for as long as he could remember. He passed it almost every single day on his way to school. Today, however, it looked even more special, maybe because he hadn't seen it in a while. It was a monument that the lifelong residents of New Salem could never fathom.

His view was suddenly blocked when Simon stepped in front of him. "So, this is Las Vegas." The vampire's head tipped upward at the skyscraper hotels on either side. "It's exactly how you described it, my friends."

"It's the most beautiful city in the world." A grin crossed Zack's lips. No offense to New Salem, but it was nice being back in the world in which he grew up.

"If I may ask, what are these bridges that travel from hotel to hotel?"

"That's how you cross the street on Las Vegas Boulevard," Zack explained. "There's very few traffic lights or crosswalks." Man, how could Simon not notice all the people staring at his eccentric attire as they passed by? Maybe that's exactly what he wanted, to be noticed.

"Another question." Simon removed the sunglasses from his face then raised his arms out, perhaps to make sure he had everyone's attention. "I brought enough blood to last me for weeks. But we will be here far longer. How did your former vampire and my old mentor, Luther, acquire his daily doses?"

"He rummaged through the Vegas desert at night," Isis answered. "He hunted for animals and took their blood."

"Interesting, I will certainly have to try that." Simon's head spun in all directions. "Perhaps later on, one of you could point me in the direction of the Vegas desert?"

"I'm honestly not sure which way it is," Zack admitted.

"Hey, Zack!" Isis pointed down the busy and congested street. "Look at that."

A huge neon sign hung near the top of what Zack was sure had to be The Sapphire. It was high enough and wide enough that they could see it even though it was at least two blocks away. A girl around his and Isis' age stood front and center. She looked out with a twinkle in her amber-colored eyes and a knowing smile across her face. Her pink hair swung from side to side each time she turned her head. Her red blouse was tight enough that it left little of her body to the imagination.

"Who is that?" Zack asked.

A circular white light formed in front of the girl, then another formed to the far left of the electronic billboard. When both lights disappeared, the girl was now on the left. She raised her hands, and bubble-like letters appeared on the rest of the screen. It read, *The Wiccan Circus...Now at The Sapphire Resort and Casino.*

"Whoa," Zack said, under his breath.

"I see The Sapphire replaced us with another witch theme," Sebastian said, from behind Zack and Isis.

"It looks to me like a cheap knock-off." Sacha smirked. "Unlike us. We're the real thing."

"Speaking of us," Selena called out. "We should get to the Felicity and check in. Our meeting with the manager is in less than an hour, and then we only have tonight to set up the theater and get ready. Our first show is tomorrow afternoon."

Simon spun around to face the coven. "Ooh, are we preparing for another teleport?"

"I don't think so," Sebastian answered. "This isn't New Salem where everyone is accustomed to witches materializing out of thin air."

"Yeah, it would freak people out," Sacha added.

"And that is why you use your witchcraft only on stage." Simon slapped his hands together. "That is so clever, my friends. No wonder you were such a success during your time here."

"Right." Sebastian raised a hand. His focus was on the suitcases in the alleyway. They rose from the ground and stood on their wheels. "Let's head on over. Zack, since the Felicity and the Galloway Theater were your stomping grounds, why don't you lead the way?"

Zack threw Sebastian a thumbs-up. Everyone grabbed the handles of their bags. Everyone except Simon who apparently only came with a small cooler filled with blood vials and the costume on his body. Zack rolled his suitcase next to Isis' and, with his free hand, took hers as well. At first, Isis threw him a slanted glance. Then she smiled and said, "Thank you."

Once out of the alleyway, Zack paused and took another look at the girl on the billboard as it repeated its presentation of *The Wiccan Circus*.

"Is everything all right?" Isis asked him.

"I guess."

"Come on, spill."

"It's just...I don't know." Zack shrugged. "I can't believe they copied our show like that."

Sacha rolled her case between Zack and Isis. "I guess they missed us," she said, speeding up and passing them.

Zack had to admit he missed this city. He loved New Salem and even looked forward to recreating the life that he had in a reality that no longer existed. But for now, it felt good to be back home and getting ready to perform again. Magic was once his whole life. This was like reuniting with a piece of himself.

Chapter Six

Later that evening...

Isis sat on the bed in her room, taking a deep breath. Her first day back in Las Vegas wasn't what she expected. She was hoping the day would be spent reacquainting with the Strip, and taking in some of her favorite spots, like the yogurt shop where she first met Zack. Maybe even that restaurant with the enormous ice cream sundaes. Isis also wanted to get a feel for her new home, the Felicity Hotel. It didn't have as many attractions as The Sapphire Resort, but Isis wanted to see what it did have.

Instead, her first eleven hours in their temporary home was spent going over ideas for the show and practicing them on the stage. It felt like they were in the theater for three days. It sure didn't help that, despite his enthusiasm, Simon may have exaggerated his stage experience. He couldn't take cues and was easily distracted in an empty auditorium. His gaffs during practice didn't bode well for the show itself. Their first few shows, so far, were sold out, and they had to come out strong.

Zack, meanwhile, preparing to resume his role as the opening warm-up act, practiced his card tricks at a square table in front of the stage. Isis didn't have time to watch him at work. She was too busy following her mom and dad's show plans, which doubled as her newest lessons on manipulating the energy. It wasn't easy, especially knowing tomorrow she'd have to pull it off in front of an audience. In the few moments she had to look Zack's way, he had frustration written all over his face. At one point, he tossed the cards on the table and left to take a walk.

At least the day was finally done. They all ate together at the Felicity's buffet, which was a special treat. Isis noticed Zack was unusually quiet. In all fairness though, it may have been because the one member of their show who didn't eat dominated the entire conversation. Once they returned to their suites on the top floor, it was time to finally unpack and settle in.

Isis eyed what would be her bedroom for the next ten weeks. The room wasn't as large as the one she had in The Sapphire, or in their New Salem cottage. But it was cozy and even had a walk-in closet for all her clothes. The suite only had one bathroom, which meant she had to be on a morning schedule with her folks. That wasn't a deal breaker, although she had grown accustomed over the last few months to having two bathrooms in their New Salem cottage. Oh well, they'd be back soon enough. At least here the plumbing would always work.

Now that she was done unpacking, Isis focused her thoughts on the living room in the identical suite next door. "Teleport," Isis chanted.

Her bedroom blurred as if looking through a kaleidoscope. Once everything came back in focus, she stood in front of the other suite's couch where Simon was seated and facing the television. He pointed the remote control forward with a huge grin on his face. There was movement in one of the two nearby bedrooms, which Isis presumed was Sacha unpacking.

Simon looked back at Isis. "I do miss television all too much. So many programs on at once. So many choices. I fail to see why you ever left our home country in the first place." His gaze returned to the TV.

Zack, meanwhile, stood in front of the table in the living room with a deck of playing cards in front of him. He lifted the top card and flashed it, revealing a jack of hearts. He then tapped it against his chest and slapped it onto the table next to the rest of the deck. The card was now an ace of spades.

"Not fast enough. Still noticeable," he mumbled, then shook his head. Isis had no idea what part of that amazing switch he thought was noticeable.

"Hey, Zack." Isis leaned across the table opposite from Zack and balanced on her elbows. "It's been a while since we hung out on the Strip. How about we spend some time out there tonight?"

"I can't." Zack spread the cards across the table with the faces up. His eyes never lifted from the cards. "I realized today while practicing that I'm rusty. I need to work on my speed before we go live tomorrow."

Although she tried to understand, Isis was filled with disappointment. She would have bet anything on Zack jumping at the chance to go around Vegas with her. She certainly did not want to go by herself. "Are you sure?" Isis leaned in farther and batted her eyelashes at him. "You're so good with those cards, do you really need to spend the whole night practicing?"

Zack's head popped up. His cheeks had a slight flush to them. "Magic isn't like witchcraft, Isis. If you don't use the skill, you lose it. I don't want to screw up tomorrow in front of our first audience."

One consistency between this and the other nonexistent timeline, Isis realized, was that no one was harder on Zack than himself. When he obsessed over anything, it was best to walk away and give him space. But, damn, she really missed all the times they spent after each show dancing at nightclubs and going out for a bite to eat. Well, at least they had ten weeks to make up for it; she could give him tonight. But what was she going to do to occupy her time?

Zack tossed a card in the air. He tried to catch it between two other cards that were in his left hand. The card just barely missed its target, bouncing off the edge of the top card and falling onto the table. "Damnit!" Zack shook his head. "How'd this happen in just a few months?"

"Don't worry, Hon, you'll get it. You're the best." Isis patted him on the back, but she wasn't sure Zack even noticed.

Isis straightened herself from the table and wandered into one of the two bedrooms where Sacha faced the circular wall mirror, looping an emerald earring into the hole in her right lobe. Her red hair was pulled back into a ponytail. "Hey, Sach," Isis said with a smile. "Any chance you want to hang out tonight?"

"Sorry, Kiddo, no can do." Sacha gave the earring a slight tug. "I have a date, and I expect to be out all evening."

Isis scrunched her face. "A date with who? We just got here." Not to mention they'd spent the entire day together in the theater going over the show and practicing.

"The cute desk clerk that checked us in this morning." Sacha threw Isis a sly grin. "We'll see if I make it home tonight."

"Oh. In that case, have fun."

Isis exited the bedroom as fast as possible before Sacha could elaborate on the details of what she expected on her date. So much for getting out of the hotel tonight. She eyed Simon who was stretched out across the couch with the remote control aimed at the television. He finally stopped flipping channels on an old black-and-white western. She considered asking if he wanted to hang out, but that thought lasted all of half a moment. It was a good chance his idea of a night out wouldn't mesh with hers.

"Hey, Sach!" Isis called. "Do you know where my folks are?"

"Last I saw them, they were heading back to the theater to set up for tomorrow's show. But that was hours ago." Sacha ran a brush across her left eyelash. "I haven't seen or heard from them since. I'd guess they're still there."

"I might as well see if they need any help," Isis said to no one in particular.

She threw one last glance at Zack who flipped a card in the air. This time he caught it between the two cards in the other hand. Isis shut her eyes and focused on The Galloway Theater's locker room in the back of the stage. Isis didn't expect anyone except her folks to be in the theater, but it was better to be careful than materialize out in the open.

"Teleport," she said, and then said it again. Isis closed her eyes and let a wave of the energy pass through her body.

Once she no longer felt the effects of teleportation, Isis reopened her eyes to find herself exactly where she envisioned. The tiny room offstage was set up with a clothesline that ran from one wall to the other. All their outfits for the show were wrapped in plastic and hung one next to the other. Well, all except for Simon's since he was still wearing his only outfit.

Isis exited the locker room and stepped onto the stage. She opened her mouth wide at the sight of how much work had been put into the auditorium in the time she spent unpacking. Where earlier the stage didn't have a curtain, glittering red drapes now hung from a long perpendicular rod high above. It was pulled open on both sides. Multicolored streamers wafted all over the entire theater. Midway through the auditorium, a hoop was tied to a streamer. It was there for Isis' "lighter than air" spell.

The Witches of Vegas was displayed on an electronic banner above the stage. Although they were shut off at the moment, it was written in fancy lights that would shine for the audience when they entered the theater. To their left hung *The Amazing Herb Galloway* banner as a tribute to Zack's late uncle.

Zack's table stood in front of the stage. It had a gorgeous navy-blue cloth covering with a gold lining that wrapped around the edges. A deck of cards sat in the center of the table.

"What do you think?" The voice almost made Isis jump out of her skin. She spun around to find Sebastian standing behind her. He must have just teleported onto the stage from wherever he had been.

"It's beautiful." Isis put a hand on her heart and breathed deeply. "I love it."

"The stage is a lot smaller than what we worked with at The Sapphire." Sebastian stroked the back of Isis' head. "For that matter, it's less than half the seats we had there. But we'll make do. How do you feel about tomorrow?"

"I don't know if I'm ready," Isis answered. "What you're asking me to do…it didn't go well in practice. I don't know what'll happen in front of the audience. If I screw up, it'll kill the whole show."

Sebastian patted Isis on the back. "Controlling the energy on two separate fronts is difficult for any witch. But it is a skill you can master. I'm sure you have memories of doing just that from the other timeline."

"Oh, Dad!" Isis let out a frustrated scream. Something inside her brain snapped. She was sick and tired of the philosophical discussion over if it actually was her and Zack in their memories, or a whole other version of them that no longer existed. Or if any of it happened at all. Technically, it didn't. The worst part of having those memories was the constant comparison that went on in her own mind. She really hated when others did it.

"Isis, what is it?" Sebastian asked with concern. "You know you can talk to me."

"I don't remember me using the energy like that. I remember *her* using the energy like that!" Isis stepped away from Sebastian still facing him. "It was a version of me I'm never going to become because I'm not a vampire. I won't live forever!" Her shouting echoed. "*I'm not her!*"

Isis widened her eyes. Yikes, she had never raised her voice at either of her adopted parents. She certainly didn't mean to lose her temper this time. They were too good to her and deserved better. "Dad, I'm so sorry—"

"This is a sore spot for you, isn't it?"

"I guess so." Isis dropped her head. "It's like having a big sister who has accomplished everything and I'm stuck following in her shadow. Except it's not a sister. It was actually me. I think."

"I won't pretend I can relate. No one can. But I know you're not her, Isis. You're you." Sebastian kept a calm and even tone. There wasn't a hint of hostility toward her outburst. "The training we give you has nothing to do with the potential *she* achieved. This is about bringing you to the peak of *your* potential. I know this is all within your scope. You're strong enough, you're smart enough, and you're focused enough to maintain such control."

"What if I screw it up in front of all those people?"

"Then you screw up." Sebastian shrugged. "That's not a huge issue. You'll do better the next time. You know this has never been about the performance. It's about honing our skills as witches. Just don't make screwing up your goal tomorrow, okay?"

A slight chuckle shot out of Isis' throat. "No, Sir, I won't. I promise."

Sebastian rolled his eyes. "I thought we agreed to stop with the 'sir' stuff. You know how much I dislike that."

"Sorry, Daddy." Isis did know, but it was her way of needling him with a slight tease. She wrapped her arms around Sebastian's waist, dug her head into his chest, and gave him a strong hug.

"Not that I'm complaining, but how did I earn this sudden display of affection?" Sebastian asked through a slight grin. "I'd hope this isn't just guilt over getting upset, is it?"

"No, it's for everything." Isis tightened her grip. "For saving my life when I was nine, then giving me a great one to live. For bringing me into the family. Also, for taking Zack in after his uncle's death. I appreciate that, too."

Sebastian laid a hand against the back of Isis' neck and leaned his chin against the top of her head. "It's a good thing we did. The two of you saved a lot of people, and I mean in *this* reality."

Isis looked up into Sebastian's face, placing her chin against his chest. "I guess we did have a hand in sending Valeria through that portal."

"If not for that, the entire planet would be destroyed and under her rule today. You know that firsthand, don't you?"

Yeah, Isis witnessed the repercussions of Valeria winning when *she* changed the timeline. Thankfully, that happening would never come to pass. Everyone in New Salem gave her kudos for putting time back in order, but if that really was Isis, she knew who to thank for the adult she had—and now would—become.

"If I don't say it enough, I love you and Mom so much."

A few tears rolled down Isis' cheek. She pressed her face tighter against Sebastian's shirt to wipe them from her face. Her love and appreciation for them was genuine, although she made sure not to flaunt those affections in front of Zack. Not so soon after he lost his one and only family member. Mom and Dad were good about that too.

Sebastian stroked her hair, then backed up. "We love you with all our hearts, Isis, and we're also very proud of you." He wiped her moist cheek with the back of his hand then motioned across the theater. "Your mom is in the sound booth setting up the system. How about we give her a hand?"

"Sounds good."

Isis ran ahead to the back of the theater. Now that she expressed her feelings to Dad, it was time to do the same for Mom. She deserved to hear it, too. No need to teleport—they had all night.

Chapter Seven

For Isis, everything came together in her head the
moment she stepped onto the stage. Wearing the mint-
green blouse and black slacks again helped everything
feel right, at least for the moment. Isis opened the show
with her "lighter than air" spell where she floated
throughout the theater. The focus on the energy, along
with the cheers from the audience, helped take her mind
off of the other set of memories drifting through her
head. It was her hope that performing did the same for
Zack, who rocked the card show and warmed up the
audience for the main event.

The time went by in a heartbeat. Isis had been on
stage twice already and was preparing for the third use
of her witchcraft. Peeking through the side curtain, she
watched Selena and Sacha, in matching blue blouses
and black pants, enter separate hardwood trunks on
opposite sides of the stage. Sebastian used an illusion to
make the trunks appear to be on fire. In his black
tuxedo, he looked less comfortable than in New Salem,
but far more in his element.

Once the image of flames subsided, Sebastian
opened each trunk and turned them on their sides to
show the audience that they were empty. Then, with a
motion of Sebastian's hand, the spotlight focused on a
third trunk on the floor in front of the first row. Its lid
creaked open. Selena and Sacha stood from inside, arm

in arm, and exited to the crowd's delighted screams.

The sisters bowed, which elicited a standing ovation. It was a hard act to follow, but that was exactly what Isis had to do. She pulled in a deep breath. It was her turn to take the stage again. She was in the finale, not because what she was about to do would knock the socks off all the acts that preceded, but because it was the most complicated. Isis would use the energy on a level she had never done before except in her recent practices. It was the equivalent of a mid-term exam.

The rapid beat of her heart was at an all-time high. She had sweated through her outfit. Damn, she had been through much worse. Why was this making her so anxious? Being a nine-year-old with foster parents who tried to set her on fire was real stress. So was battling the all-powerful Wiccan vampire, Valeria. At least this time Isis' life wasn't on the line, only her pride if she screwed up. She also wouldn't be taking the stage alone, but did that make it easier or harder? She couldn't be sure.

"Oh, boy!" Simon clapped his hands and leaned his elbow on Isis' shoulder. "This should be tons of fun. Are we ready to amaze?"

"Sure, let's do it," Isis said, feigning an equal level of excitement. At the same time, she backed one step. Simon's elbow fell to his side. It was only their second day in Vegas, and his costume was already giving off a smell.

"Ladies and gentlemen, I hope you've enjoyed the show so far," Sebastian spoke into the microphone. "And it is now time for our grand finale!"

Selena and Sacha took a final bow then exited the stage through the curtain. Sacha ran for one of the towels resting on a nearby table and wiped her brow. Selena stopped short in front of Isis and put a hand under her chin. "Okay, Sweetie, you're up." Selena's bright hazel-colored eyes connected with Isis'. "It's just how you practiced."

"Practice didn't go so well," Isis replied. "The first time, I almost lost the illusion. The second time, I did lose it, and the third time, I dropped Simon."

"He can handle it," Sacha called out. "He has a hard head."

Selena placed her palms against Isis' cheeks. They were warm due to the stage lights. "But the next few times, you were nearly flawless. Concentrating on two spells at once is difficult for any witch. But you're not just any witch. We would never send you out there with anything that's beyond your scope. Just do the best you can, okay?"

"Yes, I'll try to do my best."

"Don't try. Concentrate. Trust your connection to the energy." Selena winked. "You've got this. I know you do."

Selena stepped away, flashing her right hand in a thumbs-up position. Isis peeked over at Zack who was standing three steps behind Selena with his foot on a bridge chair's seat. He gave her a quick nod, showing the confidence he had in her. Isis grinned and returned the nod.

"And now!" Sebastian pointed to the far left of the stage. In response, a wooden chair slid along the floor to the center of the stage. "You saw her earlier as the girl who can fly, but she can do so much more. Please put your hands together once again for our vampire, Simon, and the future goddess of magic, *Isis*!"

Simon skipped onto the stage, bowed, and dropped onto the chair. Isis' step was a bit slower, at least until she heard the smattering of applause. Sebastian squeezed Isis' shoulder as they passed. A moment later, he joined the rest of the cast offstage. Isis waved to the audience, then strolled behind Simon.

"A quick reminder, my young friend," Simon whispered. "Although I am among the undead, I can still very much feel pain. So try not to drop me again, okay?"

"I'll do my best," Isis responded. "And sorry again."

"You will do your best," Simon repeated. "That is hardly reassuring."

Isis cleared her mind and focused on an image of the illusion she wanted to create. It was a forest like the one surrounding New Salem. But in this one, the leaves were brilliant colors and blowing in the wind. At the same time, Isis concentrated on Simon and his chair becoming light as a feather. "Illusion of forest, lighter than air," she mumbled under her breath several times. A stray thought about yesterday's screw-ups tried to find its way into Isis' brain. She quickly forced it out of her head. She only wanted two thoughts and nothing else. The illusion and the weightlessness of the chair.

The energy crackled behind Isis. She sensed it all around her. Isis could see the multicolored leaves from the corners of her eyes. She could also hear the wind rustling those leaves. The audience's "oohs" and "ahhs" meant they could see it, too. The illusion was set for as long as she could hold it, which she hoped would be the entire act. Now, it was time for the second spell.

With a raise of her hand, both the chair and Simon

rose off the stage floor like a balloon. Isis pointed forward. The energy around Simon moved in that direction, taking him just out of reach of the audience members in the front row. A few tried to touch him. When one young girl stood on her chair and stretched out her arm, Isis pulled Simon back to the stage.

The vampire hovered high in the air, swinging from one side of the stage to the other. He waved to the audience, letting them know that he was real. He also swung an arm over his head to show that he wasn't attached to wires or strings of any kind. Enchanting music playing in the background added to the effect. It was a tune chosen by Zack from his uncle's old collection.

"Okay, Isis," Sebastian called from the side. "It's time!"

She knew what he meant. It was time to make this manipulation of the energy even more challenging. She pictured the image of a huge ring of fire. It would form in front of the trees in the canvas of her illusion. It was just like how she did it during practice, but this time Isis was determined not to lose control of Simon's chair. She needed to split her concentration in half, just as she was taught by her folks.

Crackling flames formed overhead. The circle of fire reflected off the crowd, a crowd that sat at the edge of their seats. Isis' hands shook. Maybe creating an image of fire wasn't such a good idea. It brought back bad memories…it made her think of the battles with Valeria. Stay calm, she told herself. Just focus on the task. It's not real fire anyway, just an illusion.

Isis held out her left palm and pushed. Simon's chair hovered toward the circle of fire. Now came the really hard part. She had to control the motion so Simon would fit perfectly through the circle. If any part of him or the chair touched the flame, he'd pass right through it and expose to the audience that it wasn't really there. Damn, illusion was Dad's thing, not hers. But since she didn't really have a *thing*, she agreed to learning all forms of witchcraft.

Simon was probably a heavy guy, but that didn't matter, not with this rendition of her "lighter than air" spell. She levitated him back toward the circle in a slow descent. At first, Simon peeked over his shoulder, but then he made sure the audience saw his frightened expression. Of course, he had nothing to fear, but the audience didn't know that. It was hard keeping him steady while also focusing on the illusion, but the last thing Isis wanted was for it to suddenly fade away.

Simon fanned himself as he went through. Once safely on the other side, he gave the crowd a look of relief. It was a decent performance on his part convincing everyone the fire illusion surrounding him was scalding hot. Their act was almost over. Now, Isis just had to lower Simon to the floor while keeping the forest and the circular flame images intact.

The chair obeyed her mental command and lowered to the stage inch by inch until its legs touched. To the left, Isis saw Zack flip on the lights. That meant she could stop projecting the forest illusion. She let out a deep sigh of relief as the image faded and the back curtain came into view. The audience exploded in applause. Simon stood up and waved to the audience. Isis did the same. She pulled it all off with great success. Of course, she had no idea how much of that was with her family's assistance with keeping both the illusion and Simon intact. But no matter what they did behind the scenes, this was still her moment.

Sebastian ran out on the stage, microphone gripped tightly in his left hand. "Ladies and gentlemen, let's have another hand for *Simon and Isis!*"

Sebastian waved a hand at the two performers, which led to a standing ovation. Simon made a heavy bow as Isis gave the audience a slight curtsy. Sebastian waited for the applause to die down before once again addressing the crowd. "We thank you all for coming to our first show in five months. We hope you enjoyed yourselves because, as of this moment, I am happy to announce, *The Witches of Vegas are back!*" Sebastian stretched his hand forward and dropped the microphone. He exited stage left.

Once the applause died down, Isis followed Sebastian. She enjoyed the sight of his embrace with Selena and his high five to Sacha. Isis, meanwhile, stopped in front of Zack. She expected to be greeted with a huge smile and a similar embrace. Instead, his eyes were wide as he gawked over her shoulder. "What is it, what's the matter?" Isis asked.

"I think we're about to have a problem!"

Zack's gasp caused Isis and the others to turn to the stage where Simon had not yet left. The vampire bent over and picked up the microphone. Most of the audience were still in their seats. Those who had stood to leave turned back to the stage.

"What is he doing?" Sebastian whispered.

"Ladies and gentlemen, both alive and dead," Simon's loud voice screeched through the speakers causing feedback. "On behalf of The Witches of Vegas, we hope you all had a *ghoulish* time."

Simon paused. If it was for laughs or applause, he received neither. Apparently, that didn't stop him from going on. "Now, folks, I did not start with the witches' original show. I am what you may call a late broomer." His voice echoed due to the microphone being too close to his mouth.

"Broomer?" Isis asked.

"But now that they have welcomed me into their troupe, let me say that I enjoyed performing for you today. In fact, I just want to suck my fangs into all of you. However, we are The Witches of Vegas, not the vampires of Vegas, so I will make a hexception so you can leave with an en-witching experience!"

Sacha let out a loud groan. It matched the collective sound coming from the audience. Soon their groans turned into outright boos.

"Oh my, I do hope I'm not driving you batty." Simon giggled at his own joke. He was the only one who did. "I do realize that as a vampire, I can be a real pain in the neck."

The booing got louder. Isis spun around to her folks. "How long are we going to let him do this?"

"If his puns get any worse, this audience might lynch him," Zack said.

"I feel like lynching him myself," Sacha replied.

"Selena, Sacha, get ready to teleport him." Sebastian stepped forward. "I'll cover you with a smoke illusion."

"Good idea." Selena grabbed her sister's hand. "Let's do it!"

"In all seriousness, folks, I normally hunt for fresh animal blood day and night in the Vegas desert," Simon explained to the crowd. "The only time I am not hunting is when I take a coffin break."

One young male voice rose over the booing. "Make it stop!" the boy shouted.

Sebastian shut his eyes. A wave of green smoke rose from the stage floor. Once the smoke was thick enough, Selena and Sacha spoke at the same time, "Teleport Simon."

"Did you hear me? I said a coffin break— Oh my!"

The vampire faded from the stage, then rematerialized between Isis and Zack. Sebastian opened his eyes and waved a hand. The smoke disappeared, revealing an empty stage. The crowd went silent...then they clapped and cheered. A chant of "witches" broke out. Thankfully many in the audience thought it was all part of the show's conclusion.

Selena rubbed a hand against Sebastian's arm. "Okay, show saved."

"Not to mention our reputations," Sacha muttered.

Five angered glares focused on Simon.

"Oh, that was so fantastic!" He took another bow, this one aimed at his fellow stage performers. He frolicked to the dressing room door. "It was fantastic, indeed. I cannot wait for our next performance."

Sebastian pointed to the dressing room. "Moving forward, we have to keep that from happening again."

"Agreed," Selena responded.

"Oh, definitely." Sacha sighed.

Isis waited for Sacha and her folks to walk off. She closed in on Zack, leaning her forehead against his cheek. "So, now that we've had a successful first show," she whispered in his ear. "How about taking your girlfriend out on the town?"

"Yeah, I'm down for that," he said with a lot more excitement in his voice. "Let's check out the sights."

Chapter Eight

Zack hadn't felt this sense of belonging in a while. Standing in the middle of the Las Vegas Strip with the night sky lit up by all the bright lights and neon signs, it was like seeing an old friend, one that had been a huge part of his life since he was a young boy. His emotional attachment was still there. Even before he moved in at the age of six, Uncle Herb used to take him out on the town and show him the sights. It was a pleasure Zack had since experienced in a new way by doing the same for Isis.

Man, to think she lived just a few blocks away from him since the age of nine, yet she knew nothing about how much this city had to offer. After Zack's uncle was killed in the battle with Valeria, The Witches of Vegas took Zack in. After that, he spent each night showing Isis around town and taking her to all of his favorite places. Well, that actually all happened in the other timeline. Here they had only started to take in the sights for a few weeks before going to New Salem and deciding to stay. But Las Vegas was the exact same place there as it was here.

"So, where do you want to go?" Isis ran her fingers through her thick brown hair.

The question made Zack pause. He really wanted to make this time something special, especially after the way he blew her off last night. Should they hit a location they used to enjoy, or one that was brand new? He hadn't given it any thought because he was focused on his old card techniques to open their show.

"Is there a place you want to check out?" Zack threw the ball back into her court. She did have a tendency of asking where he wanted to go when she actually had an idea in her head. Maybe this was one of those times. "We have all night. We could hit a few places unless you have something in mind."

"Ooh, how about the fountain show?" Isis asked. "I remember we saw it about a dozen times. But I think this you and I only went there once."

"I get what you're saying," Zack said to answer the confused look on Isis' face. They both still suffered from the confusion of which memories came from which reality. Talking it out for the last few months with Isis helped, but the conflict in their heads still crept up once in a while. Her answer was always to talk to Doctor Mac, but Zack just didn't like the idea of being analyzed by a shrink.

He checked his watch. "If the schedule hasn't changed, the fountain show should start in about twelve minutes. Let's head on over."

They walked along the sidewalk with hands clasped. The sound of traffic was loud, at least compared to the tranquil quiet of New Salem. Being honest, Zack preferred the roar of the engines and the beeping horns over the constant mooing and pig squeals. At least the moving vehicles didn't pull him out of bed unlike the roosters' early morning wake-up calls.

Hordes of people walked in either direction on both sides of the street while cars passed at various speeds.

The Strip was always a crowded place. To think, in that other reality, the entire area was destroyed by a time-hopping Valeria. Now there was no shred of evidence it ever happened in the first place. Zack spent many nights questioning whether his memories were real or not. The only proof they had was the existence of New Salem, which they discovered in that other reality. Now it was their new home in this reality.

"You're awfully quiet," Isis said.

"Sorry, just thinking." Zack threw his arm around Isis' shoulders and gave her a peck on her temple.

After what could have been seconds or minutes into their walk, Isis stopped in her tracks, which forced Zack to stop as well. It snapped him out of his thoughts. "What is it?" he asked.

"Check out where we ended up." Isis pointed at the huge resort property with a tall building that took up the entire block. The top floor protruded from the rest of the building. In the property's front yard stood statues of ancient Greek characters—mostly in robes—and a huge screen that played the resort's commercial.

"It's The Sapphire, your old home."

Isis' wide eyes and open mouth revealed how much she missed that stage, and how disappointed she was that they couldn't return here to perform. Zack sensed it from the entire family, and he empathized with those feelings. But deep down, he was kind of giddy over the fact that The Witches of Vegas were performing in his house, and on the stage named after his uncle. The fact that Uncle Herb couldn't be here to see this was what caused Zack's disappointment.

Under the screen, a teen around their age stood behind an old wood table. His white button-down shirt and red tie didn't mesh with the multicolored doo rag wrapped around his head. There was one couple along with a young boy and a younger girl watching him place coins across the table. He covered one with his left hand, then removed the hand to show his audience that the coin had disappeared.

"It looks like The Wiccan Circus has a table for magic outside the hotel like I used to," Zack said.

Isis grabbed him by the elbow. "Let's check it out."

Zack and Isis moved swiftly to the table, standing to the right of the family of four. The table had a black drape, which hung along the edge. It said "The Wiccan Circus" in bubble letters that were clearly hand sewn onto the cloth. The magician laid four copper dollar coins across the table at equal spacing.

Zack eyed them carefully. They looked real enough although there were lots of "special coins" used by magicians that looked authentic to the naked eye.

"I would like another volunteer," the magician announced in a British accent to his small audience. His head spun to Zack. "How about you, Sir?"

Sir? Zack lifted his eyebrows. "Um, that's okay. I just want to watch."

"I'm afraid I must insist." The magician clapped his hands. "Everybody, give our new friend a proper round of applause."

The family across the table clapped. So did Isis. "Okay, sure. Why not?" Zack knew personally what it was like to get stung by an audience member who didn't want to participate. It was awkward and a momentum killer. He didn't want to stick a fellow performer—especially one of his peers—in that predicament.

Zack stepped up to the table. He caught the smirk on Isis' face just before she threw a hand over her mouth. The magician took Zack's wrist and turned it palm up. He placed one of the coins in Zack's hand and pressed a finger across it which he held for several seconds. He then closed Zack's palm into a fist. Although Zack felt the ridges of the coin indented against his skin, he was sure the magician had palmed it.

"Cheers, Mate. Now, everyone keep an eye on the coin, which is now in my volunteer's fist." The magician gripped Zack's wrist with his right hand. He picked up another coin from the table with his left hand and balled it into a fist. Then he swung his fist in a circular motion for effect. "Watch as the coin magically disappears from his hand…"

He tapped Zack's wrist, then pulled his fingers open. They revealed an empty palm; the coin had vanished. Zack feigned surprise.

"…and watch the coin reappear in my hand." The magician opened his hand, revealing two dollar coins. The other couple and their children all gasped, then applauded. Isis clapped her hands as well. Zack did the same. The magician folded his hands and bowed.

"Thank you, everyone, and I hope to see you all tonight at The Wiccan Circus. I can assure you that tonight you will be even more amazed at what we do."

The couple and the children walked off in one direction. Zack and Isis did the same but the opposite way. Isis wrapped her hands around Zack's bicep. "Do you know how he did that?" she whispered in a teasing girlfriend manner.

Zack rolled his eyes. "I'll bet even you know how

he did that."

"Hey, wait up!" the magician shouted.

The two about-faced to see the guy run out from behind the table. He rushed up to Zack and Isis. "Let me introduce myself." He held his fist straight out. "I'm Thomas. Thomas Leverton, performer for The Wiccan Circus."

Zack tapped Thomas's fist with his own. "Hi, Thomas. I'm Zack. This is—"

"I know exactly who you both are," Thomas replied with excitement. "Zack Galloway and Isis Flores Rivera."

"I prefer Isis Quinn-Santell," she answered. Her face scrunched. "How do you know us?"

Thomas laughed. "Oh, come on now. You're part of The Witches of Vegas. Your show was famous around here for years." His head spun from far left to far right. "Are Sebastian Santell and the Quinn sisters here as well?"

"Nah, it's just us out tonight." Zack threw an arm across Isis' shoulders. "Am I right in guessing you're from England?"

"Aye, Leeds to be specific." Thomas pressed two fingers against the center of his chest. "I've been learning magic since I was a wee tyke. My family moved to the states around five years ago. Soon after I got my own card, and now I'm a Las Vegas immigrant."

"Is the whole show from Leeds?" Isis asked.

"Nah, lass, just me." Thomas patted his shirt pocket with excitement. "Hey, I have a few comp tickets left for tonight's Wiccan Circus performance. You'd like to come check it out, wouldn't you?"

Isis threw a glance at Zack. While attending a magic show didn't top Zack's "to do" list for entertainment, Isis definitely looked interested, and it wasn't like he had anything in mind for the night. This may have been the answer. The price was certainly right. "Do you want to see their show?" Zack asked.

"Yeah, I'm totally down!" Isis' answer came quickly. "How about you?"

"Sure." Zack turned back to Thomas. "Thank you, we appreciate it."

"Then come right this way." Thomas turned around and waved a hand toward the theater's entrance. "And prepare yourselves for what will be a most brilliant performance."

Chapter Nine

Zack dropped into the auditorium seat next to Isis. It was against the left aisle in the last row on the floor level. Hardly VIP seating, but not bad for free tickets. There had to be at least a thousand heads in front of them, but the seats in each row were slightly higher than the row in front. The setup gave everyone a clear view of the red curtain in front of the stage.

"I'm going to put my arm around you. Is that okay?" Zack asked with a hint of levity.

"Of course it is." Isis flashed him a cheese grin. "After all this time, do you still really need to ask?"

"I guess not." Zack slipped his arm across Isis' back. "It's still weird, two sets of memories, both feel real. You know what I mean?"

"I do." Duh, of course she did, maybe better than he did.

Once his arm draped, Isis pressed the back of her head into his shoulder. Her hand clutched his knee. Despite the long history they shared, Zack still felt special that this amazing girl—a shy and humble, yet all-powerful witch—thought enough of him to fall in love. He felt the same about her. Zack hadn't been the most popular kid in school, ever. He wasn't the captain of the football team, or the center of anyone's social circle. Yet of all the girls who surrounded him in his school, both in Las Vegas and New Salem, there was no one he'd rather have at his side than Isis. She looked up at him, a message that even though she wasn't reading his mind, she knew what he was thinking, and in this moment they were on the same page. He leaned down and kissed her just as the lights went out.

Circus music blared through the speakers, although it was slower than the typical big-top theme, and it had a metal-like rhythm. A spotlight hit the curtain, which shot straight up. Zack raised his eyebrows, immediately impressed by the motif. The curtain that ran across the entire backdrop was shaped like a genuine circus tent. Red and white stripes ran from the top to the floor.

A metal swing hung from the ceiling. It reminded Zack of the metal hoop The Witches of Vegas used for Isis' "lighter than air" act except it was on two chains, one on each side of the seat. What a shame they never thought of a swing.

A sweet older female voice with a slight rasp to it echoed over the music. "The circus has been a part of our lives forever," it said. "The concept started in the sixteenth century when witches existed among us all throughout the world. They lived in secret, hiding their amazing gifts…until today, on this very stage. Prepare yourselves for amazement."

"Can we sue them for this?" Isis whispered. Zack wanted to ask the same question.

The theater lights returned, but they were dim. Three clowns appeared in the aisle next to Zack and Isis. All three were males and looked young under all that white and red face makeup and orange-haired clown wigs. They wore skintight T-shirts and multicolored pants. Zack took notice of the third clown in the row. At first he was hard to recognize, but soon it became clear that it was Thomas.

In the right-end aisle of the auditorium, three female clowns stood in the back. Like the men, they wore similar makeup and multicolored clown wigs, only theirs had long hair. Unlike the men, they wore bright multicolored bikinis. The women, who also had to be teenagers as well, were far more animated than the male clowns, waving to the audience and throwing kisses from their bright-red lips.

The two lead clowns in each row simultaneously stretched their arms out like birds. They suddenly floated high over the crowd and glided to the front of the theater. They landed feet-first onto the stage. The next two did the same. Zack leaned forward, examining every inch of Thomas just before he, along with the last female clown, took to the air and then landed on the stage. The crowd cheered.

"Isis!" Zack tapped her. "I didn't catch any wires. Plus, the women are in bikinis. There's nowhere to hide a harness."

"What are you saying, Zack?" Isis whispered back.

"I'm not sure. Are they witches like you?"

Zack expected Isis to roll her eyes at the question, and he would have deserved it. His credibility dwindled on that subject from day one when Zack suspected everyone he came across of having a Wiccan connection. One thing Zack did know, however, was stage magic. He practically grew up on a stage. Even if they came up with an alternate way of pulling off a flying illusion, there still had to be a gimmick somewhere on the performers, but one that could slip by Zack's trained eyes? And especially on the girls in those outfits that hid absolutely nothing? Possible but not likely.

"I thought I felt the energy in the room when they went up," Isis answered. "But I don't sense a connection in any of them. I must have been mistaken. They're not witches."

"They have to be."

"I'm telling you, Zack, they're not."

The performers formed two straight lines on the far ends of the stage. They pointed to the center where a clear circle of distorted air formed. The curtain in the back of the circle looked like it was a tank filled with water. Isis insisted that none of the performers were witches. But if this wasn't the work of witches, then these were stellar magicians who hid their talents in the guise of a circus performance.

"You said you sensed the energy," Zack said in Isis' ear. "Could there be another witch somewhere doing all of this?"

Isis shrugged. Her eyes never left the stage. Zack leaned forward in his chair. The circle reminded him of the portal Selena and Sacha created that led to the Other World. Had The Witches of Vegas done something like this on stage, Zack would have made sure there was a projector nearby to make sure their secret stayed safe.

Suddenly, someone stepped out, and the circle disappeared. The girl, around Zack and Isis' age, had a look of confidence he had only seen in one other face so young, and she was the president of an entire village. This girl's dyed pink hair, which hung down to her shoulders, swung as she sprinted to the front of the stage. It blended well with her strapless red dress that barely covered her ankles. The belt around her waist sparkled as the spotlight hit it straight on.

"That's the girl from the billboard," Zack mumbled.

Her eyes were wide and bright but with a slight slant and confidence that matched her grin. It was as if those orbs made contact with every single member of the audience. Zack caught her amber irises even from the back of the theater. He had a hunch they were colored contacts, but either way, there was no doubt in his mind that she was a lifelong stage performer just like him.

"Zack!" Isis nudged him in the ribs with her elbow. "That girl! *She's* a witch!"

"For sure?"

"Yes, I sensed it the moment she stepped through that portal."

The music changed into a slower remake of "March of the Wooden Soldiers." The girl raised her hands and pointed them at the two lines of circus clowns. Circular portals opened in front of the clowns who marched one at a time straight through and disappeared. Instantaneously, the clowns paraded from similar portals in the back of the theater. They marched down the aisle and back to the stage in random directions.

"Whoa!" Zack exclaimed. "That's witchcraft?"

Isis opened her mouth to respond, but no words came out. She just shook her head. Zack thought back to the way Selena and Sacha, two of the most powerful witches other than Isis he'd ever known, struggled to create one portal. This girl was making them with ease. Of course, her portals were going all over the theater, not across the world or between dimensions the way Selena's and Sacha's did.

With the clowns dancing in a circle around the stage, the girl pointed to the floor. A distorted portal opened under her feet, and she fell straight through. She reappeared near the theater's ceiling and dropped straight down. Her descent was halted when she landed in a sitting position on the swing. The crowd gave her an explosive ovation while she kicked her legs and swung. Soon the clowns hovered in the air as if the stage's gravity had suddenly switched off. Many things happened at the same time with the music blaring at ear-piercing decibels, but the audience seemed to be digging it.

"There's got to be other witches back there," Isis mumbled. "There's no way this one girl is doing all of it by herself."

The clowns floated back to the stage, landing on their feet. They formed a circle underneath the swing. The girl kicked her legs harder, causing a high arc. She leaped off the swing. The audience gasped. Yet another portal opened in front of her. The girl flew straight through and disappeared. The clowns scampered, opening up their circle which revealed the girl on the stage, safe and sound. The cheers and applause shook the entire building.

"Zack!" Isis shouted. "Check out the glowing on the stage floor!"

The glows consisted of five spots with colors shining various hues of light, each no larger than pebbles, and equal distances from one another forming a pentagon around the stage. Zack couldn't believe his eyes. Enchanted crystals were being used to enhance a witch's control within its perimeter. The Witches of Vegas used them during shows on occasion, but Zack always made sure they were placed away from the audience's view. The Wiccan Circus, however, had them out in the open.

Zack peeked back and forth, from one end to the other. Of course, there were no gimmicks anywhere to be found. This was pure witchcraft, and they weren't even trying to hide it. To think that was just their opening act. Zack had a strong feeling this show would break even more Wiccan barriers. No wonder The Sapphire didn't want The Witches of Vegas back. They had the next big thing on their stage already.

Chapter Ten

One Hour Later...

The show was over. Isis had to admit, she was impressed. The performers stood in a line on the stage, holding hands, and took their final bow. The girl with the hot-pink hair jumped in front of the line and raised her arms, acknowledging the standing ovation the audience was giving them. The curtain closed. The theater lights came on. People made their way into the aisles to the doors, two of which led to the Strip, the other to the hotel lobby.

"What'd you think?" Isis asked, although the scowl on Zack's face answered the question for her.

"It was absolutely amazing," Zack growled. "Filled with impossible illusions. The audience loved it."

"But?"

"But..." Zack waved a hand at the stage. "I put a lot of work into making sure what you do up there can be explained away through traditional magic. I protect the big secret. This show didn't bother with any of that. There wasn't the slightest attempt to cover up the use of Wiccan power. They even used enchanted crystals right out in the open."

Isis listened to Zack's rant and nodded. He was right about how much work he put into scrutinizing and camouflaging their acts. It was his primary job, to make sure there were enough red herrings in place for any magicians or skeptics in the audience to find. Better those types think they knew how the show was put together rather than stumble upon the fact that the illusions weren't illusions at all but were the creation of witches.

"I only sensed the one witch on the stage, but I get your point." Isis rubbed Zack's arm in an attempt to calm him down. "They do call it a circus, not a magic show. So maybe the magic world won't bother with it?"

"Hopefully," he replied, "but if they do, it could be really bad for your kind on a global level."

A neon sign lowered from above the stage. Isis stepped forward to get a good look. In bright orange lettering, the sign read, *Check out The Wiccan Circus Gift Shop in the Sapphire Theater's lobby.* It was a good distraction. Isis sure needed one so she could forget Zack's use of the term "your kind." He didn't say it often, but she hated when he did. Zack may not have been a witch, but he was part of her coven, and as far as she was concerned, he was every bit "her kind."

"How about we go check out the gift shop?" Isis asked.

Zack's face scrunched, meaning he was ready to protest. But he then made that curious tilt that Isis found so adorable. After seeing it, she could always forgive whatever unthinking remark he made. "Yeah, why not? Let's see what they have," he answered.

Once through the theater doors, Isis and Zack were surrounded by four long rectangular tables with red cloth coverings and a performer behind each one. Three of the tables were piled high with shirts, programs, and baseball caps with The Wiccan Circus logo on them.

The table nearest them held two open cardboard boxes. They reminded Isis of the cheap stuff she'd seen at flea markets as a young child, except these had expensive price tags.

Isis peeked inside the cardboard box closest to her. It was filled with what looked like hundreds of diamond-like baubles. "Enchanted crystals," the teenage boy behind the table said. "They're the key to our miracles on stage. Have a piece of the power for just one dollar each, or five for four dollars."

Isis picked up one crystal and held it in front of her face. It was far lighter than what an actual crystal would feel like, and she was quite familiar with actual enchanted crystals. She didn't sense even a drop of connection in whatever this cheap knockoff was made from.

Zack pulled one from the box as well, then looked toward Isis. "Let me guess—"

"Yup," Isis quickly answered. She smiled to the worker behind the table. "Maybe later, thank you." She dropped her "crystal" back into the box. Zack did the same.

Across the lobby, Thomas, out of makeup and his head rewrapped in the bandana, was speaking with the pink-haired girl from the stage. Thomas pointed toward Isis and Zack. The two walked their way. Isis' eyebrows rose at the girl's short, tight outfit. She imagined her folks would kill her if they caught her in something like that...if she hadn't already died of embarrassment.

"Ahoy, my new buddies," Thomas shouted as they closed in. He stepped forward and placed a hand on the girl's shoulder. "I'd like to introduce you to Amelia

Cross, the team captain for our fancy gig."

Amelia had a definite arrogance in her step. Her head panned down to Isis' blue jeans and lavender T-shirt. "Well, well, the famous teen couple from The Witches of Vegas show. Welcome to The Sapphire Theater, or should I say welcome back?"

"Thank you." Isis raised her eyebrows. She had never once thought of Zack and herself as a "famous couple." Did their reputations proceed them, even after a five-month hiatus?

"So, you're a, um…" Zack leaned in close. "You know—"

"A witch?" Amelia replied, rather loudly. "Yes, I am."

Damn, so much for subtlety. Zack spun his head to some of the other shoppers. Isis was sure those were his instincts kicking in to protect their secret. A woman and her young son stood at the nearest table purchasing crystals. Even if they had overheard Amelia's remark, there was no indication that they were fazed by it.

Amelia threw her hands against her hips. "So, what did the two of you think of our rookie show?"

"It's absolutely amazing," Zack answered. "But aren't you worried about exposure? There are a lot of skeptics in Vegas trying to make names for themselves."

"We're not concerned." Amelia waved a hand in the air. "No one in that audience is watching our show and thinking it might be real." She rolled her eyes. "Would you like to meet our director?"

"You have a director?" Isis asked.

"Don't you?" Thomas threw a wide-eyed glance at Amelia, then back at Isis.

"My mother runs the show from backstage." Amelia spun around, then waved everyone to follow her. "Come on back. I know she'll be hyped to meet you two."

"Your mother runs the entire show by herself?" Zack asked, as he and Isis followed from two steps behind Amelia and Thomas. "Is everything that happened out there thanks to her witchcraft?"

"Miss Cross is the creator of The Wiccan Circus. She recruited us all," Thomas said, peeking over his shoulder. "She's like a mum to the whole team."

"Yes, she also handles most of the heavy lifting." Amelia reached for the curtain and held it open for Isis and Zack to walk through. "Everything except for my parts. That's all me and my gifts."

"Your use of the energy is impressive," Isis said. "Those portals you make, they're real next level."

"At this point, they should be." Amelia smirked. "That's what my Wiccan connection was focused on since it first manifested. Portals are what I do. I was taught nothing else, so I decided to be the best at it."

The four walked through the backstage to what used to be The Witches of Vegas' dressing room. The room was empty except for a short adult lady with long gray hair that had several thin black streaks running from the scalp. She wore a white robe with a black belt.

Boxes slid across the floor, positioning themselves against the wall. Costumes on hangers levitated in the air and hung themselves on a metal rack in front of the woman. If she noticed the group entering the dressing room, she was determined to finish putting everything in order before acknowledging them.

"Zack!" Isis grabbed his arm and whispered,

"She's a witch, and a powerful one, too." Although her housecleaning made it obvious even if Isis hadn't sensed the lady's connection.

"Mother, we have guests," Amelia announced. "Let me introduce to you—"

"I know exactly who they are," the woman sang, never looking their way. It was the same raspy tone that narrated the show through the speakers.

She slowly turned to face them, and then marched across the room, bringing herself into Isis' personal space. Her deep brown eyes were wide and inviting. The huge smile lit up the room despite the heavy wrinkles that surrounded it. "It is truly a pleasure to meet you both," she said in a warm and friendly tone. "My name is Erisa Cross, but you may call me Erisa."

Zack reached out with his right hand. "It's nice to meet you."

Ignoring Zack's hand, Erisa leaned down, bringing herself nose to nose with Isis. Her heavy cigarette breath made Isis' nose twitch. "I see my suspicions about The Witches of Vegas were, indeed, correct. You are connected to Mother Earth's Wiccan energy as well." She glanced at Zack. "You, however, are not. I see your show is a conglomerate of the connected and the non-connected."

Erisa stepped back and stretched out her arms. "As you have seen, since your abrupt departure, The Wiccan Circus follows in your mighty footsteps."

Amelia stepped between Isis and Zack, placing her arms across both their shoulders. "Thanks for paving the way, guys."

It did not escape Isis' notice that she gave Zack a particularly hard squeeze, or that she placed her nose against his cheek. Zack must have noticed as well based on how red his face had become.

"Um, are you two the only witches in the show?" Zack asked.

Erisa held out an arm with her palm facing up. Her fingers were covered in rings. She motioned it to the other cast members who had joined them, Thomas and a girl on his left side, a boy a few years younger on the right. "None of my cast share our connection to the Earth except my daughter. However, for a few hours each night, they get to experience the energy directly."

"Wow," Isis exclaimed. "You control everything that happens on stage from behind the curtain?"

Erisa folded her hands and smiled. "We all have our secrets behind the curtain, my dear. Now, if you will please excuse me, I have business I must attend to. I thank you for visiting. I have a sense we will see a lot of one another in the future." With that, the word "teleport" glided off Erisa's tongue, and she faded away.

"I like her," Zack said. "She seems a bit kooky, but real cool. Well, for an older person, that is."

"Yup, that's my mom." Amelia laughed. "Kooky, but cool."

But something about her rubbed Isis the wrong way. She couldn't put a finger on it—maybe her Wiccan senses were triggered, or simply a girl's intuition, but despite the outward friendliness, something in her gut said nothing about the woman felt legit.

Chapter Eleven

The next morning...

Zack skipped the celebratory breakfast his "coven" was enjoying in the hotel's buffet. Of course, this took them all by surprise since he rarely missed a meal, especially the first one of the day. But he was on a secret mission. Isis' birthday was coming up, and he wanted to surprise her with something nice.

This should have been an easy task. Zack knew Isis better than anyone in the world, including the family that raised her. But shopping was never on his list of things he liked to do or was good at. It was hard enough walking into a store filled with jewelry and various types of products enjoyed by the more feminine of the species. Well, it was this or a clothing store, and he would not try to buy Isis clothes. She didn't even like the ones he picked for himself.

Damn, he had so many memories from the reality where they were together for almost two centuries. How come he couldn't remember any of the presents he got her during that time? Probably because for most of that history, they were vampires, so their wants and needs were different. All they ever needed in that time was blood every twenty-four hours. The clothes they wore, or any other types of "presents" they may have exchanged, were made by witches and seamstresses in

New Salem. Those didn't really stand out in his memories either.

Sebastian and Selena were kind enough to give Zack his salary from the show in advance—they were generous with his cut even though he was just the opening act and the non-Wiccan magic advisor. They also handled all his needs, so he didn't have much use for the money. Then again, between living in a hotel, and then New Salem, they didn't really need it either.

Now that Zack had a pocket full of cash, it was time to find something Isis would like. This particular store was high-end, like most of the stores in the Strip's malls, and filled with teen and preteen aged girls. They were all far more comfortable browsing the shelves than he even this early in the morning. As the only guy there, Zack felt very much out of place. He hoped to just find something, purchase it, and get out. So far that wasn't working to plan.

He suddenly saw his salvation in a display case filled with small plastic boxes with locks on them. Best of all, they were at prices that were well within Zack's range. Isis would love one of those for all of her keepsakes. They included tickets to shows they attended and their mini golf scorecards. Hell, Isis even held on to receipts from their trips to the frozen yogurt shop. Right now, she kept all these mementos from their dates in a paper bag. One of these lock boxes, or "memory boxes" as the sign above the display said, would be a perfect present.

The only issue was that there were so many to choose from. He wanted to get her one that had hearts in the design. Unfortunately, that narrowed it down to almost all of them, each with differing heart-based patterns. Wow, this was a lot harder than he expected.

Zack lifted one of the memory boxes and balanced it against his palm. It was light, although weight was probably not the best way to judge which one she would like. He opened the top to find the box had decent room inside. "Okay, which one of you should be Isis' birthday present?" he asked the display case. "Maybe you or one of your friends?"

A female voice spoke from behind. "Do you always talk to inanimate objects like they're people?"

Zack's head popped up. He recognized that high-pitched voice immediately although he hadn't noticed her anywhere in the store when he walked through.

"Hey, Amelia. How are you this morning?"

Did she actually teleport into a store full of people? Based on all that happened last night, Amelia and her mother were reckless when it came to hiding their witchcraft. But was she that brazen? Of course, she could have just walked in, or perhaps she was already shopping in the store and Zack just didn't see her. Anything was possible.

"Oh, I'm good, real good." Amelia grabbed Zack's arm and turned him around so they could look eye to eye. It took him a moment to take Amelia in. For some reason, he expected her to be in the same skimpy outfit she wore on stage. A ridiculous thought, he realized, as he looked over her grey sweat suit. It was damp and pressed against her body, which Zack took as a hint that she had just finished a run or a jog.

"You look lost," she said. "I'm betting this isn't your usual hangout locale."

Zack shook his head and let out a sigh. Lost was a good way to describe his predicament. "Isis' birthday is in a couple of days, so I'm trying to find a nice memory box for her. To me, they all look the same."

Amelia took the lockbox from Zack's hand. "It sounds like you need a female perspective."

"I think that would help a lot, yeah. I know she likes heart designs, but that's as far as I've made it so far."

"For starters, why one of these things?" Amelia placed the memory box back on the display case. "They're mushy, but bland. Why not get her something really special? There's an awesome lingerie store a few blocks from here right off the Strip."

Lingerie? Zack's cheeks went warm. "I don't think Isis would be into that. She's more the traditional type."

"In other words, lame and boring, just like these boxes. Gotcha." Amelia eyed the display case with the scrutiny of an expert. After several moments, she reached into the back and pulled out a silvery one in the shape of a heart with five tiny diamond-shaped crystals. Although Zack was sure these crystals weren't enchanted like the ones witches use to enhance their Wiccan power, they certainly had a lot of similarity, at least in appearance. The five crystals were even at the ends of the box forming a pentagon shape. Whoever designed it must have had some knowledge of the Wiccan world.

"This one's cute." Amelia held out her hand with the memory box displayed on her palm. "You think Isis will like it?"

Zack leaned in and examined the box. He definitely liked it, especially the way the store's ceiling lights made it shine. Isis would like it, too. But how did he not catch it after examining every inch of the display case?

It was all the way in the back. Maybe he wasn't looking as carefully as he thought.

"Yeah, okay, I think that one will do." Zack reached out for the lockbox. "Thanks a lot."

"Anytime." Amelia pulled the box back just before Zack's fingers touched it. "I'm hanging with some of my crew after our show tonight at The Sapphire's nightclub lounge. Why don't you meet us there?"

"That sounds like fun," he answered. "I'll see if Isis is up for it."

Amelia held out the lockbox again. This time she allowed Zack to wrap his fingers around it, although she kept a solid grip on her end. "Interesting that you need to check with Isis before you can commit. Is she in charge of you or something?"

Zack's head popped back. "I'm sorry, what?"

"Like, if she's not up for hanging out tonight, you can't come?"

"No, no, it's, um...not that, not at all," Zack stammered. "We like to do things together. We're a couple, and we make plans together."

"So you consider her before making a decision. That's so sweet, Zack." Amelia's amber-colored eyes connected with his. Her hands had wrapped around both his hand and the memory box. She squeezed tight. "You really are a good boyfriend. She's such a lucky girl."

Zack always considered himself the lucky one, and that's exactly what he wanted to tell Amelia. But the words wouldn't roll off his tongue. Looking in her eyes, it was like swimming in a pool full of honey. He felt both intrigued and intimidated by her. All he could say was, "Thank you for the help."

"Anytime, Zack." Amelia released her grip of his hand and the lockbox. She leaned in and whispered, "Hold on to that present and don't let the others know you have it. You don't want her to find out before you're ready to give it to her, right? So keep it on you all the time."

Zack suddenly found himself staring at the curves along Amelia's face. They were about as perfect as her smooth skin. Of course, she wasn't Isis. She was different. Maybe a bit cooler. How long had he been staring? A moment? A minute? Did she notice? Maybe. Damn, what the hell was he doing?

Finally, his head cleared. "Um, right. Okay. Thank you." Zack pressed the small box against his chest. For a moment, he forgot he was holding it between his sweaty palms. "Maybe I'll see you later tonight?"

Amelia finally stepped back. "I sure hope so, Zack."

She winked at him, then walked off. As much as he tried, Zack couldn't stop watching her stroll through the store and out the door. Zack stared down at the memory box...the one he chose thanks to Amelia. The wink and her smile...they were flirtatious and flattering. Her perfume still lingered around him. It smelled like fresh flowers covering his nostrils and flowing up to his brain. Of course he wasn't interested. His one true love was Isis. Isis was the girl he had been through hell and back with, a memory only they shared, together. He'd never even consider giving his love to someone else, especially someone he just met.

Still, no one had ever looked at him like that. It gave him a warm and fuzzy feeling inside. Well, no one except for Isis. "Just be flattered and move on," he told himself. "She probably didn't mean anything by it, anyway."

Chapter Twelve

Isis had lived in The Sapphire Resort from the age of nine to fifteen—or sixteen depending on which version of herself her mind was thinking about at the moment. In all that time, she had never entered the hotel's night lounge even though they did allow underage patrons until eleven p.m. No matter how many teens hung out in there, the place never had a teenage sort of feel to it. It was more of a smoke and alcohol motif with hard metal music that gave Isis a headache even when she walked past the doors.

Frankly, she didn't want to come this time either. The Witches of Vegas performed twice today, an afternoon and an evening show. She was exhausted and wanted to get some sleep. But Zack was excited about the invitation to hang out with fellow performers their age. For him, she changed into her most comfortable jeans and white T-shirt, then teleported them to The Sapphire.

The place was exactly how Isis remembered it—with so many people puffing on cigarettes, cigars, and a few illegal substances that made her eyes water. It was a miracle that the smoke detectors weren't blaring throughout the room. It would certainly be a better sound than the music shooting out of those speakers.

This place, to Isis, was a lounge in name only. It was really just a bar with a small dance floor and a few old-looking couches against the wall. Amelia sat on a stool in front of the bar with Thomas seated on her left and another girl seated next to him. Apparently, Thomas gave up the doo rag for a white "Wiccan Circus" baseball cap. So far Isis and Zack hadn't been noticed by the three, which meant there was still time for a discreet exit.

"Hey, Zack?" Isis tapped his shoulder. "I'm getting real itchy in here. Maybe we can see them another time, and definitely somewhere else?"

"Come on, Isis," Zack pleaded. "This could be a great thing for us. We could be fast friends with Amelia. We have a lot in common with her, and we don't remember her, or any of her crew, from that other time. We can't have that in New Salem."

"I guess." Isis shrugged. Outside of the fact they performed on her old stage, she thought the "having a lot in common" was a stretch.

Amelia spun on her stool and, noticing Isis and Zack, waved them over. Zack took Isis' hand and scurried across the dance floor. For Isis, it felt like she was being pulled by a leash until they stopped short in front of their destination. Amelia's friends rotated around on their stools. The girl next to Amelia looked Isis and Zack all over.

"Good evening, my friends," Thomas greeted them. "Allow me to make the introductions. Zack and Isis, you've already met Amelia. The lass on my left is Meghan, the lead clown on the ladies' side of the theater."

"Are you two brother and sister?" asked the girl with dark-blonde hair in pigtails and way too much eye shadow. With her hand on Thomas's knee, Isis had a feeling they were far more than just friends.

"What? No!" Isis exclaimed. She couldn't imagine where that question had come from. They didn't look anything alike. They didn't even have the same complexion, but they had, over time, picked up each other's habits. "We've been together for a long while."

"How long is a long while?" Amelia asked.

Zack let go of Isis' hand. "We've been together for about five months and a few days," he said through a grin.

"Wow, five months *and* a few days?" Amelia spun a finger in the air. "Yeah, I guess that's a long while, at least for our age." She leaned back, resting her shoulders on the bar. "Grab seats. I'll order us some drinks."

Isis peeked around the club. There were no free chairs to pull up. Maybe she meant it as a figure of speech? Ugh, the loud music screeching through the speakers made it hard to concentrate. Hopefully she wouldn't need to use a spell to lower the volume of that ear-piercing bass. Their new "friends," however, didn't seem bothered by it at all.

"How are you, Amelia?" Zack asked with an enthusiasm that made Isis' eyebrows squint.

"I'm super, Zack." Amelia spun back to the bar and signaled the bartender, a husky man in a sleeveless button-down shirt. "Five colas in glasses, please."

The bartender placed five glasses in front of Amelia and used the fountain gun to fill each one to the top. "On your mother's tab?" he asked.

Amelia flashed a thumbs-up. The bartender tapped the countertop, then strolled across the bar to help other patrons. Meghan and Thomas each grabbed a glass. Isis covered a slight grin. She never would have pegged Amelia to be a simple soda drinker. Then again, it wasn't like she could order an alcoholic drink. Even if she had a fake ID, they all looked way too young to fool any server on the entire planet.

Zack reached past Amelia with both hands and grabbed the two remaining glasses. He handed one to Isis, who brought the glass to her lips for a sip. Amelia reached out and grabbed Isis' palm, stopping her from taking that sip.

"What's up?" Isis threw Amelia an icy stare.

Amelia turned the glass in her hand upside down and let the contents spill on the tiled floor. A few drops splattered onto Isis' sneakers. Thomas and Meghan did the same.

"What are you doing?" Isis asked.

"We're not children." Amelia spun back to the bar. "We need the glasses, but for something way stronger. How about we try the bourbon tonight?"

"Go for it." Meghan patted Amelia on the back. "I'll keep an eye out."

Amelia's gaze focused on the bottles along the rack attached to the bar's mirrored wall. A small circle of blur formed under one dark bottle on the top shelf. It was big enough for the bottle to fall through, which it did. Amelia caught it from another hole above her. She yanked off the cap and filled her glass.

"All right, here we go. Let's party!" She poured bourbon into Thomas's and Meghan's glasses. Her eyes flashed to Isis and Zack. "How about you two?"

"I think we're good with the soda," Isis replied.

"Suit yourself, square." Amelia reached out and cupped her palm against Zack's elbow. She stared at him with those widened off-colored eyes. "How about you, handsome? You want to live a little?"

Amelia's hand on Zack's elbow annoyed Isis a lot more than she wanted to let on. Zack peeked down at his soda, then straight at Amelia with that curious look on his face. Isis liked that look, but only when it was aimed at her. For a moment she felt selfish about that, but damn, Zack was her soulmate, and Amelia was someone they just met.

"Um…yeah, sure. Why not?" Zack turned his glass upside down and let the soda pour out. "I want to live a little, too."

Isis focused her thoughts on Zack's mind. *You're not seriously going to drink that stuff, are you?* She aimed her question directly into his thoughts.

I don't know, came the response into her own mind. She couldn't understand where his confusion was coming from. Then again, Zack always had a thing about wanting to fit in. Much of his time in school was spent getting bullied by people much like Amelia and her friends.

Amelia filled Zack's glass from the bottle. She, along with Thomas and Meghan, downed their glasses. Zack eyed his carefully. For a moment, Isis thought he was going to back off. Then with a shaky hand, he took a huge swig. His upper body lunged forward while a dry heave shot out from his throat. The rest of the bourbon in his glass spilled out.

"Damn, it tastes like liquid wood!" Zack shouted. It elicited laughs from the others. But not from Isis.

"Congratulations!" Amelia shouted. "You're officially a man. We'll have to celebrate with another drink."

"Hey, can I talk to you?" Isis whispered in Zack's ear. She placed her glass on the bar's countertop, then pulled at Zack's wrist.

"Sure. Um, we'll be right back," he said, placing his glass next to Isis'.

"Don't take too long," Amelia called out. "Or we may finish the bottle without you."

"We wouldn't want that to happen," Isis muttered under her breath. She led Zack across the dance floor and near the entryway.

"Isis, what's the matter?" There was a slight annoyance in his tone. It took her by surprise.

"Zack, I-I want to go." She let the sob in her voice be heard. "I'm not comfortable here."

"Why not?" Zack shot back. "They're cool people, and they're just having some fun. Lighten up."

Lighten up? His words felt like a punch to her gut. It had to be the heat of the moment; he couldn't have meant it. Zack had said insensitive things before, but he always realized it immediately after the words flew off his tongue. It was almost always followed with an apology. But not this time…at least not yet.

"Zack, I'm heading back to the Felicity. Are you staying, or will you come with me?" Isis widened her eyes and looked into Zack's. It was her way of connecting with him on a romantic level, by flashing her "boyfriend, please" face. She was hoping it was enough to get him to come with her. That look usually worked. Her mouth dropped when he pulled his gaze and peeked over his shoulder…at Amelia, Thomas, and Meghan.

"I'm…I want to stick around a while longer. I'll walk back later."

"Okay, Zack. I'll see you in the morning then."

Zack took off and returned to the group. Amelia handed him his glass, which was refilled with bourbon. Isis watched them for a few moments from across the dance floor before turning around and walking out. As hard as it was for her, she was willing to make new friends. But not with this group. Definitely not with them.

Chapter Thirteen

Isis peeked at the digital clock on her nightstand. It was one fifteen in the morning, and even though she was in bed, she hadn't slept a wink. Her eyes were wide open, focused on calling to Zack inside her mind. She had received no answer so far. With their natural connections, he should have been able to hear her thoughts. If he did, her pleas went unnoticed or ignored.

"Where are you?" she mumbled over and over.

Isis stood from her bed and paced around the bedroom as she had done several times throughout the night. Something had to be wrong. But what? For a moment she considered changing out of her pink pajamas and teleporting back to The Sapphire lounge. She thought better of it. Showing up like a controlling girlfriend wouldn't help if everything was fine. But what if everything wasn't fine?

A voice suddenly ran through her head. *Isis, are you up?*

The familiar voice was older and female, obviously not Zack's. "Sacha?" Isis spoke out loud. "Everything okay?"

Not at all. Get to the hallway. Now.

Isis ran for the bedroom door. *Should I wake Mom and Dad?*

Not yet. Just you come.

Isis' mad dash became a tiptoe through the suite's

living room. She slowly opened the door to the hallway and stepped outside. Once outside the suite, her mouth dropped. The door a few feet across was wide open with Sacha and Simon staring down and gawking at Zack. He lay face down on the hallway's gray carpet, moaning.

Isis eased the door behind her shut so she wouldn't wake up her folks. This was the last thing she wanted them to see. "What happened to him?" Isis whispered.

"Are you asking *us?*" Sacha shot back. "I thought the two of you went out together."

"I came home early." Isis dropped to one knee. "Zack stayed."

"I'm surprised the huge thud didn't wake up the entire hotel." Simon put his hands on his hips with his lips squeezed tight. "I'm missing the end of my detective show for this. Now I'll never find out how Sergeant Benson catches the perp."

Isis leaned down so she could whisper in Zack's ear. He smelled like bourbon. "Zack, how many glasses of that stuff did you drink?"

He lifted his head with his eyes shut tight. His head turned, but it was clear he couldn't focus on Isis. There was a puddle of liquid on the carpet under his bright-red cheeks and nose. "Not just bourbon," Zack muttered. "Amelia stole another bottle. Whiskey. It tastes…yuck."

"Then why did you keep drinking it?"

"I don't know." His face dropped back into the puddle that had to have come from his mouth. Isis had a hunch spitting it up probably saved him from alcohol poisoning.

"Poor boy took in far more of the hard stuff than

his body could hold." Simon leaned by Zack's side and reached under his armpits. "I've experienced that many times before my death. The best thing we can do is take him to his bed so he can sleep it off. Isis, if you will please grab his other arm?"

Sacha clutched Simon's shoulder before he could lift. "You realize Isis and I are witches, right?"

"Indeed, you are correct. No need for the heavy lifting." Simon jumped to his feet. "A spell of yours will make things so much easier."

"Sach, please." Isis pointed a thumb over her shoulder at the opposite suite's door. "Before they wake up and hear us out here."

"It's best you do the honors," Sacha said. "You know my connection and your mom's are intertwined. If I use it, she'll sense it."

"Right." Isis dropped to a squatting position and placed a hand on Zack's back. "Zack's room," she chanted. "To Zack's room in his suite."

The hallway pixilated into a blur, then just as quickly came back into focus. Isis and Sacha now stood over Zack's bed where he lay above the covers with his face in the pillow.

"Are we...are we telling Mom and Dad about this?" Isis asked her normally cool aunt.

Sacha snickered. "Nah. I remember the first time I came home drunk from a night out. Big Sis and Sebastian read me the riot act, but the real punishment came the next morning. Hangovers give great lessons, which I'm sure Zack will discover quite well when he wakes up."

"Thanks, Sach." Isis let out a sigh of relief, although she didn't know why. Rage toward her love's uncharacteristic behavior ran through her veins. This wasn't something she ever expected out of him, no matter how much he wanted to be accepted by that group. The peer pressure got the better of him. Isis felt a moment of guilt in her stomach over leaving him alone. But only a moment's worth.

The bedroom door swung open. "I think you ladies forgot about me," Simon bellowed.

"I'm sorry, Simon," Isis responded.

"You're just in time to let our intoxicated coven member sleep." Sacha strolled around the bed. She hooked Simon by the arm and exited the room, taking the vampire with her.

Isis grabbed a blanket from the top of the closet and placed it over Zack. She headed for the door but stopped in her tracks when Zack mumbled her name. His voice was muffled from his face still being pressed in the pillow.

"I'm here, Zack." But she couldn't bring herself to turn around and look at him. At least not yet.

"I-I've never felt this way before." Zack's head lifted, then fell back down.

Isis forced herself to turn around and face him. "We don't drink, Zack. That's not us. It's not you."

"I know it's not." His words slurred. "I didn't want more, but I couldn't say no. She was like...in my head."

"Really? In your head?" Was Amelia using some sort of influence spell on Zack? Amelia claimed her connection was focused only on opening portals. But that could have been a lie. There was no reason to question her claim, at least not at the time. There was no reason to believe it either. "I think we both learned a lesson today. They're not people we want as friends."

"She…she wants to hang out again tomorrow night. I said yes."

"You're going out again with them?" Isis exclaimed. "After this, why would you?"

There was no response. Zack had fallen asleep. Isis rubbed her temples, trying to make sense of this. The boy she knew better than anyone else in the world questioned everything, even the little things. He analyzed every situation to death. Sometimes it was an annoying habit, but it led to him figuring out how to send Valeria back to the Other World and save their lives. Sure, Zack had a desire for new friends, but was it so strong that he let his guard down that easily? Or was something with Amelia and her friends amiss?

"We'll talk in the morning," Isis said, although she knew Zack was no longer listening. He was out like a candle that ran out of wax. Isis left the room. It was time for her to go to bed as well. Hopefully The Sapphire's staff would pass by and clean up Zack's mess in the hallway before Mom and Dad woke up and saw it.

Chapter Fourteen

Early morning...

Isis strolled past the New Salem cottages with a bright sun beaming down on her. She glanced at the moss and corrosion that had formed on each circular wall. It was out of place considering how well maintained the village was kept. She did, however, remember the cottages had suffered from neglect in the far future of the other timeline. Isis was supposed to be in Vegas right now in a hotel bed getting much needed rest. Somehow, being here at this moment made sense in her head.

Her bare feet were covered in mud and left footprints across what was normally well-maintained grass. What day was this, and how did she get here in the first place? Isis knew her way around the maze of cottages better than anyone else except maybe for Zack, yet she found herself taking far more turns than she remembered needing to take. The path was longer than ever before and completely different. She was lost.

But Isis was also a witch. There was a much easier way to get through this maze. "Teleport to the quad," she chanted.

Her vision didn't blur. Her surroundings didn't fade. Instead, she stood at the quad's edge in front of the school building without any sense of teleportation at all. Six teens stood at attention in a straight line. Isis blinked several times. This group—she didn't expect to see them in her lifetime. Each of them she knew so well even though they'd never met, at least not technically. They were her Wiccan students. Well, not her students, but rather the Wiccan vampire Isis before she changed the timeline. This was the far future. None of those six would be born for another two centuries, if at all.

Cameron and Cindi, the sixteen-year-old redheaded twins, were side by side in the center of the line. They were the tallest of the group by at least two inches. One girl, Kim, stood on Cameron's right while a boy and a girl—both with pitch-black hair and similar jaw structures— stood to Cindi's left. Elian, the youngest of the group at thirteen, paced back and forth. Whether due to nerves or excitement, he was incapable of standing in place. With each step Elian twirled his baseball cap so the visor pointed in a different direction.

Two bodies materialized in front of the line. The sight of them made Isis wince. She knew who they were even though she only saw their backs. The girl was her, or the other her, if that was an accurate description since they were the same person. The boy one foot ahead of her was Zack, but a far more seasoned and mature Zack, that was clear from the perfect posture and shoulders pulled back. The skin on his hands was white like chalk. That was because he was a vampire.

"Everybody, listen carefully!" Zack announced. He walked forward with confidence. His head turned from the far left of the line to the far right, making eye contact with each of their trainees. The other Isis had disappeared as if she was never there. "Mother Earth has chosen us for our special gifts to keep the world safe. It is what you have been training to do. I believe in you. Represent New Salem well."

The students all cheered. A smile formed on Isis' face. Zack spoke with such persuasive poise just as her dad displayed on stage. In front of her was the man Zack could grow up to become. Granted, he'd never become a two-hundred-year-old vampire in this new reality, but he would be an adult in the not so distant future—

"Then what are you waiting for?" a deep voice rumbled from behind.

Isis' heart nearly jumped out of her chest. She spun around as fast as her body would allow. The sight of an albino-skinned man with the sun glistening off his egg-shaped bald head was an even bigger shock than seeing Zack and herself. The wind picked up, flapping the man's black cape like a bullfighter's muleta.

"Luther," she said to the former vampire mentor of The Witches of Vegas. Isis never thought she'd see him again, let alone in the black suit he wore on the stage during their performances. "I don't understand. You're in the Other World with Valeria—"

"Never mind where I am." Luther's thin squinted eyes glared at Isis. He stood at least seven feet. That was far taller than Isis remembered him. "You need to save the boy."

"I want to, I really do." Isis' eyes dropped to the grass around Luther's black boots. "But I don't know what's wrong with him."

"Lie to me if you wish," Luther scoffed. "But do not lie to yourself. You know exactly what is wrong with him."

"Yes, I do." Isis widened her eyes. "I do know what's wrong with him—"

A loud ring suddenly echoed all throughout New Salem. Luther hunched over and pressed his hands to his ears. "What is this?" he shrieked. A second peal shook the ground.

"It's the telephone," Isis shouted over the ringing.

Her upper body shot up into a sitting position. Her head spun in every direction. Luther was no longer there. Neither was New Salem. She was in her bed surrounded by the hotel room's walls. The green blanket had rolled to her feet. Isis' eyes flashed to the oak nightstand next to her bed where the phone rang a third time. She grabbed the handset and pressed it against the right side of her face.

The computerized voice spoke into her ear. *"This is your…seven thirty a.m.…wake-up call, courtesy of the Felicity Hotel. It is currently seventy-eight degrees with a high today of eighty-nine degrees. Have a wonderful day. This is your…seven thirty a.m.…wake-up call—"*

Isis hung up the phone, rubbed the sand from her eyes, then climbed out of bed. Yes, she did know what was wrong with Zack. It was the only explanation as to why he'd become obsessed with Amelia. Zack was under a spell. A Wiccan spell. Isis shook her head and damned herself. Her instincts saw red flags from the start, so why didn't she act on them? Zack's sudden shift in personality was so extreme that she should have trusted her suspicions in the first place.

Now that she had figured out the problem, Isis had to come up with a way to fix it. At least she was halfway there. She ran for the door with renewed determination. She reached for the doorknob, ready to face the day, and Zack. Before pulling the door open, she stopped and eyed the ceiling. "Thanks, Luther. Well, sort of."

When discussing dreams with Doctor Mac, he'd explain how the mind uses images in the same way a therapist uses back and forth conversation. Dreams help a person come up with answers they already knew but needed it spelled out from another source. Isis' dream made her see what she knew deep down but she didn't want to admit. It brought her face to face with the truth of what happened to Zack. A damn Wiccan spell.

If only her dream lasted a little longer and told her what to do about it. She'd have to figure it out on her own, and that was exactly what Isis planned to do. She would break Zack of that spell one way or another.

Chapter Fifteen

The next day...

It was almost time for The Witches of Vegas'
afternoon show. While her folks and Sacha were setting
up behind the curtain, and Simon was practicing facial
expressions in front of the dressing room mirror for
some reason, Isis made her way to the front. She
wanted to check out the show's opener with her own
eyes. Although he missed breakfast, Zack was up and
ready to go. He took his spot behind the table in front of
the stage and signaled a dozen audience members to
form a semicircle in front of the table. Once they
surrounded his table, Zack whipped his playing cards
from his shirt pocket. He was ready to begin.

It was apparent ten minutes into his act that he
wasn't himself. Besides the fact he was at the table
performing in his dirty jacket, the
performance...lacked. A lot.

Zack had a card sitting face down on the open palm
of a young girl in a pink dress. He offered a smile to
both his audience around the table and to the camera,
which broadcasted his performance on the big screen
above the stage. "Okay, so far we found the first
selected card, the ace of spades, which we placed in my
young volunteer's hand." He waved a hand at the
facedown card. "Now that it's out of the way, let's see

if we can find the second card."

Zack spread the deck across the table. "I don't see it here in the deck. That's because the card..." Zack lifted it from the girl's palm and showed it off to the camera and his close-up audience. "...is right here, the eight of hearts. She had it all the time."

The little girl giggled. "That's not my card."

"No?" Zack's mouth popped open. But he quickly straightened his back and grinned, letting his experience take over. "Which card was yours?"

The girl's father rested his hands on the back of his daughter's shoulders. "It was the two of clubs."

Isis slapped a hand over her mouth. "The eight was from the trick before this one," she whispered to herself. That was Zack's third mess-up during his performance, although the other goofs were minor. None were so blatant where he actually forgot the card, then revealed the wrong one.

Zack, not missing a beat, scooped up the cards and then cut the deck. "You're right, it was the two of clubs. Please place the eight on the top of the deck." The girl did as instructed; she placed the card at the top. "But the two of clubs is smart, and it can disguise itself like any other card. As it did right now. Let's see its real face."

Zack picked up the top card, revealing the two of clubs. "Sure enough, it was the two all along."

The crowd gave him a smattering of applause. Isis caught Zack's "double lift" as he called it. But catching him lifting two cards instead of one wasn't something she could ever do, even after he taught her the technique. Zack was distracted to the point his hands were unsteady, and even a bit sweaty. This wasn't just a simple hangover. It was happening because her suspicions were correct. He was under a spell, and it was throwing him off.

"Okay, folks, my time is about up." Zack stowed the cards into the empty box and placed it in his vest pocket. "But, if you enjoyed my act, then please return to your seats and get ready for something really amazing. It is time for The Witches of Vegas!"

The audience applauded. The group in front of the table spread out around the theater to find their seats while the screen above went black. Zack rubbed a hand across his face and then made a beeline for the side door.

"Zack!" Isis called, which made him stop in his tracks. "Where are you going?"

His head dropped. A confused expression crossed his face. "Amelia…and the others…they're off tonight. She invited me to join them once my part was done."

"Join them to do what? Drink more of that stuff?" Isis took Zack's hands. "After last night, do you really want to go through that again?"

"Not at all," Zack snapped. "I learned my lesson. Amelia promised me no alcohol tonight. We're just going to hang out in The Sapphire Theater. She said there will be others from her cast there, too."

"Zack…" Isis moved in close until her nose pressed against his upper lip. "I was hoping we could hang out after the show. I'd like us to spend some time together." That would be her opportunity to help him realize what was happening.

Zack's eyes shut. But then they reopened as his lips stretched into a huge smile. "Maybe you could meet us there after the show. We never hung out in The

Sapphire Theater while it was empty. Now we can do that with other performers like Amelia. It'll be great."

"I meant just the two of us. Something low key, like a place where we could sit and talk?"

Zack's head dropped again. Isis had never known him to be so indecisive. That meant subconsciously he was fighting the spell. "Amelia…she really wants me to be there. I wouldn't want to let her down."

"Let *her* down?" Spell or not, Isis suddenly felt a sudden sense of betrayal. "What about us, Zack? You don't really feel something for *her*, do you?"

Zack's eyes went wide. "You and I, we have a lot of history together—"

"That doesn't answer my question!"

"It's not like that, not at all." Zack shook his head. "Of course I love you. It's just…"

"It's just what?" Isis put a yard of distance between them. Maybe she couldn't wait until after the show to let him in on what she had figured out. It was time to make him confront it now. "Think about it, Zack. Why are you acting so confused all of a sudden?"

Zack's head picked up. Somewhere inside, he was giving the question some thought. If he couldn't come to the conclusion himself, Isis needed to help him along. "Zack, please hear me out—"

"Isis!" Sebastian shouted while peeking around the curtain. "It's time. Your mom and Sacha are in position. I need you on stage as well."

"I'll be right there," Isis replied, never turning around or taking her eyes off Zack.

"Now, Isis!"

"I'm coming!" She waited until Sebastian returned to the stage before going on. "Zack, promise me you'll stay until the end of the show. Please?"

Zack peeked back at the door, then into Isis' eyes. His hands were shaking. Finally, he uttered, "I promise."

"Thank you."

Isis dashed for the stage. Her spot was in front and centered between Selena and Sacha. As the music blared and the curtain opened, Isis peeked over at Zack who never left the proximity of the door. She knew he wouldn't keep that promise. Helping him back to his senses would have to wait until later. Hopefully it wouldn't be too late.

Chapter Sixteen

Zack had made a promise to Isis, and it was one he truly wanted to keep. The last thing on his mind was breaking her heart. In fact, Zack was sure if he waited until the end of the show, he could convince Isis to come with him. Once they were in The Sapphire hanging out with Amelia and The Wiccan Circus cast, she'd see there was nothing to worry about. Amelia's wit and charm would win her over, too.

He really did want to leave after the show. But something inside pulled at him. He couldn't wait the full hour to get over there. But why? Was Isis right about him falling for Amelia? She didn't seem like his type, yet every time Zack shut his eyes, he saw her face. That was the case even when he tried to focus on Isis' face. Zack kept repeating in his head that he only saw Amelia as a friend. They couldn't be anything more because Isis was his true love. Yet Amelia was so intoxicating he had an urge to be around her all the time. She was easily the coolest person Zack had ever met.

He jogged the entire way from the Felicity to The Sapphire. He was breathing heavily, but he made it under fifteen minutes. To his surprise, Amelia was standing outside the resort's front doors. She was in a tight white tank-top with her hot-pink hair tied in a bun. Her lilac pants looked like they were painted on.

Zack jogged up to her. "Where's Isis?" Amelia asked.

He checked his watch. "Probably preparing for the final act."

"Oh. So sorry she couldn't make it." Amelia wrapped her hands around Zack's arm. "But I'm glad you're here. Let's head in."

A portal formed in front of them. Amelia led Zack through. Stepping through was different from teleporting. The blur was immediate, and it didn't cause a sense of tingling throughout his body. On the other side was The Sapphire Theater. Four teens—two guys and two girls—were dancing on the stage to loud techno music. Four others were in the front row, spread out in the seats, looking on and cheering. There was also a couple with arms wrapped around one another in the floor level's back row. Their heads popped up and looked Zack's way. It was Thomas, with a plain black doo rag on his head, and Meghan.

The theater's spotlight was on and illuminating the stage. Once Zack stepped out of the spotlight, he realized there was one person in the upper level standing in the front row with hands pressed against the guardrail. Erisa watched the proceedings from high above like a hawk examining its field. Zack waved a hand to greet her. Without an acknowledgment of his greeting, Erisa walked through the aisle and left the auditorium.

Thomas trotted to the stage steps and walked up to Zack. "Hey, mate, nice of you to come." He wrapped his hand around Zack's and shook it. "I was at the Felicity the other day checking out your skills. You're real impressive."

"Thanks." Zack hadn't noticed Thomas in his audience. Good thing he wasn't there for today's show. "If I knew you were coming, I would have gotten you in for free."

"No worries. Any chance you'd be willing to share some of those impressive card-handling techniques of yours? From one magician to another, it would be much appreciated."

"I would, sure," Zack replied. "Maybe you can help me improve my sleight of hand with coins. You're amazing at that."

"I reckon we can work a deal."

"Thomas has been waiting for someone on his level to work with for a long time," Amelia said, stepping between the two.

"So have I," Zack said, more to himself than to anyone around him.

"Actually, I'll bet you'd be able to improve everyone's game around here," Thomas said. "We could use someone of your stature."

Amelia threw Thomas a side glance that clearly meant for him to shut up. Zack raised his eyebrows to the statement. Were they trying to recruit him? Was that the reason Amelia asked him to come over tonight? Not that he'd want to leave The Witches of Vegas, especially after they invited him into their family—or coven. But man, the offer was flattering. He felt the pull inside of him.

"I'd be happy to exchange some tricks of the trade, Thomas."

"That'd be wicked, mate." Thomas reached into his pants pocket and showed off what at first Zack thought was a cigarette...until he realized it wasn't. "Maybe along with that, we could get this party going with some of your city's best spliff."

Zack's tongue almost slipped down his throat. "Um, I'm not really into that stuff, but thanks anyway."

"Suit yourself, mate. More for the rest of us." Thomas pulled a lighter from his left pocket and sauntered off the stage.

"Hey." Amelia tapped Zack's arm. "You want to do something fun and exciting?"

"I think this is fun and exciting."

"This is boring, and you still have that worried look in your eyes." Amelia stepped toward the side door exit. "I have something even better in mind. Let's you and me take a field trip."

Zack's feet stayed in place. "I really don't want to drink tonight." His head still pounded like a conga drum from last night. He couldn't even remember how he got back to the Felicity, let alone onto his bed.

"No drinking. I have something else in mind." Amelia turned to face Zack. She placed a hand on his cheek. "You can trust me."

Zack barely knew this girl, yet a warm feeling in his brain told him that he could trust her. He couldn't understand where that feeling was coming from since she hadn't exactly given him good reason. His instincts told him to ask for more information, find out where she was taking him and what she wanted to do. Or he could simply decline and go back to the Felicity. That plan would certainly make Isis happy, although he'd have to explain to her why he broke his promise and left so quickly. He didn't have a good explanation for that discussion.

Yes, going back, that was exactly what he wanted

to do. But when Zack opened his mouth, the warm feeling took over and the words "I trust you" popped out.

"Then follow me."

"Another portal?"

"Nah, let's walk. I feel like breathing some fresh Vegas air." Amelia yanked open the door and stepped through. Zack couldn't help himself or stop his feet from following. The door led to the alleyway on the side of The Sapphire.

"Where are we going?" Zack caught up to Amelia and walked side by side with her. "What are we doing?"

"Something real witchy." An ear-to-ear grin formed across her face. "I think you'll be impressed. Of course, with your whole group being witches except for you, I'm sure they do impressive stuff all the time, am I right?"

"They can, but they usually don't."

"Bummer."

Amelia turned left at the corner. Zack did the same. Wherever she was leading them, it was off the Strip. In all the time Zack had been a Vegas resident, which started when he was six, he rarely veered off Las Vegas Boulevard.

"Mom and I haven't run across a lot of witches since we came to Vegas, or even before then." Amelia's pace quickened. Zack pushed himself to keep up. "I honestly wondered if any others existed outside of her stories. Well, that was until I found out about The Witches of Vegas."

Man, Zack wanted to tell her all about New Salem, but that was something in all good conscience he couldn't do. He pushed the urge down to his stomach. Better to listen to her stories—he really did like her voice. He wanted to learn all he could about Amelia. He could always share his own stories with her later.

"Where did you grow up, Amelia?" Zack asked.

"My mom dragged me all over the place." Her eyes rolled. "City to city, town to town, even country to country. Vegas is the first place we ever settled down. At least for now."

"Do you expect to stay?"

"Maybe." Amelia shrugged. "I get the sense Mom finally found what she's been looking for with The Wiccan Circus. Hopefully this all works out for us how she expects."

Zack did a double take. "What does she expect?"

"Enough small talk. We're here."

Amelia had led them seven blocks into an area Zack had never walked through before in his entire life. They stood on the corner across the street from a bodega and what looked like an abandoned pizzeria. The area was a lot less crowded than what Zack ever experienced in Vegas. Few people walked the streets, and only a couple of cars had sped along the road.

"I love this area," Amelia said. "It's so real, unlike resort row where we live."

"What are we doing here?"

"Something I've often thought about but haven't done, until today." Amelia rubbed her hands together. "Just give it a few minutes."

After a long while of silence and just staring at the bodega, Amelia finally spoke up. "Zack, what's it like being the only non-witch stuck in a coven of witches?"

Zack shrugged. "It's not really something that

comes up. They treat me as an equal." He never before saw himself as stuck. Did he give off that sort of vibe?

"I'm glad they see you as an equal," Amelia said. "But do they really?"

"What do you mean?"

She placed a hand on Zack's shoulder and squeezed. His entire body tensed. It was a powerful sensation he had last experienced during the battle with Valeria. "Say there's a dispute between you and Isis and it leads to her using witchcraft on you to settle it. Which side would the rest of them take?"

"I…I think they'd be fair," Zack responded. "I do get that Isis is their adopted daughter. They're her family, but they've never made me feel like an outsider if that's what you're getting at."

Amelia's amber eyes met Zack's. "Who is *your* family, Zack?" she asked with a voice filled with sympathy.

A chill ran down Zack's spine. He tried to step back, but the grip Amelia had on his shoulder kept him in place. "It was my uncle, but he passed away. Now they are."

"I get it," Amelia replied. "I think of my cast as family, too. But my mom and I, we stand out as the only witches in the crowd. They understand the pecking order. How do you stand out in your crowd, Mister Opening Act?"

Zack wanted to argue the point. His job went far beyond being the opening act. In fact, he had the most important job of all, making sure the performances looked close enough to traditional magic that their secret would be safe from skeptics. That happened behind the scenes, but they were the most important details when planning out their shows. Zack's opening act was something extra, and something he wanted to do, not his primary job.

He didn't expect Amelia to understand. She didn't know The Witches of Vegas, or his relationship with any of them. She couldn't know what they had gone through together. How could she? Of course he could never utter a word about it to her. That was knowledge that belonged in New Salem and would stay there no matter what. But Zack still wanted to tell her everything. If he did, maybe it would make her even fonder of him. He wanted that in the worst way.

Zack opened his mouth to speak, but he couldn't bring the words out of his throat. Even though he knew Amelia was dead wrong in her assessment, he felt an insatiable urge to agree with her. That suddenly felt more important than getting her to understand his role. He let out a deep sigh, then shook his head back and forth. "I guess I don't stand out," Zack mumbled. Those weren't his true feelings. He knew better than that, but he stated it nonetheless.

"That sucks, Zack, it really does." Amelia leaned in, her eyes never wavering from his. "For what it's worth, you stand out to me."

Zack braced himself. He sensed that Amelia was about to kiss him. A random thought inside his brain screamed at him that this was wrong. She wasn't Isis, so he shouldn't be doing this. But he couldn't pull away no matter how hard he tried.

Before their lips touched, Amelia's head spun away. Her face lit up at the sight of a black Thunderbird pulling up in front of the bodega. "Ooh, he's here!"

Amelia screeched. "Okay, Zack, get ready for some real fun."

Chapter Seventeen

"Ladies and gentlemen," Sebastian announced into the microphone to the hundreds of fans in attendance. "Please welcome back to the stage, the youngest member of The Witches of Vegas. She is the future goddess of magic, *Isis!*"

The crowd cheered as Isis stepped from behind the side curtain. She walked to the middle of the stage and faced the audience. Once again, she had to focus the Wiccan energy on two separate tasks at once, a tough chore for her under normal circumstances. The difference was that this time she'd be the one floating in the air while creating wind throughout the auditorium. It was an idea Zack came up with before their first performance. Mom and Dad saw it as a good test for Isis' witchcraft while Zack said, if done right, the audience would think they were using wires and hidden wind machines to create the effects.

Isis peeked offstage. Zack was nowhere to be seen, which meant he chose not to wait. Even though she was using his idea, he didn't stick around to see it in action, which was uncharacteristic for him. He was probably at The Sapphire. With Amelia. *Focus, Isis.*

The soft ballet-like melody played. Isis raised her hands in the air. "Wind," she chanted. In response, a breeze blew past her, ruffling the hair of audience members in the first few rows. Now she needed to keep her attention on that breeze while utilizing the energy for her second spell.

"Lighter than air," Isis said. "Lighter than air."

A sense of weightlessness flowed through her body, which then lifted her off the stage. She hovered three feet, then five feet, above the stage floor with her arms spread out. Isis' clothes fluttered around her body from the wind against her back. A hoop lowered from the ceiling in the middle of the theater. Isis' next task was to fly from the stage and through the hoop. It was a use of her Wiccan control she had done many times before, but never with her concentration on the energy split.

If only Zack was still here to see this. His presence always brought Isis strength. She enjoyed being around him as much as she sensed his pleasure in her presence. But right now he was distracted and obsessed by Amelia. What if this wasn't a spell? What if he really did like her and the feelings were his? Wow, was the throbbing in her temples what jealousy felt like?

No, it had to be a spell. In all their time together, throughout both realities, Zack never so much as looked at another girl. Not once. That was especially the case with the wild and crazy ones. From what Isis could see, that defined Amelia. Zack had nothing in common with her, in no way would she ever be his type. It had to be Amelia's doing, Isis was sure of it. The only thing she couldn't figure out was why. What interest did Amelia have in Zack—

The wind under Isis' control picked up, perhaps sensing her rage. It pushed against her back and nearly flipped her over. Audience members were being pressed against their chairs. A murmur filled the theater. Suddenly, her lighter than air spell broke.

Isis fell straight down. She needed a spell quick, but panic prevented her from summoning the energy in the split second available. She landed on her right foot, then her body tipped over, and she tumbled onto her backside. A stinging throb shot straight up her right leg. The crowd gasped in unison.

"Damnit!" Isis reached out and grabbed for her ankle. Her foot wouldn't obey her non-Wiccan mental command to wiggle.

Selena and Sebastian ran onto the stage. Selena kneeled at Isis' side and touched the right ankle. Isis cringed. The audience shrieked. Sacha and Simon looked on from offstage with the same worried expressions Isis' parents had. The music stopped.

"Just relax, Sweetie," Selena screamed over the blaring music. "We'll fix you right up."

"Let's get her to the back," Sebastian said. "Heal her there."

Sebastian and Selena took one of Isis' arms and pulled her to her feet. She leaned on Selena for support while hopping to the back. The crowd applauded. Isis' head pointed down. Her eyes were shut but more out of embarrassment than pain.

Once in the back, Selena lowered Isis onto the floor. Simon passed Sebastian the microphone. He sprinted back onto the stage and faced the nearly quiet audience.

"Well, that's what happens when we're live, folks," Sebastian said into the mic. "There's always an element of danger in what we do, so do not try this at home. We hope you enjoyed The Witches of Vegas. Sorry to cut the show a few minutes short but we do hope to see you again real soon."

About the half the audience applauded. The rest still suffered from stunned silence. The curtain closed. Sebastian ran to the back. "How is she?" The microphone dropped from his hand.

"I'm okay," Isis replied.

"It looks like a sprain," Selena said. "Sacha and I can heal it. We just need a moment."

"Isis, what happened?" Sebastian asked.

"I don't know...I guess I lost concentration."

Selena stroked her daughter's hair. "Maybe we need to take a step back? Focusing the energy on two tasks at once may be a bit much for her, at least at this point."

"I'm fine. I can do it," Isis responded. "I just had a moment up there. I'm sorry."

"I was impressed," Sacha said. "Way to make a big splash in front of the crowd, kiddo." If her goal was to use levity to get a smile out of Isis, she failed.

"I can't believe I lost control." Isis rubbed her temples. "And in front of everyone. That was so lame."

"It's okay, Isis," Sebastian replied. "Remember the point of these shows is to practice our control of the energy and find out where we need to improve."

"I guess." But Isis still kicked herself inside.

"Sach, are you ready to do this?" Selena asked.

"Sure, let's heal her up." Sacha cracked her knuckles then knelt by Isis' ankle. Her head spun from one direction to the other. "Hey, where's Zack?"

It was a good question. Isis knew the answer, unfortunately. He was with Amelia, the witch who had him under a spell. Once Mom and Sacha finished healing her, Isis was determined to break him from her control.

"I know what I have to do," Isis mumbled.

"What is that, sweetie?" Selena asked. "What are you talking about?"

"Nothing. Never mind." But it wasn't nothing. It was a sudden spark of revelation. Once they healed her ankle, Isis planned to get right back to her feet with a renewed purpose. It was time to stop being mad at Zack and help him find his way back.

Chapter Eighteen

A rugged and burly man stepped out of the driver's seat of the black Thunderbird and entered the bodega. With his leather vest, long beard, and tattoos all over his arms, Zack thought he'd be a better fit on a motorcycle than in a sports car. Actually, he fit in well in this seedier part of Las Vegas. For all Zack knew, he could have been a good person. There was no way of knowing anything about him, but the intense look on Amelia's face showed that she had a great interest in the guy.

"Okay," Amelia sang once the man was inside the bodega. "Now's our chance."

"Our chance for what?" Zack peeked around. Except for a homeless guy sleeping in front of a high rise and a couple shouting at each other on a bench, there was no one else around.

Amelia gripped Zack's arm and tugged him. "Every day at this time, that man pulls in front and leaves the engine running while he runs in to buy a pack of cigarettes. I picked up on his pattern with one grand idea poking around in my brain. Today, we satisfy the urge."

"I don't understand. The urge for what?"

"I want to see the inside of that vehicle." Amelia ran across the street toward the car, pulling Zack by the arm along with her. "But we have to move fast, so come on."

"Hold on. Wait a second!" Zack stopped in his tracks, which also halted Amelia. They were midway along the street. "We can't just get into someone's car. That's wrong on so many levels. Besides, I'm sure the doors are locked."

"Sometimes we have to live a little." Amelia stepped to Zack's right side, never letting go of her grip. "I want to feel the upholstery."

"But Amelia, it's illegal—"

"It'll be fine. Trust me!"

Zack did trust her, although for the life of him, he couldn't understand why. What she was proposing went against every moral principle his uncle drilled into him as a child. He needed to stand firm and tell her "No." But her smile, her touch, it was like Isis' but different in a way he couldn't explain. He couldn't bear the idea of Amelia ending their friendship. Damn, his thoughts should have been on Isis. In fact, he should have been with her right now. She was the only girl in his life that he found so intoxicating. At least until he met Amelia, and that thought filled him with guilt.

Zack reached into his jacket pocket. His hand touched something square and solid with a smooth surface except for the five-crystal pattern. It was Isis' birthday present. The memory box was still in there. It fit in the palm of his hand. Isis would never break into a car. For that matter, neither would he. Yet when Zack tried to envision Isis' look of disappointment, he could only see Amelia's face filled with excitement. The only thing that could wipe away that excitement right now would be if Zack said no.

"What exactly are we going to do?" Zack dropped

the memory box back into his pocket.

"Just hang tight, partner!"

A portal opened underneath Zack and Amelia's feet. They dropped straight down and landed in the Thunderbird, Amelia in the passenger's seat and Zack behind the wheel. The car vibrated due to the engine's hum. Amelia glanced around the car, from the backseat to the dashboard covered in blinking lights. Foam dice hung from the rearview mirror.

"Not bad, huh?" Amelia slapped Zack's knee. "I totally want one of these when I get my license."

Zack's heart pounded a mile a second. His body was filled with sweat underneath his clothes. It leaked out of every pore in his body. "Okay, Amelia, we've seen it, we're even sitting in it. Now let's get out of here before the guy comes out of the store. Sound good?"

Amelia's head spun toward Zack. Her eyes were wide above the cheese-faced smile. "I think we should see how this baby handles!"

"What?" Zack shrieked. "No, we...we can't do that. I've never driven before. H-how can we just take the guy's car—"

"He's stepping out of the store!" Amelia stretched her foot to Zack's side of the car and pressed down on the gas pedal. *"Let's ride!"*

Zack's back squashed against the seat once the car took off. He grabbed the steering wheel as tightly as he could, taking deep breaths and trying to get everything around him to stop spinning. They zipped by another car on their right, which had stopped once the traffic light turned red. Horns beeped and tires shrieked while they raced along the street.

"Hard right!" Amelia screamed with her foot still tight on the gas pedal. "Turn right!"

Zack twisted the steering wheel right until it wouldn't turn anymore. The tires screeched along the road, speeding through block after block. He wanted to shut his eyes, but he dared not even blink. He spun the steering wheel left, then right, narrowly avoiding two much slower vehicles. Through the rearview mirror, Zack watched the two cars stop short and pull to the side of the road.

"A-Amelia, we have to stop! I've never driven—"

"*Go left!*"

Amelia grabbed the wheel and spun it, forcing the car to skid left. They barely missed hitting a minivan strolling along in the middle lane. The Thunderbird zipped by several cars on either side, including one in front that shifted lanes to avoid them. They passed one hotel after another.

"Oh my God, we're on the Strip!" Zack cried out.

"I know. Isn't this exciting?" Amelia shouted with glee.

Zack's hands tightened on the steering wheel to the point he no longer felt his fingers. Lucky the Strip was always moving, except for a few sporadic traffic lights, one of which was directly in front of them, and it was red. Three cars were lined up in front. There was no room to get around them.

"Hit the brakes!" Amelia shrieked, taking her foot off the gas.

Zack slammed both feet on the brake pedal, but it wouldn't push down. Instead, the brake ground and the car kept moving forward. The vehicles' trunks and rear bumpers grew closer at a massive speed. Zack threw his arms in front of his face. There was nothing he could do to prevent what would surely be a massive impact and the end of his life…

He suddenly felt himself fall, then land on something soft. There was no pain, and he could move his fingers and toes. Was he just killed? Was this what death felt like? Couldn't be; the afterlife wouldn't smell like rotten fish and urine.

Zack opened his eyes and realized he was in a dumpster on top of several smelly garbage bags. The side of The Sapphire Resort faced him. At least they weren't dead. But what happened to the people in those other cars? He didn't hear a crash or commotion, but they were also now several blocks away. He looked at Amelia through wide eyes that refused to blink.

"Was that a rush or what?" she asked, seated in the dumpster next to Zack.

Zack's breathing had increased to the point he thought he would hyperventilate. Finding control of his arms and legs, he dragged himself to his feet and climbed out of the dumpster. His foot slipped on the way down. He tumbled to the ground.

"Zack, you okay, hon?" Amelia climbed out with little trouble.

He wanted to scream, make it clear that none of this was okay. They drove for what must have been miles through town, and although Amelia pulled them out in the nick of time, the Thunderbird must have crashed into one or more of those cars. Those people could be injured, or dead. Bystanders could be dead, and he was responsible. He, and especially Amelia, were responsible.

Zack opened his mouth to speak, but no words

came out, only air.

"Get ahold of yourself, Zack." Amelia grabbed Zack's arm and yanked him to his feet. "We're safe, and we had an adventure. That's the best we can hope for, right?"

"This isn't me," he mumbled. "I don't do things like this."

"It doesn't hurt to let your hair down once in a while." Amelia patted him on the back. "It's good for you to live a little."

"Isis would be disappointed. In fact, the whole family would—"

"You don't have to worry about that, not anymore." Amelia reached out and grabbed Zack by the shoulders. She looked directly into his eyes. "Maybe Isis is jealous because you're making friends and she's not."

Zack pulled himself from Amelia's grip. What she just said, it made sense, but if the statement was right, why did he feel wrong about having that thought? But it wasn't his thought. It was Amelia's. Wasn't it?

Zack's head pounded. "I-I…I have to go."

"I understand." She flashed him a huge grin. "I'll see you soon."

Zack spun away from Amelia and ran. His destination was the Felicity. He needed some space and a chance to figure out what was going on in his brain. Mostly, he needed to get away from Amelia, at least for now. Yet, a part of him looked forward to seeing her again. Maybe he was just overreacting. Yeah, what else could it be? He'd have to make it up to her the next time they saw each other so she wouldn't be upset at him.

Chapter Nineteen

Isis teleported into the huge Sapphire Theater, ready for wherever this confrontation would take her. She was careful to appear in the locker room as opposed to the middle of the stage so she wouldn't draw attention to herself. She expected to find the entire Wiccan Circus cast partying to loud music and plenty of alcohol that none of them were old enough to legally drink.

Instead she found the theater empty and dark with a spotlight shining from the ceiling on the huge auditorium's sole occupant. Erisa was seated in the middle of the stage with her legs crossed, her eyes shut, and her hands clasped together. She faced the back curtain while her lips moved at a rapid pace. Isis couldn't make out a word she was chanting, or praying. She tiptoed closer, unsure if she should disturb the woman.

"Please, just a moment," Erisa said, never opening her eyes or looking Isis' way. She resumed her silent speech. After several moments, she turned her head toward Isis and opened her eyes. "If you are here for the get-together, I'm afraid you are too late. The last of my crew dispersed a while ago."

"I'm actually here to speak with Amelia," Isis explained. "Is she around?"

Erisa levitated inches off the stage floor. Her legs

were still crossed. "She departed earlier than the rest."

"With Zack?" Despite her best efforts, Isis couldn't hide the bitterness in her tone.

"I do believe the two left together, yes." Erisa let her legs drop so the soles of her bare feet landed on the stage floor. "I presume from your brash response that this troubles you."

"If Amelia is trying to take him from me, then yes, it troubles me."

Erisa's head tilted. "Does Zack not get to choose for himself with whom he spends his free time?"

"Of course he does. It's not that." Isis' jaw dropped. Why would she even make such a suggestion? "It's just…"

Erisa placed her hands on Isis' cheeks, forcing her mouth to shut. Her fingers had a slimy glaze to them. "Please share with me your concerns, child. Let's see if I can alleviate them for you."

Damn, this lady gave Isis chills. She couldn't tell if Erisa was being genuine or if she was mocking the problem. Either way, if the woman had the slightest suspicions about her daughter, Isis wanted to get them out in the open. "I think Amelia has done something to him, something Wiccan. Zack hasn't acted like himself since we met her."

Erisa let out a loud cackle, which echoed throughout the empty auditorium. "I know my daughter can be a wild spirit, but her connection is exclusively in the creation of portals. She can do no more or less. It is where I have focused and guided her even before manifestation."

"I'm not sure I believe that."

Erisa's grip of Isis' cheeks tightened. She forced

her to look up. Until that moment, Isis hadn't realized that she was staring at the corns on the elder witch's naked feet. "Do you believe that I am deceiving you, Isis?"

"No, I'm not saying that," Isis answered, ignoring the large pocket of air that dropped down her throat. "It's just, I don't think…I *know* she's not Zack's type, yet he's suddenly obsessed with being here, with her. It doesn't feel natural."

"Although I am not without faults," Erisa explained, "I do not lie. I speak only in truths, and I am well aware of my child's limitations."

"Is it possible you're being deceived?"

Isis' question elicited an angered glare. Erisa's lips repositioned into a smile. Her narrowed eyes opened wide while her hands slid off Isis' cheeks. "Let me assure you that what you accuse Amelia of doing, she truly cannot. It is something she hasn't learned and could not pick up on her own."

The elder witch folded her hands across her chest. Her eyes closed once again. "Perhaps this is something more. Perhaps the boy simply finds solace here among the diversity of Wiccan and non-Wiccan mortals his age. The pull of being surrounded by likeminded people—in his case, show performers—can be invigorating."

"I hope that's all it is. But if it's not—"

"Enough! I will speak with my daughter and discover if anything is afoot," Erisa said. "You have my word, Isis."

"Thank you." Isis backpedaled and then spun toward the side door.

"Isis!" The elder witch calling out her name made

Isis stop in her tracks.

Once again, Erisa sat on the stage floor facing the back curtain. "Try to understand that people, particularly the young, do not reveal their true inner selves in a short period of time. And even if they do, their wants and needs can change quickly. Our perspectives are directed by the experiences that surround us. Zack's recent behavior could be him redefining himself. I am sure that someday soon your tastes and behaviors will change as well."

Isis highly doubted that theory. She knew Zack, and herself, far better than Erisa could ever understand. Of course she couldn't let the witch know that. Instead, she nodded, then left The Sapphire Theater as fast as her legs would allow.

Chapter Twenty

With her ankle healed thanks to Mom and Sacha's spell, Isis decided to walk back to the Felicity. She could have easily teleported, but this was a chance to clear her head. The Strip was amazing once the sun dropped under the horizon and the sky lit up like a Christmas tree thanks to all the neon billboards and headlights. Vegas at night was a beautiful sight, and it helped put Isis in a better mood.

Her stroll lasted an hour, but that was due to her constant stopping to check out the displays in the store windows and to watch a few of the street performances along her route. A new magic shop had opened a block away from the Felicity. Isis hadn't seen a magic shop in town since she was a child. She took that as a good sign that the craft was finally reemerging in Vegas.

Hopefully Mom and Dad weren't up this late worrying about her. They never liked the idea of Isis walking the area by herself despite the fact that she was a powerful witch. They did seem less concerned when she stayed out with Zack. He was always a source of safety and confidence for both Isis and their entire coven. Never once did she even consider that, when returning here, he would become her biggest worry. But that's where they were at.

Isis' dream made clear what she had already figured out but was afraid to confront. Zack was under a spell, and despite Erisa's assertions, it was one that had to be created by Amelia. If Isis could use her connection to break it, she would. But that was the problem with influencing spells—they couldn't be broken unless the recipient didn't want to be influenced in that way. Was that the case with Zack? Deep down, did he want the spell broken? Maybe this was exactly what he wanted, a group of friends with a common interest and where he wasn't the only non-witch in the group. At least that's what Erisa suggested.

This was not a problem she could solve with witchcraft. To pull Zack out of this spell, Isis would have to appeal directly to him and hope he truly wanted out of Amelia's influence. Easier said than done. In their time together, Isis had never felt so cut off from Zack, and that was in either reality. When problems came up, they were always able to talk them out. There was never a time where she felt him avoiding her. *It has to be the spell. God, please let it be the spell.* This wouldn't be an easy conversation, or the type of talk she and Zack were used to having. The thought of it gave Isis a bellyache.

She finally made it home, or what passed for home for now. The Felicity lobby was quiet at this time, unlike The Sapphire, which was hopping twenty-four hours a day. Isis hit the elevator button and waited. While the double doors spread open, she felt a presence behind her. A Wiccan presence. Her hands trembled.

The last time another witch snuck up on her, it was Valeria. That wasn't her experience, though. It was the other Isis, the one who no longer existed, yet all the trauma from the battle that came after that moment stayed with her as if she did live through it. To Isis' brain, it was her memory. Technically, it really was, and it still bounced around somewhere in her head.

Isis spun around with her hands up in a defensive position. It wasn't Valeria behind her, but this intruder wasn't much better. Amelia stood inches away. A huge sneer filled her face. "Boo!" she said.

"What are you doing here?" Isis screeched. "What do you want?"

Amelia charged, shoving Isis a step backward. Everything blurred, but it didn't feel like teleportation. A cold breeze blew into Isis' face. She was no longer in the elevator, a realization that hit the moment everything came back into focus—Isis had been pushed through a portal of Amelia's making. She stood at the edge of a rocky cliff. A second shove by Amelia sent her plummeting over the precipice. The wind suction pulled on Isis' arms and legs, taking away her ability to control them. Time to stay calm. She just needed to concentrate.

"Lighter than air," Isis chanted while focusing on the energy. "Lighter than air."

Her descent slowed until it came to a halt. She could freely move her arms and legs. Isis hovered like a balloon. Amelia, standing at the edge of the cliff, glanced down at two huge rocks by her feet. A portal opened underneath one of the rocks, and it fell straight through. Another portal opened above Isis. The rock dropped from the static-filled circle. Isis focused on the rock and changed its trajectory. Another portal opened in front of her. The second rock shot out like it had been fired by a cannon. It was aimed directly for Isis.

"Explode!" Isis shouted and pointed both hands forward. In response, the rock shattered into thousands of pieces and plunged to the ground below.

"I heard you were looking for me!" Amelia shouted from high up. "Here I am!"

"What did you do to Zack?"

"What makes you think I did anything?" Amelia's words echoed throughout the night sky. "Maybe you're the one who has been doing something to him all along! Am I right?"

Isis scoffed at Amelia's accusation. She knew what it was meant to do, shake confidence, but it wouldn't work. Isis was determined not to let this girl get into her head as well.

"*I know what you did!*" Isis pointed a hand at Amelia and sent a wave of energy her way. It wasn't strong enough to rip through her, but it would knock her down...if it hit. A huge portal formed behind Amelia. She leaped back into it before Isis' blast could connect.

Amelia was suddenly behind Isis with an arm across her throat. The abrupt weight broke Isis' "lighter than air" spell, and both girls dropped straight down. They hit the dirt-covered ground hard and rolled. Isis lifted her upper body and glanced in every direction. They were surrounded by rocks, cactus, and mountains. The air was cold and dry—Amelia had taken them to the heart of the Nevada desert.

"Look at you being the jealous girlfriend," Amelia said, through a huge grin. She jumped to her feet. "Here we are, two women fighting over the love of a boy you're losing, and you don't even realize it. Talk about a reversal of gender roles, huh?"

Wow, was this all a joke to her? "What do you really want with him, Amelia?" Another portal opened in front of Isis. She formed a clear shield in time to deflect another huge rock. "He's not even your type!"

"You're right about that. Zack's way too much of a tightly wound Boy Scout for my tastes." Amelia charged, stopping short in front of Isis' shield. "But I'm sure I can break him of that attitude once *you're* out of the picture."

"That still doesn't explain it," Isis roared. "Why are you doing this to him?"

"Wouldn't you like to know?"

A small portal opened. It was just big enough for Amelia to put her hand through. Isis was suddenly yanked back by her ponytail. The hard pull forced Isis onto her backside. So much for the shield. Isis focused on the ground underneath Amelia and willed it to shake. Throw her opponent off-balance, then figure out what to do. But Amelia, never missing a beat, opened a portal big enough to jump through. Amelia popped through another portal in the air, landing on top of Isis' legs. Isis sat up. She needed to attack. But before anything came to mind, Amelia wrapped a hand around her throat.

"Face it, little girl," Amelia growled. "I'm too damn fast for you. Whatever you try, I'll see it coming. My whole life has prepared me for this."

Isis widened her eyes. What did Amelia mean by that? Her whole life prepared her for what? No time to figure that out. The fingers around Isis' throat tightened. She needed to do something to escape before this damned witch choked all the air out of her in the middle of the cold and dark desert...

Wait, the desert. It was dark with only the stars high above for light. Isis' eyes had adjusted to the dark, and so did Amelia's. That was something she could use. "See *this*," Isis snarled and held her palm out inches from Amelia's face. "*Light!*"

A bright flash like that of an old-fashioned camera shot from Isis' palm. Amelia's grip of her throat released. She stumbled back and rubbed her eyes. "Okay, that was good," Amelia said, shaking her head. "I see you can do a lot with your connection, but I dare you to do that one again."

"This is over." Isis lunged forward. "Teleport!"

Amelia's face blurred. The back of her head came into focus. Isis, from several feet behind, held both hands forward. "Force blast," she commanded the energy.

A transparent wave ripped from her hands. Amelia peeked over her shoulder. A portal opened, and the energy ripple shot straight through. For Isis, it suddenly felt like she had been socked in the lower back with a sledgehammer. The energy knocked her onto her face. Isis pushed her upper body off the ground, her vision filled with stars. A sense of nausea ran through her throat.

"You were saying?" Amelia grabbed Isis by the back of her hair and pointed her face up. Isis stared deep into her eyes. While they were an amazing yellowish color, they were also psychotic. Amelia shook her head in disgust. "You know, for a witch who can do just about anything, you're not all that creative. Your connection is wasted on you."

A portal opened on the ground under Isis' chin. Amelia clutched the top of Isis' head and pushed down. "I, on the other hand," Amelia shouted, "can be very creative with what I can do. Ever feel the heat of an active volcano?"

Isis struggled, but Amelia's grip was tight. No question, there really was a volcano underneath that hole. She couldn't see it, but she felt the intense heat. Steam smacked her in the face. To answer Amelia's question, yes, Isis had felt such heat…when she battled Valeria over a volcano two hundred years from now in a defunct future. Memories of those events haunted Isis' dreams more times than she cared to remember. She didn't want to live though another experience like that ever, let alone in this moment.

Amelia pushed Isis' head closer to the portal. Isis needed to escape. If she phased her body then Amelia's hands would pass right through her. It was a way out, but she couldn't tap the energy. Isis could only feel her body tremble. "Come on," Isis mumbled. "I have to focus—" But she couldn't escape the memories of that night, a night that would never be, but was so real, so horrible…

A loud roar nearly deafened her. It didn't sound like an animal, but it wasn't exactly human either. The portal closed. Amelia's hands left Isis' head. Isis pushed away and rolled across the ground, putting some distance from her adversary.

A rotund body landed between them, kicking dirt up in all directions. The eyes were pure black. Two slim fangs protruded from either side of his mouth. It took Isis a moment, but the green camouflage-patterned pants and the white cape with gold trim were a dead giveaway. It was Simon. Nice to see he did some clothes shopping since their arrival.

Amelia leaped to her feet and jumped a step back. "What the hell are *you*?" she shrieked.

Isis let out a deep sigh of relief while Simon flashed his fiercest vampire face. He raised his long fingernails at Amelia and roared again. Amelia glanced at Isis, then opened another portal and ran through. Simon's black eyes faded back to his natural brown irises. His small fangs retracted.

"Friend of yours?" he asked, offering his hand to help Isis off the ground.

"Not exactly." Isis took his hand and was pulled to her feet. She stroked her face, which was still hot from the volcano's steam. "What are you doing out here?"

"You told me how our old mentor, Luther, used to come to the desert and hunt wild animals for blood, so I thought I'd give it a try. Good thing, too, it seems. Right now, I think *you* should be answering that question. What did I just intervene in, a juvenile dispute of some sort?"

"She's a witch from that other show. The one at The Sapphire."

Simon's eyebrows rose. "Ooh, so this is a rivalry between performers?"

"She's trying to attract Zack." Isis rubbed the sweat from her neck as she spoke. "And I know she's doing it with bad intentions."

"That is a concern." Simon's gaze shifted to the stars. "What did Zack have to say when you brought it to his attention?"

"Well, I…haven't. Not yet."

"Really? I'm surprised to hear that." Simon scratched his chin with one long fingernail. "You and Zack have such a special relationship. I don't think he'd allow himself to be wooed by the smell of another femme."

"I don't either." Isis threw her arms up in frustration. "That's why I'm sure he's under a spell of some kind."

"Perhaps, but it sounds like you cannot know this for certain." Simon's attention shifted from one end of the desert to the other. "He is a teenager, after all, prone to teenage impulses...spell or otherwise."

Isis narrowed her eyes. Was that meant as a dig at their age? "Not Zack. He's always been in control of himself. Until now."

"Yet you haven't spoken directly to the boy?" Simon asked, still studying their surroundings like a detective searching for clues.

"I didn't get the chance." Unless she counted that moment after they dropped him in his bed. But it wasn't the right time. He wasn't sober. "I want to—"

"Then perhaps you should put it on your agenda." The vampire about-faced, once again looking directly at Isis. "Through conversation, you are likely to get a better feel for the situation."

"That was exactly what I was on my way to do before I was ambushed by—"

Simon cut her off. "What about our coven leaders? I would presume you've caught them up on the situation. What is their take?"

Damn, she knew he was going to bring that one up. "I...haven't spoken to them at all on it."

Simon gasped. "Really? Why not? They strike me as very smart people. Perhaps they could help you figure all this out for sure. Then you will know how to proceed."

Isis opened her mouth to respond, but Simon's glance shifted to a coyote running along the desert.

Mark Rosendorf

"Have to go. Best of luck." He took off, following the animal's path.

"Thanks for the advice, Simon," Isis called out. "But I can handle this on my own."

Simon's abrupt exit was almost a relief. His insistence that she didn't know for sure what was wrong with Zack couldn't be more wrong. Of course she knew for sure. Still, Isis owed Simon a debt of gratitude. Lucky that he happened to be in the desert tonight and heard the commotion. Now she was free to head back to the Felicity and have that confrontation with Zack, as uncomfortable as it would be.

She had to let Zack know he was under a spell and make him confront it. Then he could break through. It was the only way, and they would beat that spell together. They'd always looked out for one another with most of that responsibility falling on Zack. This time it was Isis' turn to look out for him.

Chapter Twenty-One

The portal opened. Amelia sashayed into The Sapphire Theater, which was empty except for three people. Her mother sat on the stage with her legs crossed, facing the back curtain. Thomas, who had his multicolored doo rag back on his head, and one of their younger recruits at thirteen, Milton, sat in the front row's center seats. Their eyes were also shut tight with their heads pointed down. If Amelia dropped a pin, it probably would have echoed off of every single wall.

"I'm back from my date," Amelia shouted. Sure enough, her voice did echo.

Erisa floated off the stage floor. Her body rotated so she faced the seats. She dropped her feet into a standing position. "Young men," she said in her sweet salesperson tone. "Let's finish our session later. Right now, I must speak with my daughter privately."

"Understood." Thomas stood up and tapped Milton on the shoulder so he could do the same.

"See ya, guys," Amelia sang out.

Thomas turned back and gave her a wink. The two exited through the theater's side door.

Amelia skipped up the theater stairs with a pep in her step. "Mission accomplished," she said with pride. "We had a good time tonight, and it was a great bonding experience—"

"I know exactly what went on tonight, Amelia."

Erisa's sweet tone had disappeared, replaced by what sounded almost like a ferocious dog's barking. "You know that nothing escapes my sight."

Amelia's smile melted off her face. "I did the job, Mother."

"You stole a vehicle and sped through Las Vegas!" Erisa's narrowed eyes stared daggers into Amelia. "It was discussed on the news for all to see. The vehicle was found abandoned in the middle of an accident. You were lucky you did not leave behind fatalities. The authorities are still at a loss."

"That's because I got us out of there before—"

"You may have fooled the non-Wiccan population out there, but did you really think I would not recognize your careless handiwork?"

"Careless? Really? It was *your* instructions to bond with Zack." Amelia pointed an accusatory finger forward. "That's exactly what I did. It was a bonding session. We shared an adventure, just the two of us—"

"*Enough!* You took him out of his comfort area, Amelia, and put his life at risk. You could have lost him." Erisa's fists clenched. "He is the next step in everything we are doing here. This is the closest we've ever come. We cannot afford to have you chase him away for the sake of flaunting your rebellious nature."

"As I said from the start, Mother, I can handle it. Leave the recruitment to me." Amelia pressed a hand against her chest. "I need to help him loosen up, get him to drop some of those brainwashed morals he has from hanging with Isis and her coven. Then he'll be a willing participant. Trust me, by the time I'm done, Zack Galloway will be a wild adventurer who will be up for anything."

Erisa looked up at the ceiling and shook her head. "Goddess, help me, she just does not understand."

"Hey, I'm doing the job," Amelia screeched. "But I'm doing it my way. I don't need a lesson in—"

"*But you do!*" Erisa flung her hand outward. An energy blast hit Amelia in the chest. Her entire body convulsed as if she was having a seizure. Amelia could no longer feel her legs. She hit the floor face-first. Her eyelids closed from the sudden striking pain. She wanted to fight the urge, stay conscious, but darkness took over…

Amelia's eyes opened. Her body shivered from intense cold that stung her skin. She pushed herself up onto all fours. Her arms and legs were pressed in snow. Her fingers were somewhere under all that white. Amelia tried to wiggle them, but all she could feel was the bitter burn of frostbite. Erisa hovered inches above the ground, encased in a clear circular dome, which must have protected her from the elements around them.

"Your inability to understand triggers me, my dear." Amelia could barely hear her mother's voice over the howling wind. That could have been because her ears went numb.

"What? What don't I understand?" Ice cracked around Amelia's jaw when she spoke.

Her body shook. She couldn't make it stop. Everything around Amelia spun as if she had been on the teacups at an amusement park for three days straight. She managed to yank her arms from the snow. Wrapping them around her body offered no warmth. Amelia tried to suck in some air, but it was so cold and thin it tasted like liquid tin foil. Was this all an illusion, or did Mother really teleport them to some frozen mountaintop?

"Listen very carefully." Eriza floated closer to Amelia. "The boy is on the fence. He is close. I am sure of it. You must act fast. Understand, he is not just our best chance to succeed, he is also our only hope. You must not lose him."

"What…" Amelia spoke through a jaw that felt like it was about to fall off her mouth. "What do you want me to do?"

Erisa brought her hands together. "Finally!"

Everything blurred, a sign of teleportation. Once Amelia's vision cleared, she was back on the stage in the warm Sapphire Theater. Her body was still shivering. Her hands had turned an ugly shade of blue.

"Go apologize to the boy, Amelia," Erisa said. "Win him back into your charming graces. Then issue the invitation. It should be easy at this point, even for you."

Amelia forced herself to stand. Her knees were still shaking, and she couldn't feel her toes. "I hate you," she growled through numbed lips and jaw. "I've always hated you."

"Your personal feelings are irrelevant, only that we succeed." Erisa faced the back curtain, sat down, and placed her hands together. "The world is counting on us, even if it does not realize it yet."

Amelia was finally able to feel her fingers and toes. She opened a portal and ran through it. Her destination was supposed to be to Zack. But first, a fifteen-minute detour to the hotel spa's jacuzzi and sauna called to her. They were closed at the moment, but that never stopped her before. All her body wanted, all it needed, was warmth. Then she could get back to work.

Chapter Twenty-Two

The Felicity hallway between the two suites came into focus around Isis. She faced Zack's, concentrating on who was inside. Simon was still on the hunt in the desert. Sacha was out doing whatever it was she did to occupy her free time. Isis sensed Zack in the living room alone. Something was definitely wrong. She wouldn't read his thoughts, but she could tell that they were erratic.

Isis rapped her knuckles on the door, then waited. Zack was still in the living room, yet he wasn't answering the door. "X-ray eyes," Isis chanted. The spell let her see through the door. Zack was slumped in the middle of the couch. His eyes kept closing and reopening, never wavering from the television. After a second knock, she watched him look to the door, but he didn't get up or make a move to answer.

This conversation needed to happen. Isis canceled her spell, then focused on the door. She called upon the energy to allow her to walk straight through and into the living room. To her surprise, the television was turned off. Zack must have been in that spot for a while, evident from his slumped position, yet he still had his jacket on with his hands thrust in its pockets.

"Zack," Isis said in a tone barely above a whisper.

His head spun her way. He was breathing heavily as if he was just awakened from a nightmare. His hair was a ruffled mess. "What are you doing here, Isis?" he asked.

"I was hoping we could talk." Isis strolled to the couch and sat next to him. She flashed widened eyes his way. "Please?"

"Okay." Zack sat up. His eyes dropped to her jeans, which were covered in dirt. "What happened to you?"

"Amelia tried to kill me," Isis answered.

"Kill you?" Zack's head dropped. His head shook. "No…that can't be. She wouldn't do that."

"She *did* do that, Zack!" Isis caught her voice raising. "From the moment we met, Amelia has been manipulating you while trying to get between us and steal you away."

"Why would you say that?" Zack's threw a hand on top of his head. His eyes, pointed at Isis, were filled with blame. "Amelia is just being a good friend."

"She's not a good friend! She's changing you, Zack, and…I believe she's using witchcraft to do it. You're under a spell."

"What? Under a spell? That's crazy!" Zack jumped off the couch. He grabbed a clump of his hair with his left hand and spoke fast. "I just…I like the fact that I was invited to their party. Amelia is a really cool person who likes spending time with me. It's nice hanging out with normal, non-Wiccan people our age…and Amelia, she's really nice. I'm not surrounded by witches where I'm the only one who can't teleport or control the weather."

"New Salem is filled with people our age who aren't witches."

"I know. We were there for nearly six months, and

we never hung out with any of them." Zack's arms flailed in the air. His hands were balled up into fists. "We don't hang out with anybody, Isis! Now we have a group of performers our age just a few blocks away. I fit in well with them. I can be myself."

"Be yourself? You got drunk last night." A sob slipped out of her throat. She breathed deeply, determined not to let her tear ducts open like broken faucets. "And I don't know what happened tonight, but look at you. You're filthy and shaking all over. You used to like spending time with me. But since we've been back to Vegas, you've spent more time with Amelia. This isn't you, Zack. If you're not under a spell, why are you letting her make you do things you'd never do?"

Zack's eyes were wide and unblinking as if he had just seen something that disoriented him. He shoved his hands deep into his jacket pockets. "I don't know what to say. I guess I feel good around Amelia. The way she looks at me, I like it. No one else has ever looked at me like that."

Despite her best efforts, two tears snuck out of Isis' ducts and rolled down her cheek. "I-I look at you all the time like that."

"Yes, you do," Zack said in a whisper. "That's not what I meant, at least I don't think it is."

Isis sank farther onto the couch. All the Wiccan energy in the world couldn't keep her from sobbing like a rainstorm. She was still convinced these weren't his true thoughts or feelings, but hearing him say those words, even under a spell, they were her deepest fears come true. Zack squatted and put a hand on Isis' knee. His face was filled with guilt, but also confusion.

"I don't know why you're upset," Zack said.

Isis' eyes opened to the size of grapefruits. This boy knew her as well as she knew him, yet he didn't know why she was upset? "You like how another woman looks at you?" She spoke slowly and loudly. She wanted Zack to hear his own words repeated back to him. "How could you say that? How could you even think it?"

"Isis, I-I..." His head dropped. "I mean, besides you."

"Is that supposed to make me feel better?" Isis swatted Zack's hand off of her kneecap.

"I don't want to make you feel bad."

Isis sat up straight. She needed to pull herself together. Fighting and arguing wouldn't help the situation. She needed to make him understand what Amelia had done to him. So far she was failing miserably. Zack could break through her witchcraft if he really wanted to, but first Isis had to get him to confront it.

"Zack, please, come back to me." She wiped a hand over her eyes to dry them. "I want the boy I'm in love with. I want you to break out of her *spell*."

"Spell..." Zack jumped to his feet with narrowed eyes. His facial expression morphed from sympathy to rage. "I am not under a spell, Isis. I've been under a spell before. I know what it feels like. I'd know if I was under one now. I'm sure I would."

"You're not acting like the Zack I knew for two hundred years."

"Two hundred years?" Zack took two steps back. His teeth ground between his red cheeks. "We don't know if any of that even happened." His eyes glazed over. His jaw shook. "The reality is that we've only known each other for not even half a year. I'm not under a spell, Isis. I haven't changed. Maybe *you* have. Maybe Amelia's right that you're jealous because I'm making friends and you're not."

"Amelia said that?" Isis gasped. They had both been through so much together, and to hear him say these things, spell or not, broke her heart. "And you're listening to her?"

"No, I'm not listening to her! I'm—" Again, Zack grabbed his head with his left hand while his right was still thrust in his jacket pocket. Zack's face cringed. His mouth opened, but no words came out.

"Finish your thought, Zack," Isis said. "You're what?"

"I don't know what I am, Isis. I just…I need time to think." Zack about-faced and went for the bedroom.

"Am I losing you?" Isis called out. "Are we still together, or is that all over?" It was a cruel and insensitive comment, but she was upset, too. Maybe he needed to hear it in order to wake his brain.

Zack stopped in his tracks. He looked over his shoulder at Isis. All that confidence he had, at least in their relationship, was gone. All Isis saw in his face was a boy who was lost. "I just…I want to be left alone right now," he said. "Please?"

"All right, Zack." Isis covered her face with her right palm. "We'll talk another time."

Zack ran into his bedroom and slammed the door. Isis stood from the couch and slapped her hands at her sides.

Damn, that didn't work out well at all. But at least she achieved something. From his constant confusion, she was now sure he was fighting Amelia's Wiccan spell. Unfortunately, the spell may have been more powerful than Isis realized, which meant it would take a lot on his part to break through, if he even could. Her attempt to help that process by making him confront the spell might have made things worse. She had one solution left, and that was to follow Simon's advice. He was right, and damn her for not doing so earlier.

It was time to admit she was in way over her head. She needed adult experience, which meant it was long past time to call in the big guns. Isis focused on her suite past the front door and across the hallway. Mom and Dad were both awake and probably waiting on her arrival. Sacha was still on her date, but if she reached out and asked her to come home, she would.

That was exactly what Isis needed to do. She needed all of them together for a much needed family meeting. She needed their input and their assistance before it was too late.

Chapter Twenty-Three

Zack slumped at the edge of the bed with his head down. His insides spun with emotions from anger to guilt and confusion all at the same time. He had never made Isis cry before, and it wasn't something he ever wanted to do. Why did he tell her that he didn't believe that other reality actually happened? Why would he ever hurt her that way? He might as well have taken a knife and stabbed her in the heart.

Maybe because, deep down, he wasn't one-hundred-percent certain it did. Sure, the memories felt real, but there was always a lingering doubt that he had never shared with anyone. He certainly never expressed it to Isis. How could he? It was the key to their bond, memories that said they had been together for over two centuries. Everything he knew about Isis, and she knew about him, came from those experiences together. But they were experiences she put in his head. He wanted to believe they were real—Isis certainly did—but how could he really be sure? Witchcraft was like real magic; it could do just about anything.

A voice inside Zack demanded he apologize and make amends to Isis. He needed to reassure her that their relationship was real, that their bond was true. Hell, maybe he needed to reassure that to himself as well. Yet every time Zack closed his eyes and tried to picture her face, he saw Amelia's. Instead of seeing those deep and loving brown eyes, his mind replaced them with that confident, yellow-tinted stare. In fact, every face he tried to picture, from Sacha's to his late uncle's, they all turned into Amelia's.

Was it possible he was developing feelings for her? Of course, Zack's loyalty was to Isis just based on everything in two realities their love had survived, real or not. They had a deep and solid connection, at least they did until recently. Isis aside, Amelia was bad for Zack, and he knew it. Today proved that sentiment. She almost got him killed. Other people probably did get killed. That he was a part of such a horrible fiasco would haunt his dreams for the rest of his life. So why couldn't he get her out of his mind?

Maybe it was her charisma, her personality, or that she was really pretty. How could he not be turned on by her? Anyone his age would be. If she went to school in Las Vegas, Amelia would be the most popular girl there overnight, and she'd probably never look at Zack twice. But she did look at him and even seemed turned on by him.

The question he needed to answer for himself was whether or not he was turned on enough to end what he had with Isis. His brain said that couldn't be the case. Isis was right for him in every single way. Their relationship was the one thing in his life since he joined The Witches of Vegas that made sense. Yet, the way Amelia made him feel…he couldn't explain it if he tried. Of course, he knew how Isis would explain it. "You're under a spell," she'd insist.

Was she right? Was it possible he was under a spell? Nah, not a chance. Zack was a magician, and he lived with witches. He'd seen and lived through more supernatural magic than anyone else his age. If anyone could pick up on an illusion, it was him. Plus, Zack had been under a spell before. He knew the difference. His feelings had to be his own. Weren't they? What if he was wrong?

Zack let out a scream then dropped his head into his hands. If only Uncle Herb was still alive. He would lead Zack to the right answer—he always did. But Uncle Herb was gone. He sacrificed himself so Isis' family could save the world. Everything since then had been a whirlwind of new information, and emotions. Witches, vampires, alternate realities where Zack was a vampire. New Salem. Man, he thought he was handling it so well. At least that was the attitude he liked to give off. Yet there was always another turn in his road. This one, Amelia, may be the most puzzling of them all. He just couldn't get her out of his head. If that image was indicative of his true feelings, why was he such a confused and conflicted mess?

There was a knock on the bedroom door. Damn, Isis was still out there. Didn't she get that he wanted to figure things out for himself? He just needed time to think. "I told you to leave me alone, didn't I?" he grunted.

"Doubtful since I just got here."

Zack lifted his head. That wasn't Isis' voice. It was Sacha's. "Sorry. Come in."

The door pushed open. Sacha waltzed into the bedroom. From the look in her eye, it was clear she knew there was a problem. Did she hear the argument he had with Isis? "I thought you were out with that desk clerk," Zack said.

"I am. I went to use the bathroom, but the toilet at

the nightclub was filthy, so I teleported here to use our much cleaner facilities. Ironic considering I share our bathroom with two men, although the vampire only really uses it to stare at himself in the mirror." Sacha placed a hand under Zack's chin and lifted his head. "Are you all right? You look like someone just kicked over your birthday cake."

"I don't think you'd understand."

Sacha scoffed. "I've been a confused sixteen-year-old." She smacked him across the shoulder. "It wasn't too long ago, either. Hey, I got you through your math homework, didn't I? Maybe I can help with this, too. Why don't you try me?"

Zack had a momentary notion of asking Sacha to give him some space, but he thought better of it. He didn't want to be rude, especially since she had been there for him since the moment he joined the coven. In that time, Sacha's help had been invaluable. While Sebastian and Selena were focused on Isis, Zack was sure Sacha's goal was to take him under her wing. He did find her to be the one member of the coven he was most comfortable trusting after Isis.

Right now Zack felt more lost than ever before. Might as well take Sacha up on the offer. "Have you ever been so sure of something, then all of the sudden you weren't so sure about it anymore? Then you were sure about something else, and suddenly, you're not even sure about that?"

"Sounds like most of my life." Sacha sat next to Zack on the bed. "That's come up more times than I care to admit."

"How did you handle it?" he asked. "I thought everything finally made sense, yet now I'm more confused than ever. Everything just feels…unclear, you know what I mean?"

"I didn't realize your problem was philosophical."

"No, it's not philosophical, it's…I don't know what it is." He knew what Isis thought, but she had to be wrong.

Sacha stood from the bed and turned to face Zack. "Maybe you need to take a step back and ask yourself why it's suddenly confusing. Did something change, did you change, or is there another reason behind it?"

"Is that what you did?" Zack looked up at Sacha. "Did you figure out why things were confusing for you?"

"With me, it was mostly due to underage drinking." Sacha chortled. "That's probably not your problem, except for that one night. Hey, I left my date standing outside the restroom, I should get back. We'll talk more in the morning, okay?" Through a sly grin, she said, "Don't wait up."

Sacha faded away, leaving him all alone with his confusion. But he wasn't alone for long. A circular distortion opened in the exact spot Sacha was standing. Amelia stepped out. The portal closed behind her. "About time. I was starting to think that annoying tramp would never leave."

"That's not right to say, Amelia."

"Just being honest." Amelia shrugged. "That's how she strikes me, and I'm usually a pretty good judge of character."

Zack wanted to tell Amelia to get lost, especially after her rude comment about Sacha. For some reason, he couldn't bring himself to say the words. He had no problem telling Isis he wanted to be left alone, so why not Amelia? Because he really wanted to connect with her, and offending her wouldn't make that happen.

After several quiet moments, he looked up and asked, "Why are you here?" At least he could muster out that question.

Amelia took Zack's hand and pulled him off the bed. He didn't appreciate being forced to stand up, but her hand wrapped around his was so soft. A warmth rolled through his body. "I came here to apologize," she said in a slow and sweet tone. "Taking that car with you was wrong. I should never have forced you to come with me and do that."

"It was wrong with or without me." Zack's gaze stayed on the floor. He didn't need to look at Amelia to see her face. "You can't just take something the way you did. It's stealing."

"I get that, but being a witch, I sometimes confuse what I can do with what I should do." Amelia placed her hand on Zack's chest. His eyes shifted to her fingers massaging his pectoral muscle. "Maybe the best thing for me is a partner who can remind me of my sense of morality."

Zack's eyebrows rose. His body tensed. "What are you saying?"

"I should think that's clear." Amelia placed her free hand on Zack's cheek and leaned in. "I'm inviting you into my coven, Zack Galloway. My mother has given her blessing to offer this invitation. I know we can grow closer, and you'll fit in so well with everyone else."

"That would mean leaving The Witches of Vegas." That wasn't something he had ever thought to do. Something in his head told him to say no. Yet the offer also meant more to him than it should have. Mainly because it came from Amelia. This was his chance to be with her forever. But there was someone else he had to consider. "What about…Isis?"

"The invitation is just for you, Zack, not Isis." Amelia stroked the side of his head above the ear. "You mentioned the two of you were an item for what, six months?"

"Just over five but…it's more complicated than that." He didn't want to lie to Amelia, but technically it was the truth, at least in this reality that timeframe was correct.

"Five months," she repeated. "That's not a long time, Zack. We are offering you a purpose in life, which will last far longer. With you, we can change the world for the better. You are our missing piece."

Zack tried to look away, but he couldn't. He was sucked into her gaze. He shut his eyes and tried to picture Isis' face. Again, he couldn't. He could only see one face. His eyes popped open as if he had just woken from a dream.

"What do you say, Zack?" she asked.

"I don't understand. Change the world? How?" Did she mean that metaphorically?

"You seem unsure as to what you should do." Amelia flashed him a pearly white smile.

"I am," he answered. "More unsure than ever before."

"Then let me help." Amelia leaned in close and whispered, "Let me rid you of your uncertainty."

Her lips pressed against his. Zack's heart fluttered, and his body went cold. Part of him enjoyed this more than he thought possible. Yet, another part felt regret.

He didn't want to hurt— Oh man, in the moment he couldn't remember her name. Because she didn't matter. Nothing mattered, only the life he could have with Amelia. At least that's what his heart told him. His brain, however, kept registering that aura of confusion.

After a long embrace, Amelia pulled back her head and rubbed her hand across her mouth. "Come to the theater tomorrow morning at eight o'clock. I promise everything will be made super clear."

Zack dropped onto the bed. He touched his bottom lip with his left hand. He shut his eyes again, but he still couldn't picture anyone other than Amelia. He had tons of questions, starting with what would be made clear to him? How were they changing the world? But he couldn't will his mouth to move. He couldn't focus on a single question long enough to let it fall from his tongue. All Zack could do was nod.

"We canceled our morning practice." A portal Amelia's size formed behind her. "Everyone will be there. I promise you'll begin a journey you won't soon forget. Trust me, trust us, and I will be forever grateful to you."

Amelia stepped through the portal. It faded away. Zack's body shook like never before, not since the day he met Isis. He never fawned over anyone before meeting Isis, and he never considered anyone other than her in either reality. But Amelia was different. She left Zack in a flustered and confused state.

But that confusion finally passed. The muddled thoughts in his brain cleared up, and his next move would be dictated by his emotions. First was the hard part. He needed to tell Isis and her family. He needed to explain it from the beginning and get them to understand. It wouldn't be an easy conversation, but it was necessary so he could move forward.

Zack stood from the bed with his hands thrust in his jacket pockets. He still had Isis' birthday present in that right pocket. The plan was still to give it to her, but that wasn't his biggest concern, not right now. Zack marched out of the bedroom like a man on a mission. He paused at the sight of Simon sprawled out on the couch watching another detective show. Apparently he had come home early.

"You look like you're off to somewhere important," Simon said. "And at this late hour?"

"I need to speak with the others," Zack answered on his way to the front door. "You should probably come too. I'm not keeping it a secret. Not anymore."

"Ooh, that sounds juicy. I'll be in at the commercial break." Simon refocused his attention on the big flat screen.

Zack stepped into the hallway. The door to the opposite suite was wide open. He entered to see Isis in a chair at the end of the open kitchen's marble table. Sebastian and Selena were at the opposite end in seats facing her. Sacha leaned against the counter. Isis' face was red, her cheeks moist. "There's a problem," she said. "With Zack."

Selena answered, "What kind of—" She was cut off by Sacha loudly clearing her throat. Her gaze fell on Zack. Soon, all eyes zoomed onto his entrance.

"Come on in," Sebastian said. "Talk to us. Are you okay?"

"I...I need to tell all of you something." Zack tiptoed toward the table. "It's important."

Chapter Twenty-Four

The next morning...

Although Zack had entered The Sapphire Theater at least a few dozen times in the past, today it was as if he was walking in a stranger. Nothing about the auditorium seemed familiar. A small voice inside told him to turn around and run back to the Felicity. But it was too late for that. The deep conversation he had with Isis and The Witches of Vegas left him on this path. He told them what he wanted to do, and they reluctantly understood. Well, maybe not understood, but accepted. It was too late to go back now.

Amelia stood in the center of the stage looking out at the nearly empty auditorium with her arms spread wide. Four of the cast members, two on each side of Amelia, floated several feet above the stage floor. Another three were in the front row looking on. Before them stood Erisa, facing the stage with a glow around her hands. Circus music blasted through the speakers.

Amelia's eyes met with Zack's. She waved a hand his way. "Mother, he's here," she announced.

Erisa lowered her arms. The music came to a sudden stop. The four teens in the air—a boy and a girl on each side of the stage—lowered to the stage floor. Thomas, his head uncovered and his long brown hair hanging down to his shoulders, was seated next to

Meghan. They left their front-row seats and ran up the aisle to greet Zack. "It's good to have you here, mate." Thomas patted Zack across the back. "We actually took bets on whether you'd show."

"Nice to see you again, Zack," Meghan said.

The warm reception was touching. It was the only time he had ever been in a room filled with people his age, and his entrance was embraced by the majority. It sure never happened in school, not once, even from those who saw him perform with his uncle in their theater.

"Zack!" Amelia stepped between Thomas and Meghan and placed a hand against Zack's front jacket pocket. "You no longer have Isis' memory box?"

"That's right, I tossed it. I don't need to hold on to that for her anymore," he replied. "I'm not going back to them. I belong here with you."

Amelia threw her hands around his neck. "I'm surprised to hear you say that, but I'm also glad. It means you're ready, just as I told Mother you would be."

"Ready for what?" Zack asked.

Amelia wrapped an arm around his waist and escorted him down the aisle past the others. She then pushed him to Erisa's side.

"You are ready to be enlightened." Erisa's words were for Zack, but her attention stayed on the curtain. "To become part of something bigger than all of us. You will see how history will change for the better thanks to what we do today. Thanks to you, Zack Galloway."

"I don't understand," Zack said. "This is just a show, isn't it? I mean, I know what we do is important, but I wouldn't say it changes history."

A couple of giggles filled the group. One of them came from Amelia. Erisa snatched Zack's left arm and led him up the stage steps. "Your former coven, The Witches of Vegas, they performed on this same stage. Yet, this canvas was but a surface for their true role, was it not?"

It was. "Your show is a cover? For what? Is it also to practice your witchcraft?"

"Like your former coven, The Wiccan Circus is but a means to an end as well." Erisa positioned Zack in the middle of the stage facing the back curtain. "Our mission is a divine one, Zack. It began hundreds of years before any of us were born. But, on this day, our patience has been rewarded. Now we have the key."

Zack peeked over his shoulder. All eyes, including Erisa's, were on him. "Me?" Zack tapped his chest. He had never been so perplexed in his life, and that included when he learned about the existence of witches and vampires. "What am I the key to?"

"What has been discussed for generations all throughout the world." Erisa took hold of both Zack's hands. She leaned in. Zack smelled the nicotine on her breath. "Although their specifics are inaccurate, most religions believe in a savior sent by a higher power to lead us on a righteous path. It is believed this savior walked among us, only to be taken from this plane of existence. It was a sacrifice so that the rest of us may inherit a better Earth."

Erisa's eyes closed. Her voice was loud, meaning she spoke not just to Zack, but everyone in the theater. "But we, as a people, have not done well with it. The world, historically, has been arrogant and hostile to what it doesn't understand. We now wait for this savior to come back so that we may be led on the proper path of peace and prosperity. It will be a road to nirvana."

Another peek offstage revealed Amelia and the rest of the cast kneeling along the center aisle. Zack never believed much in religion, although his mother took him to church on a regular basis before her death. As he aged, curiosity did get the better of him, so he read the Bible. Even if he wasn't necessarily going to follow it, he could still learn what he could from the book's content. It didn't sound like Erisa followed a specific religion either, but it was clear her belief was unwavering.

He suddenly couldn't feel his hands. Erisa's grip had slipped to his wrists and tightened. "So, you believe this savior is coming?" he whispered.

"We believe she already has returned, Zack," Erisa answered. "But she was misunderstood. She was forced back to her purgatory by the misguided. It is now left to us, the enlightened, to free her from that prison and bring her back to our world. Then, we will be the first to welcome, and follow her on the path to righteousness!"

Zack jumped at the sound of many voices from the theater's floor shouting together, "Amen."

"My God," he muttered. "You're fanatics."

"We are believers, Zack," Erisa replied. "We are respectful of history, but its true nature has been taken from us. But now, we will free our savior so that she may return once again and lead us in cleansing the evil that has corrupted our world."

Another "amen" came from the small crowd behind him. Amelia's was the loudest.

Erisa faced the back curtain and dropped to one knee. She waved to Zack to do the same. Seeing no other choice, he complied. Erisa wrapped an arm across his shoulders. Her eyes let out a yellowish glow. "We have waited on this day for generations. Today, our savior returns to us, and it will be all thanks to you, Zack Galloway. Realize that you are here today because it is your destiny, as it is ours."

The curtain rose, revealing a picture of their savior. "Holy crap," Zack whispered at the sight of the image. His body jerked backward, knocking him out of Erisa's grip and off his knees.

The image was clearly hand drawn, then colored in, and not by a professional artist. But despite the crude artwork, Zack knew who it was meant to be even before the curtain had made it to the top. The brown hair that hung down to her waist and the long black dress were on point. The eyes were a far brighter purple than what Zack remembered, but there could be no doubt who the picture depicted. The sneer was a dead giveaway.

Valeria.

Chapter Twenty-Five

Isis felt the comfy wool couch against her body, but her mind was somewhere else. She needed to focus on one person and less on her own frustrations. Of course, that wouldn't be easy. Each time she tried to put her emotions aside, one question popped into her head. Did they make a huge mistake coming back to Vegas? They certainly wouldn't be in this position if Isis could have just made New Salem work.

At least she wasn't dealing with it all on her own. "Sweetie, can you sense him?" asked Selena, seated next to Isis on the couch. Her fingers ran through Isis' hair.

"I can. Something just frightened him. Badly." Isis opened her eyes. "I think he's okay, but I'm worried. I think we should bring him back, now."

"Hey, the boy made his choice," Sacha replied while leaned against the back of the easy chair on which Simon was planted. "He wanted to go."

"I know he did. But still…"

"Don't worry. We'll get him back." Selena gave Isis a squeeze.

Sebastian walked over from the kitchen area. His ruffled hair and sweaty collared shirt made him look like someone who had just been through a battle. "Okay, I just hung up with the hotel's entertainment manager. This afternoon's show is officially canceled."

"How'd he take it?" Sacha asked.

"Oh, he was pissed, especially over the short notice." Sebastian's eyes went wide. "I've never heard so many profanities in one conversation before. He expressed his understanding as to why The Sapphire didn't want us back."

"You gave him our excuse?" Selena asked.

"Yes, but I don't think he believes that we all came down with a sudden virus that will be better by tonight."

Simon raised a finger, finally turning his attention away from the TV, which was muted. "If I may, perhaps I could provide our audience with a one-man show. I should think a night of comedy from an actual undead vampire would be worth a look from a sold-out crowd."

"That's probably not the best idea," Sebastian responded.

"I don't see why not. I can be quite humorous—"

The conversation went on, but Isis' thoughts were obsessed with worry over Zack. Yes, it was true that he went there willingly and by choice, but if something happened to him, she'd never forgive herself. Their lives were too intertwined despite what recent bumps in the road may have come between them.

None of what happened was Zack's fault. He was hit with a Wiccan spell, one that made him trust Amelia unconditionally. Without even knowing her, he believed his trust was genuine and real… Hmm…

"Hey, guys," Isis said to everyone in the room, interrupting their conversation. "Can I ask you all something?"

"Of course, Sweetie," Selena responded. "What's

on your mind?"

"When you first took me in, I remember I was so nervous with you being witches, Luther was a vampire, and finding out I was a witch." Isis stretched her lips into a nervous grin. "You were also the first white people I ever really knew. I'm not saying that in a bad way."

"I didn't think you were," Sebastian replied. "But where *are* you going with this?"

"Right. My point is you were strangers, and different from anything I'd ever known. But I had nowhere else to go. I was such a mess. Then, I calmed down real fast, and I was comfortable around you. I saw you as the first, and the only, family I ever really had. After a while, I was even crawling in your bed between the two of you whenever I had a bad dream."

"Yes, I remember we'd wake up and find you there." Sebastian's head tipped to the side. "Isis, what are you asking us?"

She wasn't sure how to approach the question, except just to ask. "Did you, um, do something to make me trust you?"

"Are you asking if we put you under a spell?" Sebastian asked.

"Well, yeah, I guess I am." Dad did on occasion use a charisma spell on their audiences. At that point, Isis was their audience of one.

Selena stroked the back of Isis' neck. "No, Sweetie, we never influenced your thoughts, and we never will. With that said, you were nine years old, and you'd been through so much horror, you were traumatized. You couldn't sleep or keep food down—"

"I remember you also jumped at every little

sound," Sacha added.

"Those first few days were rough, but we understood," Selena explained. "We needed to help, so we used the energy to create the Wiccan equivalent of a sedative."

"You did that?" Isis asked.

"It was necessary to calm your nerves," Sebastian said. "It helped you relax. After that, your trust came from you and your own instincts. That's the honest truth."

"Okay, good to know." Accepting their answer, Isis gave her mom's knee a gentle pat, then stood from the couch with her back perfectly straight. It was time. "I'm ready to get him back!" Isis spoke with a conviction she hadn't heard out of herself, maybe ever. At least not in this timeline.

"You're sure you want to waltz in there by yourself?" Sebastian asked. "We have no idea what may be waiting for you."

Isis nodded. She knew how dangerous Amelia was. Erisa was probably even more so, and they had allies there, a slew of non-Wiccan people Isis could never bring herself to hurt. But she needed to show everyone, especially herself, that she was not afraid. Isis needed her family's help, but she was ready to do her part as well.

"If you're sure, then head over there and bring him home," Selena said to her. "We'll be right behind you."

Sacha threw a playful punch into Isis' shoulder. "Go get him, Kiddo."

189

Chapter Twenty-Six

"Um, Erisa, can we speak in private?" Zack whispered.

"Of course. I am sure you have many questions, and I do seek to answer them all." The witch stood from her kneeling position and waved a hand at Zack. "Please, come this way."

Erisa glided across the stage to the dressing room. Zack followed her in at a rabbit's pace, almost bumping into her when she stopped short midway. The room was actually a lot tidier than when it was the dressing room for The Witches of Vegas' show. That was despite having several more outfits hung on hooks along the walls.

"You are agitated, Zack. Why?" Erisa asked.

The door slammed behind him, forcing him to spin around. Amelia was inside with them, her back pressed against the door. "It's okay, Zack," she said. "I'm here by your side."

"The woman in the picture…who you say is your savior…" Zack's head flipped back and forth from Erisa to Amelia. "Are you aware of who she is?"

Amelia let out a loud laugh. "We know exactly who she is, Zack. We've been waiting for her return all our lives."

"Valeria's purpose has been known to my family for generations." Erisa stretched her arms out and looked up to the ceiling. "Of course, our knowledge is limited to tales and long-standing beliefs. We have not yet met her directly like you have. Is that correct, Zack?"

Zack's jaw nearly went through the floor. They were more aware of him than he realized, which meant they also knew about Isis and her family. No point in keeping what he knew a secret anymore. "Yes, I have met Valeria. She's a psychopath who murders witches like you and enslaves non-Wiccan people like me." He pointed a thumb over his shoulder at the door. "Or like them out there. She does it all to flaunt her power—"

Erisa held out her palm, a signal to Zack to stop speaking and listen. "No, Zack, you have been horribly misled. What you claim to know is due to the manipulation tactics of your former coven. My knowledge of her plan and her message is far more direct."

"How?"

Erisa walked up to Zack in what he took as an attempt to intimidate him. She was a tall woman who had at least a foot on him. She also smelled of tobacco. Zack wanted to stand his ground, but instinct, and the odor, knocked him back a step.

"How much did they teach you about Valeria's history?" Erisa clutched both of Zack's shoulders and pulled him closer. "Did they tell you about her life before she was imprisoned the first time?"

Zack's body tensed up when a hand pressed against his upper back. It was Amelia's. She had wandered directly behind him. "A lot," he answered. "They told me that witches stood against Valeria. That their combined connection sent her to another dimension."

Erisa shook her head, then raised one finger in the air. "Yes, there were many witches who resisted the vision Valeria had for Mother Earth's future. But there were others who understood. There were those who embraced the peace and prosperity that Valeria wanted to bring. They worked with her to make such a magnificent dream possible. Unfortunately, they were overwhelmed by those who could not accept her vision and would not embrace change."

Zack's eyebrows rose. "Don't tell me you were one of those witches."

Erisa's laugh filled the small room. "Of course not. I am not immortal. But Amelia and I, we had an ancestor, a witch named Belinda. It was she who fought in vain for the future of our kind throughout the world."

"They murdered people," Zack exclaimed. "Lots of people."

"There are always casualties in war, Zack." Erisa turned her back. "But in the end, we lost. Valeria was taken from us before her work could unfold. She was a casualty of the world's resistance to a better path. That is, until recently."

"What happened recently?"

"You really are cute, Zack." Amelia slapped his rear end, which only confused him further. "Do you know that?"

Zack wasn't sure how to respond. But Amelia, leaning her chin on his shoulder, gave his nose a strong whiff of her pink hair. It reminded him of the fresh flowers in New Salem's garden.

"I was there in the crowd to witness Valeria's return!" Erisa raised her hands. She spoke loudly as if she were in front of a congregation. "I watched as a new generation of witches, misguided and blasphemous—along with you, Zack—participated in sending our liberator back to her prison through a portal in the sky. She was dragged through against her will by what I believe was an undead vampire. It confirmed all I had been taught of Valeria's whereabouts. They are beliefs I have known my entire life, which is why I focused Amelia's gift on creating her own portals."

Erisa pointed to the door. "Now we can finally free Valeria and bring her back to this world where her followers will be waiting to meet her arrival."

"My God, no!" Zack tried to back away, but Amelia had a tight grip on him. "Neither of you understand. Valeria is a cold-blooded killer. She tried to kill us, more than once—"

"No, Zack," Erisa cut him off. "She was simply fighting against resistance to the cause. She will appreciate us, Wiccan and non-Wiccan alike, for bringing her back so she may resume her role as a direct advocate for Mother Earth."

Zack squinted past Erisa at the outfits hanging from hooks against the walls. It was the first time he had noticed that most of those outfits were white robes like Erisa's. They were all different sizes, meaning they were meant for the other performers. "Is this a cult?" The words flew from Zack's tongue before his brain could register the comment and stop him from being so blunt.

"Zack!" Amelia shrieked.

Erisa laughed. "That is such a harsh word, and it is not fitting in this situation. Our beliefs are not marred in hearsay and fictional stories. The tales we know of Valeria were a part of history long past but still relevant. Our connection to Mother Earth confirms those beliefs. It is why we stand together here in the Church of Valeria."

"The church of—" Zack's heart almost dropped into his stomach. It now made sense. He was correct when he said their show was used in much the way The Witches of Vegas used theirs, as a cover. But what they were covering was something far more sinister. Zack wanted to run out of the theater, go back to Isis and her family, and let them know what was going on. But it was too late for that. He was here now. There was no turning around at this point, and he did want to keep the trust of Amelia and her mother. At the moment, they were accepting him, which is what he needed if he was going to stay in their good graces. His future might depend on it.

Amelia moved in front of Zack. She pressed her hands against the back of his neck and looked him directly in the eyes. "Please, Zack, we can free her, but only with your help. I know it's a huge ask, but I need you to do this for us. Can we count on you?"

"I'm not a witch, I have no Wiccan connection at all," Zack said. "How, exactly, can I help?"

Erisa folded her hands against her chest. "We need you, Zack Galloway, to attract those who do have the power to aid us."

Now it made sense. They wanted Zack to be bait at best, a manipulator at worst. Everything about this was wrong. He knew that. But as he stared into Amelia's intoxicating eyes, he knew there was only one answer he could give. It may not have been the right answer, but he didn't have much choice. The scheme was a dangerous gambit. Still, he had no intention of tucking his tail between his legs and running.

"I guess I'm in," he said. "What do you need me to do?"

Amelia's lips stretched into a huge smile. "You see that, Mother? I told you we could count on him."

"Wonderful. Then we have no time to waste." Erisa cupped her hands together and glided to the door. "Amelia, inform Zack of what we need of him. Meanwhile, I, and the others, will prepare for our final private performance."

The door creaked closed. Amelia planted a peck on Zack's cheek, and then one on the lips. "Let's get ready." Amelia took his hand and flashed a devious grin. "We have a lot to set up for our guests."

Chapter Twenty-Seven

Twenty minutes later…

Isis teleported outside The Sapphire Theater, making sure to appear at the end of the hallway in front of the double door entrance. That hallway was only filled with people before a scheduled show. Since it was early morning, Isis could teleport in without a crowd to see her appear out of nowhere. It was time for the confrontation she couldn't avoid, not without losing Zack. Isis wouldn't let that happen. She needed him as much he needed her, now more than ever.

The theater doors should have been locked; at least they were during downtimes when she performed here. But they were unlocked. She was expected, not that Isis couldn't have walked through the door even if it was locked. She entered the dark theater. The door slammed shut behind her as if a strong wind had taken hold of it. Yeah, she was definitely expected.

"I'm here!" she shouted at the empty auditorium. "Come out, come out, wherever you are!"

The lights flipped on. Isis was ready for anything, at least that's what she thought before she saw the setup on the stage. It made her gawk. The right side of the stage floor had a large circle drawn in white chalk. A smaller circle was drawn on the left side, and it was just big enough to surround a steel cage. The cage wasn't for a human being; it was barely large enough to fit a German shepherd inside. Five crystals lay along the chalk outline. They weren't fakes like the ones sold at their souvenir stand. Isis sensed the energy emitting around the diamond shape, meaning those were genuine enchanted crystals.

It wasn't the cage, the crystals, or the circles that made Isis pause in her step. It was the image on the back wall. Not a perfect depiction, but she knew who that was supposed to be. It was the face that haunted Isis' nightmares. Their worst battles took place in that other reality. It was through sheer luck that Isis outsmarted her and this new timeline now stood. How in the world did they even know about Valeria?

Rustling from all sides pulled Isis from the drawing. Damn, she should have been paying attention. Ten teens all in white robes moved through the aisles and closed in on Isis from each side. Three marched to the theater doors and stood in front of them. She recognized everyone as the non-Wiccan cast members of the show.

"You know I'm a real witch, right?" Isis said to the small crowd that had surrounded her. "I don't want to hurt any of you."

On the stage, Amelia stepped out from behind the side curtain, also in a white robe. "Don't worry, hon," she shouted. "You won't."

The floor opened underneath Isis' feet. There was no time to conjure a spell before she dropped through the portal. Isis landed on all fours. Although it was quick, her brain spun as if she had fallen from miles above. Isis tried to stand, but the back of her head slammed against something solid and unmoving. A clanging noise echoed. The back of her head stung. She reached behind. There was no blood, but she did feel a bump.

Isis groped with her right hand. It touched a metal bar. Her blurry vision cleared. She was inside the cage on the stage. Isis yanked on the door, but it wouldn't open from the inside. She tried to call upon the energy to escape, but she sensed no connection. Then she realized why.

"You're using the enchanted crystals to cut off my connection," Isis said to Amelia. "I didn't think you could control them."

"Me? I can't, but we both know who can." Amelia looked over her shoulder. "I'm also not the one who set them up around the cage. That task belonged to my new assistant."

Isis held a hand in front of the bars, taking in the vibration of energy around them. She knew exactly the witch who controlled those crystals even before the side curtain flew open. Erisa walked out dressed in a white Geneva gown. She wasn't alone. Zack stared down at Isis with a hint of concern. At least he wasn't in a white robe as well.

"You promised you wouldn't hurt her," he said from Erisa's left side.

"Don't tell me you still care about this one." Amelia walked up to Zack and wrapped her arms around his waist. "Do you care about her, Zack?"

"No, I...I only care about you, Amelia," he answered. "But that doesn't mean I want her to get hurt."

"Oh, aren't you just the sweetest? I'm so lucky to have you." Amelia stared down at Isis, throwing her a teasing grin. She placed a hand on Zack's chest. "Do you have the rest of the crystals so you can finish the job?"

"I do." Zack reached into his jacket pocket and pulled out a set of five enchanted crystals resting in his palm. "I'll put them all in place. You can count on me."

The ten members of...whatever this was...made their way to the front row and sat at the edge of their seats with wide eyes pointed at the stage. If she didn't know better, Isis would have thought each of them were in a trance. Might as well find out for sure.

"Thomas, look at me!" Isis shouted. He was seated directly in front of her. His head popped up, then he stood. "You're such a good guy. How can you be a part of this? How can any of you?"

"We are believers." Thomas walked up to the stage and leaned forward. "From the moment Erisa showed us that real magic exists in the world, we understood that we are part of something greater than ourselves."

"It's true, real magic...witchcraft...it does exist. But everything else she's told you are lies. She's using one shred of truth to brainwash you."

Meghan jumped up from her chair and grabbed Thomas's arm. "Don't listen, Thomas! Erisa warned us that she would try to mislead us." Her words were filled with venom. "That she would come here and test our faith."

"That won't happen, Luv," Thomas responded. "This day has been written, and we all know how it ends."

"Please, you don't know what you're talking about. She's playing you—"

Thomas and Meghan about-faced and returned to

their seats. They shared the same tranquil look in their eyes as the others on either side of them. Maybe they were all under a spell, or maybe these were just teens who needed something spiritual to believe in. Whatever the reason, this was a group being manipulated, which meant Isis couldn't look to any of them for help. The one person she wanted to look to, Zack, followed Amelia around the other circle and placed crystals on the floor.

Erisa knelt in front of the cage. She faced the picture of Valeria with her hands folded. Isis expected her to speak, but it looked like she was praying. Guess she had to start the conversation.

"What do you want with me?" Isis shook the cage door. It wouldn't dislodge.

"Despite what I perceive as ego on your part, Isis," Erisa said with her eyes shut tight, "this isn't about you. It never has been. But, like Zack, you are instrumental in bringing those we do need to our theater."

"My family," Isis realized. "Why?"

"Not all of them," Erisa answered. "From my observations of the battle earlier this year, it was the Quinn sisters who created and directed the portal which took our goddess, Valeria, from this plane of existence. I could see that they did this to save you. Now, to do so again, I will need them to reconnect with that world so we can assist in Valeria's return. Then our savior can resume her mission."

Was she serious? Isis' eyes flashed to Zack, who returned her unspoken question with a nod. "Opening a portal, especially to another dimension, is complicated," Isis said to Erisa. "It took everything they had. They probably couldn't do it again, even to save me."

"What matters is they know how to access Valeria's prison." Erisa's head shot Isis' way. "The portal itself is taken care of. They need only to connect it to the precise location."

Amelia walked across the stage, stopping in front of her mother. She peered down at Isis. "Years of training, and we're finally here. I'm looking forward to opening that portal."

"What about you, Zack? Are you okay with all of this?" Isis snarled like a scared dog. "Do you still think you're not under a spell?"

Zack never looked back at her, although there was a slight tremble in his lower lip. "I'm fine," he said, although his eyes were on Amelia, not Isis. He refocused on the large circle and dropped the fourth enchanted crystal in its place.

"Enough wasted talk. We have all waited long enough!" Erisa slammed a fist against the bars. The cage vibrated around Isis. "It is time for you to summon your coven. Bring them here to participate in the rapture so that an error in judgment made hundreds of years ago can now be rectified!"

Thomas, and a few others in the front row, shouted, "Amen!"

Chapter Twenty-Eight

Zack held the fifth crystal between his forefinger and thumb over its designated spot along the circle. It barely had any weight yet it was about to play a role in something big. Deep down, none of this felt right, but he also understood there was no choice. Despite the feeling in his stomach that reminded him of the time he ate uncooked chicken, Zack was committed to this path and determined to see it through. It was the only way forward.

Erisa and Amelia were intent on rescuing Valeria and bringing her back to planet Earth. From what his natural senses told him about their followers, none of them had any trepidations about meeting and following the Wiccan vampire. The only way to satisfy everyone in this auditorium was to give them what they wanted. Zack's only hope was that it didn't blow up and incite a battle that would destroy all of Vegas. At this point, he had to trust the plan and keep the faith.

"It is time, Isis." Erisa backed away from the cage. "Summon your family and bring them here."

"Not a chance," Isis roared. "Do what you want to me, I won't help you."

Amelia leaned in front of the cage, which brought her to eye level with Isis. "Look at your former beau over there." She waved a hand in Zack's direction. "Do you still love him even after he broke your heart? I'm only asking because if you don't do as we say, we plan to kill him right in front of you."

"Amelia?" Zack exclaimed.

"It's for the cause, Babe," she replied, never looking at Zack. "Besides, I'm sure Isis won't let that happen. We're relying on her resolve not being as strong as ours."

"She won't call them, not even for me," Zack said. "Isis won't willingly put her family in what she perceives as danger. But I can get them here without her."

"Zack, are you crazy?" Isis screamed. "You can't!"

"How?" Erisa asked. "Do you have a Wiccan connection I cannot sense?"

"I don't need witchcraft to make a phone call." Zack reached into his back pocket and pulled out his phone. He was sure the excitement resonating in his body displayed on his face. "I can reach them and say we're in trouble. They'll sense where we are and come right over."

"A shrewd plan. Destiny always finds a way." Erisa turned to the picture of Valeria and cupped her hands together. "Do it, my child. Summon our soon-to-be apostles."

Members of the seated onlookers shouted, "Do it!" following Erisa's lead.

"Okay!" Zack held the phone up for all to see. "I will do it!" His announcement was met with cheers and applause that were far more explosive than any he had received during a show.

"Damnit, Zack, how could you?" Isis muttered.

"You just got really lucky," Amelia said to Isis. "Zack's betrayal may have saved his life, and you a lot of pain."

Zack pressed the speaker button, then a speed dial button on his phone's screen. It was programmed to call the house phone in the Galloway Theater's dressing room. That's where he expected they would be at this time. While he waited for the phone in his left hand to ring, the crystal in his right palm suddenly felt heavy, like it had just quadrupled in weight. He wanted to let it go, but it wasn't the time. Not yet. He had to stick with the plan.

The phone didn't ring, it only gave off blank noise. But suddenly the area in front of Zack—the space inside the large circle—blurred. Erisa's lips stretched into a huge smile. As expected, they came as soon as Zack called. They trusted him wholeheartedly, like family. A pang of guilt ran down his chest over what he was bringing them into without so much as a warning. But to keep the trust of everyone in the room, he had little choice.

The blurriness cleared, revealing Selena and Sacha with Sebastian between them. As expected, their confused faces zipped from one end of the stage to the other. Sacha pointed at the image on the wall in front of them. "Whoa," she shouted. "Is that who I think it is?"

"Zack, what's going on here?" Sebastian's eyes dropped to the floor, at the white chalk circle surrounding them with four enchanted crystals equally apart from one another. "What in the world—"

This was Zack's cue. He dropped the last crystal in its place. The ball was in motion. Whatever happened now, however it ended up playing out, it was too late to stop it.

"Isis!" Selena screamed. She grabbed Sebastian's

arm and turned him to see their charge trapped like an animal in a cage across the stage. "Did they hurt you, sweetie?"

"Zack, what is this?" Sebastian's voice roared. He stepped forward. "Don't tell me you're part of this. Even under a spell you would know better—"

"Sebastian, I need you to listen to me!" Zack threw a hand forward, a signal to Sebastian not to come any closer. "Those enchanted crystals around you are emitting an invisible force field controlled by Erisa. If you touch it, you will be electrified until your heart stops. It will kill you!" Yeah, no more doubts. Zack was all in.

Sacha's head turned from the ten people in the front row to the salt-and-pepper-haired lady in the robe walking their way. "What the hell are you?" Her eyes dropped to Erisa's white sandals. "And in what century did you get your outfit?"

"I take it you're Erisa?" Selena asked.

"The time has finally come, my friends and followers!" Erisa's voice echoed throughout the theater. "The Church of Valeria is about to experience the rapture we have awaited for hundreds of years!"

"The Church of *Valeria*? Zack, what the hell is she talking about?" Sebastian asked, a narrowed glare pointed outward.

"Please, Zack." Erisa waved a hand to the cage. "Right now, you speak for all of us. Inform them of their role in today's proceedings."

Amelia threw her arm around Zack's shoulders. "Go ahead, Hon," she said in his ear. "Lay it on them, and lay it thick." She flashed a smirk at the three in the circle.

"Amelia is going to open a portal," Zack explained as clearly as he could. "They need the sisters to direct it to the Other World so Valeria can return to Earth."

Sacha's eyes went wide. "You want us to do *what* now?"

"Zack, you know how dangerous Valeria is to this world," Selena pleaded. "She needs to remain there for everybody's safety."

"No!" Zack shouted even louder than he thought himself capable. "Valeria's destiny is to save everyone with us following her. We were wrong to stop her in the first place." He glanced at Amelia who gave him a nod of approval. "Today, we bring her back with your help."

"As you see, Zack understands," Erisa said. "He has broken through your brainwashing and has come to terms with a renewed enlightenment."

"Why would we ever cooperate?" Sebastian roared like a lion.

"Because if you don't—" Amelia's huge grin filled with determination. "—we are ready to persuade you."

Sebastian's angry eyes turned to Zack. "So, this is what you left us for? For all we've done for you, for all we've been through with you! You're going to undo it all?"

"Sebastian, be careful." Zack gasped, catching Sebastian inching his way. "Remember what I told you about the crystals—"

"You betrayed us!" Sebastian screamed with a rage that lit up the room. "You betrayed Isis! You little son of a—"

"Sebastian, the force field!"

Sebastian lunged forward. His hands shot past the

crystals' perimeter. His body shook in place. Then it convulsed. Static covered the clear crystal-created dome.

"Sebastian!" Selena screeched. She reached out for him, but Sacha grabbed her by the waist and yanked her back.

"Dad!" Isis slammed a right fist against the cage door. She quickly clutched her knuckles with her left hand and cringed in pain.

Soon, Sebastian's body stopped convulsing. His eyes rolled to the back of his head. He stumbled back, then collapsed like a discarded toy landing face-first on the floor. Selena and Sacha dropped to their knees at Sebastian's side.

Selena placed a finger against his carotid artery and gasped. "He's not breathing. He's dead. My husband is dead."

"Oh, no." Sacha crawled away from the body.

Zack stared down at the man who tried hard to fill that missing father figure in his life. He should have been a lot more upset over the scene that had just played out in front of his eyes. But Zack only felt detachment. He just hoped everyone would understand his lack of emotion in the end.

Erisa, Amelia, and their followers certainly understood. There was no remorse in any of them either.

Chapter Twenty-Nine

Isis turned her head away from what she had just witnessed. If she wasn't stuck in a cage that kept her on her knees, she would have run as fast and as far as she could. Her father's body lay lifeless. Mom and Sacha backed away making sure to stay in the crystals' perimeter. Meanwhile, Zack stood over them, watching without an ounce of guilt with another girl's arm around his waist. This was Isis' worst nightmare come to life. Amelia's demented grin sure didn't make it any better. Wow, Isis hated that girl so much.

Her head dropped as a tear rolled down her cheek. That's when she focused on the enchanted crystal in front of her just beyond the cage door. It would have been easy to touch it with her mind, especially now while Erisa was distracted. If she moved it just an inch, the pyramid formed by the five crystals would be broken. Then Isis could walk through the bars and unleash the full extent of her Wiccan connection on her captors. She'd expect the rest of the family to follow suit and end this right away.

But what if it went bad? What if her actions led to making things worse? Then all hope would be lost. She had no idea how powerful Erisa truly was, but she did know how fast Amelia could be with her connection. It was Sebastian who taught Isis at a young age not to attack blindly when in trouble. That at times she'd need to wait for her moment. Maybe this was one of those times to hang back and wait, let the adults in the coven take the lead. They'd know the best moment to strike. At least that's what she counted on.

"What happened just now was unfortunate." Erisa spoke more to her congregation than to Selena and Sacha. "Your coven leader's temper got the better of him, but know it was not our intention for him to die at this point."

"You brought us here," Selena cried out. "Because of you, my husband is dead for no good reason!"

"There's a lot of good reason!" Amelia shouted back. "Besides, we didn't do it. He killed himself—"

"Enough!" Erisa raised her arms in the air. In response, the lights flashed. "You were brought here to make amends for your past transgressions and right a historic wrong. *The time has come, we will wait no longer!*"

The ten members of the congregation cheered. They looked to Erisa, perhaps seeking approval for their convictions. In that moment, Isis wondered about each of their lives outside this theater. They were her age, but did they have families who loved them? Were they victims of abuse, or neglect? Were they spurned by the boy or girl from school that they fancied? What could have led each of them to getting coerced into a cult that worshipped an all-powerful psychotic killer who hated their kind? Isis didn't find Erisa to be that persuasive, yet not a single one of them questioned her insane goals even as they played out in front of their eyes.

Sacha stood. She walked to the end of the chalk circle's perimeter, keeping just enough distance from where they guessed the electric force field stood. "Listen up, lady," she shouted at Erisa. "If you think we have any intention of doing what you want, then you're even loonier than you look!"

"I'm afraid you don't have a choice," Erisa replied.

Sacha pointed a finger forward. "We're not about to free someone who is even more psycho than you!"

The congregation responded with a chorus of boos. Erisa turned her back on Sacha and walked to the circle around Isis' cage. "Your coven leader's death was due to his own actions. Do not blame yourselves for his fate." She waved a hand at Isis. "However, if you refuse to cooperate, the death of your youngest member will be your responsibility."

Sacha backed up. The resolve melted from her face. "You'd kill a fifteen-year-old in front of an audience her age?"

Black smoke filled the cage until Isis could no longer be seen. The smoke then cleared, leaving just the cage's shell-shocked prisoner. Isis rubbed her hands over her eyes, coughing smoke out of her throat.

"I'd rather not," Erisa replied. "But we've come too far. If you force my hand, I will instruct the crystals around her to fill with fire until she burns to death."

"No!" Isis screamed. "You can't bring Valeria back! Let her do her worst, I'm not afraid to die!"

"You hear that?" Sacha's head spun toward Zack. "She's going to kill Isis."

Zack replied with a cold "I know. I'm sorry."

"That's all you have to say? You're sorry?" Sacha shook her head in disgust. "I'll tell you now, this bluff isn't going to work. We're not letting Valeria destroy this world no matter—"

Selena jumped to her feet and stepped in front of Sacha, facing Erisa. "All right," she shouted through grinding teeth. "We'll do it."

"Sis, are you out of your mind?" Sacha's jaw fell to the point it almost hit the ground. "Valeria's wrath on this world is exactly what we were trained to prevent!"

"I can't lose both of them today," Selena sobbed. "I just can't. I won't."

"Mom, it's okay," Isis shouted. "We can't let them win!" But her screams were ignored. No surprise here. Isis knew all along it would come to this moment.

Selena grabbed her younger sister's arm. "Sach, I beg you. Please. I can't watch Isis die, too. Let's open the damn portal and then deal with the repercussions later."

"Okay, fine," Sacha exclaimed. "I guess we're bringing her back."

"A wise decision," Erisa replied.

Amelia slapped her hands together. "It looks like I'm up." She pushed against Zack's chest. "Why don't you wait at the end of the stage? I have a feeling this will all be over soon."

"Not over," Erisa said as she sat between the two chalk circles with her legs crossed. "It will be a new beginning, one we helped create for our entire world."

Isis leaned forward and watched Zack jog to the right side of the stage. He grabbed the side curtain, which was wide open, and yanked it closed. "Zack," Amelia said. "What are you doing?"

"I know Valeria," he explained. "When she comes through, she'll be confused and disoriented. If she sees that open doorway down the hallway, she may bolt. We can't let that happen. If she leaves before your mom can speak with her, then everything we went through to get her here would be for nothing." Zack eyed the sisters. "I'm betting that's what they are counting on."

"That makes sense," Amelia said to her mother. "Once she's here, we need her to stay."

Erisa waved a hand toward the side curtain on the opposite side. It also led to an exit. The curtain closed on its own. She pointed at Amelia who made her way to the back of the stage, facing the sisters from several feet away.

"All right, go ahead," Sacha said to her with resigned defeat in her voice. "Form the portal, and we'll do the rest."

"Be warned," Erisa said with emphasis. "Do not try to be clever, or there will be dire consequences."

"For Isis' sake," Selena replied, "you can trust us."

Amelia stretched her arms as far as she could. A circle of static formed in front of her.

Chapter Thirty

Zack couldn't stop staring at Isis. Inside, he could only imagine what was going on in her head with a front-row seat to the chaos in front of her. Sebastian's body lay on the floor, facedown and unmoving. It was a visual that had to be ripping her apart. Selena and Sacha faced Amelia who had her back against the oversized drawing of Valeria. A pang of guilt filled Zack's insides, although he knew there was no reason to feel that way. He was only doing his part.

This was the moment his new coven—or "family" as he now saw them—had prepared for. Zack had never gone through the experience of being on a stage without knowing how events would play out, but that was exactly the case right now. Despite the potential danger, not knowing what would happen made it even more exciting. Besides, he was pretty confident that everything would work out for the better. They knew what they were doing.

Selena and Sacha clutched hands, ready to begin. Across the stage a round blur formed in front of Amelia. The sisters jumped into a lengthy and fast spoken chant. It was impossible to make out, but to Zack's ears it sounded like a spell. Then again, it could have been gibberish; he really had no idea. Erisa watched them with excitement and intrigue. If anyone could understand their chant, it would be her.

After several long seconds, the center of the portal fluctuated. "Oh wow, something's happening here," Amelia said, from behind the blur.

"Of course it is!" Erisa called while waving her hands in the air. "Come to us, Goddess! We anxiously await your arrival!"

The center of the distorted circle turned into pure-white static. Soon, the static turned into a blinding light that forced Zack to look away. The entire congregation did the same. With a squint, Zack spun his head back to the portal. This was the moment. Time for Erisa and her congregation to meet Valeria.

An arm popped out of the bright light. It was followed by a leg and then an entire body. Zack stepped back, an instinctive reaction to seeing those dark eyes and fangs protruding from either side of her mouth. Her red fingernails were even longer than how Zack remembered them and were sharpened to the point they looked like butcher knives. Seeing Valeria standing outside that portal in the same dress she wore on the Vegas Strip shot Zack's anxiety through the roof to the point he almost lost his balance. He could only imagine what this was doing to Isis and the witches.

"Oh, no!" Isis screeched. Her head spun to the congregation. "All of you need to run! Now! You don't want to stay here!" None of them budged from their seats.

Valeria's head rotated across the auditorium. Her long grayish-black hair stayed in place. Her gaze focused on the congregation sitting in the front row, all with their mouths hung open. "You are not all witches," Valeria growled. "What is this?"

"Goddess Valeria!" Erisa shouted from her knees

while facing the immortal witch. "We are among the followers who have worshipped you for hundreds of years! We have brought you back from damnation so you may lead us in rebuilding this broken world and recreating your vision of a new and prosperous era for witches. It is they who will take their place at the top of the chain, around the world!"

Meghan grabbed Thomas's hand. "For witches?" she said, with two raised eyebrows. "That's not what she told us."

Valeria stared down Erisa with an annoyed scowl. "Why would you presume I wish to be brought back?"

Erisa's head twisted as if she had just received a right cross to the jaw. "What are you saying, Goddess?" she shrieked. "We have risked everything for this moment. We give our lives to your cause. By bringing you back, we offer you the world!"

"*You are a fool!*" Valeria snapped. She waved a hand at the portal. "I have a world back there that I can call my own with no need ever again of this dimension."

"But, Goddess, your mission—"

"*Quiet!*" Valeria's eyes narrowed. "I have no need of a mortal witch such as yourself determining my mission!" She lifted her head over Erisa's shoulder to the congregation. "And as for all of you, be glad I am no longer obsessed with said mission, for you would be the first non-Wiccan casualties I would incinerate in my one-time pursuit of cleansing this planet for my fellow kin."

"Um, Mom?" Amelia's voice squeaked. "I closed the portal. I felt it close, but it's still open. I'm not in control over it anymore."

"Goddess Valeria," Erisa pleaded from her knees. "I have devoted my entire life to you. My mother did the same, as did her father before her—"

A bolt of lightning shot out of Valeria's palm. It rose up, then fizzled. "You have wasted your fleeting lives in a fruitless pursuit." She spoke with an eerie calm. "My parting advice is that you all leave this place and do something productive with the brief time you have. Just make sure you do not waste *my* time with such foolish nonsense ever again."

Valeria about-faced and reentered the portal. She disappeared, as did the bright light that shot through it. Erisa let out a deep gasp as the portal closed.

"Mother?" Amelia screeched. The wide-eyed look on her face said she was lost on what to do next. It may have been the first time Zack saw the confidence sucked out of her.

Erisa stood up. She was in the center of the stage with all eyes on her. That included her prisoners and the congregation still seated in the front row. "This cannot be," she shrieked. "How could it?" Her upset gaze stopped on Selena and Sacha. Her eyes narrowed. "You...you did this." Her screeching echoed throughout the auditorium.

"Don't look at us," Sacha replied. "We did exactly what you made us do. I guess you didn't know her as well as you thought."

"I don't understand." Erisa's hands covered her face. "After generations, our plan to bring back Valeria worked. How could she forsake us so easily? Why would she voluntarily return to her prison?"

Sacha's scoff echoed. "Because she's not interested in your mission, or in *you!*"

The theater went silent. Isis banged on the cage's barred roof. The loud clang shook the ten members of the front row's congregation out of their collective daze. "You heard what she said," Isis screeched in their direction. "You're wasting your time here. Valeria doesn't want you to free her; she doesn't want to lead you. She wants you to move on with your lives." She sounded like a mother scolding her children.

The ten teens, looking back and forth at one another, broke into random murmuring. Thomas and Meghan stood from their seats. They eyed Isis, then each other. Soon the other eight stood as well. Without a word, the group turned left and headed for the theater's door.

"Hey!" Amelia shouted at them. "Where are you going?" She opened a portal and sprinted through. The second portal formed in front of the door. It blocked the group's exit from the theater and into the world. Amelia ran out and stood in their way.

"You can't just leave." Amelia held her palms pointed at the group as if to tell them to back away. "We are a team here. We have a common cause...you took an oath when you joined us—"

"We agreed to a goal, and we just succeeded," Thomas said, cutting Amelia off. "We brought your witch back and then heard her words. She doesn't want to be rescued. We were told to get lost and to get lives. So that's what we're off to do."

"Sorry, Babe," Meghan added. "It was fun and stuff, but I'm done with the whole supernatural witch thing. In fact, I think we all are." Heads among the group nodded in agreement.

"No-no-*no*!" Amelia stuttered in a way that was

uncharacteristic for her. Her head shifted from Erisa on the stage to the ten teens standing in front of her. "We need to stick together! We have to...you're *not* abandoning me!"

"Amelia!" Zack leaped off the stage and pushed through the crowd. He made it to Amelia's side and spoke in her ear. "It's over. Just let them go. They need to live their lives."

"They pledged to stay! They can't just walk away like this..." Amelia picked up her head and looked over the congregation. Zack did the same in time to see Erisa hovering in the air. Her hair spread in every direction as she floated their way.

The crowd backed off and formed a semicircle. Erisa landed in the middle, facing her daughter. "Come with me, Amelia. Immediately," she demanded.

"But, Mother, we were so close! We can't just accept defeat—"

"Heed me!"

Erisa clasped Amelia's shoulders, one with each hand. They blurred, then faded. The portal evaporated, leaving only the doorway out of the theater. Now, only Zack stood between the ten former members of the congregation and escape. He pulled open the door and stepped out of the way.

"Go ahead." He waved his arm to the hallway.

One by one, the teens exited through the doorway and spread out. The hall split into two corridors; one led to the parking garage while the other went to the hotel lobby. Both would take them to the Vegas Strip, away from The Sapphire and along their own paths. Now it was just Zack and The Witches of Vegas left in the theater.

On the stage, Selena kneeled over her husband's body. Sacha made her way to the cage holding Isis. Her eyes were locked on Zack who jogged back to the stage and up the steps.

"Okay," he said, through a wide grin while wiping a hand across his brow. "They're gone. It's over."

Chapter Thirty-One

Isis no longer sensed the energy swirling around her cage. That meant Erisa had truly left with Amelia. Sacha reached for the cage door's handle and pulled. Isis wasted no time crawling out. Zack offered a hand, which she took, so he could help her to her feet. Once upright, Isis stretched her back, which had gone stiff due to her being stuck hunched over for what had to be hours.

"Sebastian, honey, we did it," Selena called, standing over her husband's supine corpse. "Sebastian, can you hear me?"

Sebastian's body faded away as if it was never there. The side curtain, which Zack shut earlier, scuffled, then pulled open. Sebastian stepped onto the stage with a hand across his stomach and breathing heavily. "Sorry, everyone. But creating an illusion that complex and for that long of a time…it takes a lot of out of a witch."

Selena ran up to Sebastian, wrapped her arms around her husband, and gave him a tight hug. Her head sank into his chest. "The plan worked. Crisis averted," she exclaimed, with a sigh in her voice.

"It looks like the two of you were right," Sacha said to Isis and Zack. "They were definitely up to something major over here. We just didn't realize how major of a something."

Sebastian rolled his eyes. "The Church of Valeria. Were they serious?"

Selena released her bear hug on Sebastian and turned toward the rest of the coven. "That was timely, Zack, the way you tipped us off on what she was trying to do with the crystals. It was good thinking."

"I know you were listening in through me," Zack replied. "But I wasn't sure how long you were listening before you arrived. I didn't know if you caught that last piece of info."

"We didn't. Lucky we're damn good at improvising." Sacha picked up one of the crystals from the large circle. "Phony enchanted crystals." She held it in front of her eyes and gave it a close inspection. "I'm surprised that crazy witch didn't catch on."

"The ones around me sure were real," Isis said.

"I remember you once told me that a witch would struggle to control two enchanted crystal formations at once," Zack replied to Sacha. "I took a chance that, with her attention divided, Erisa wouldn't realize she wasn't actually controlling energy within them, especially if you made it look like they were doing exactly what she wanted."

Zack reached into his jacket pocket and pulled out a fist. He opened it to show five tiny crystals glistening along his palm. "Here are the real ones. I swapped them out before placing them around the circle."

"Very clever," Sebastian replied, between breaths. He and Selena strolled their way while he leaned on her for support. "Where did you get the fake ones?"

Isis pointed to the stage doors in the back of the theater. "They sell tons of them in the show's souvenir shop."

Zack poured the five enchanted crystals into Sacha's cupped hands. She eyed them before transferring them into one hand and ruffling Zack's hair with the other. "How come *we* never had a souvenir shop?" she muttered.

Isis let out a deep breath, relieved this entire crisis was over. She just needed to satisfy the one lingering worry that bounced around her brain like a ping-pong ball. She jumped in front of Zack and took his hands. "So, are you really you again?" She looked him in his bright-green eyes. She wouldn't read his mind, but she wanted to know for sure whatever answer he gave was genuine. "Are you free from her spell?"

"I'm pretty sure I am," Zack said, returning her gaze. "I have been for a while. Since the moment Amelia kissed me."

Isis gasped and dropped his hands. "She kissed you?"

"She did. But when it happened, it didn't feel right. After, I closed my eyes and, finally, I could only see you."

Isis flashed him her widest and cheesiest grin. "In that case, I'm glad I'm in your head. I like it in your noggin."

"I needed you in there to bring me back to reality."

"Well, aren't you two the sweetest thing?" Sacha said, through a sarcastic smirk.

"*Zack!*" Isis shrieked.

"Honestly, I knew in that moment that something just wasn't right—"

"*Zack, stop talking!*" Isis jumped back. She grabbed his arm and yanked him, trying to pull her confused boyfriend away.

"Isis," Selena gasped. "What is it?"

"There's a hole!"

Isis pointed to the tiny circle of blur behind Zack that hovered in the air. It couldn't have been more than an inch wide. It was barely noticeable, but Isis' stare just happened to wander its way. Now it had everyone's attention.

"What the hell is it?" Sacha exclaimed.

"It's one of Amelia's portals," Zack exclaimed. "We're being spied on—"

The tiny circle faded away. Then two much larger ones opened on the floor, one under Isis' feet and one under Zack's. Both dropped as if they were standing in a dangerous amusement park ride. Selena screamed their names.

Isis landed on all fours. Every limb shook after hitting the ground. She gasped for breath. Above her were clouds and a blue sky. Nearby, Zack was on his knees also, clutching his stomach and struggling to catch his breath. A peek revealed the rooftops of buildings, which were at least a story or two lower. They were at the highest point in Vegas, which explained her sudden light-headedness. This was The Sapphire's rooftop.

"Isis, look out!" Zack screamed.

She tensed at the sight of Amelia charging across the rooftop. Isis jumped to her feet. "This time, I'm ready for you," Isis shouted, although the statement may have been far more menacing if her body weren't still so wobbly.

"That right?" Amelia replied. "Well, this time, I'm pissed off."

Another portal opened under Isis' feet. But she was

ready for that trick. Isis focused on her lighter than air spell. Her body floated over the blurred hole. "That's slick," Amelia scoffed. "But not really."

Amelia's head darted to the left where a flock of seagulls flew a distance from The Sapphire's roof. An evil grin crossed her lips.

A portal formed in the birds' path. The seagulls flew straight through, disappearing in the blurred circle. A moment later, they exited straight up from the portal underneath Isis, who swatted her arms in front of her face for protection.

The birds flew in every direction around Isis, squawking as they passed. Most avoided her. But one clipped her knee while another made full contact with her chin, then reversed course and flew off. Both portals closed as Isis landed on her feet. She swayed to keep from losing her balance, a tactic that worked until she noticed Amelia's right hand had disappeared. Isis was suddenly yanked by the hair from behind. She dropped onto her backside. "Ouch," Isis screeched.

"I told you, witch," Amelia roared. "I'm too fast for you. There's nothing you can do that I won't see coming."

"Amelia, that's enough," Zack called to her. "It's over. There's no need—"

"*Shut up, Zack!*" Amelia's slanted eyes, filled with rage, returned its focus on Isis. "This is for killing all my mother's beliefs."

Amelia raised her arms over her head. A large portal formed high in the air above Isis. A huge wooden staff plummeted. At first Isis thought it was a tree severed from its limbs, but as it neared, she saw wires flailing in the air. It was a wood telephone pole. Isis braced herself, calling upon the energy for protection, but could she summon it before getting impaled by this huge and heavy projectile?

"Isis, no!" Zack cried out.

Before Isis could react, Zack, now on his feet, lunged in front of her. He threw his hands in the air, a futile attempt to protect them from the huge and heavy object that would most likely shoot through both of them like an oversized bullet. Isis couldn't imagine what Zack was thinking to put himself in such danger for no reason. Even if he acted out of love, it was a bad move...or maybe it wasn't.

"What the hell?" Amelia shrieked. "How?"

The pole shattered off of a clear dome of energy that suddenly encased Isis and Zack. Wood chips flew in every direction, filling the air. Amelia froze in place, staring dumbfounded at the energy crackling around the dome. Zack stared at his hands, which were now glowing.

Chapter Thirty-Two

Zack couldn't feel any sort of energy coursing through his body, not that he knew what Wiccan energy would feel like. Maybe feeling nothing was normal. It wasn't like he had any direct experience with it except for what he was told secondhand. All that mattered to him in the moment was that Isis was on her knees and a telephone pole was about to plummet through her like a rocket from the sky.

Amelia was actually going to kill Isis, so Zack reacted. Irrational instinct made him jump in the way and ask the Earth's energy for help to save his girlfriend. He didn't know why he asked. He never expected anything to happen, but it was a desperate situation. Somehow, the energy reacted and saved both their lives.

Euphoria filled Zack's body. But it may have been from the shock and awe. Or it could have been from the bubble of energy he created although he had no idea how it happened. The witches always insisted that the energy wasn't controlled simply by instinct, it was why they trained nonstop, so they could consciously master their Wiccan gifts. Yet the proof to the contrary surrounded both himself and Isis.

Based on the face staring at Zack, he wasn't the only one surprised by this occurrence. "You're a witch?" Amelia screeched.

"The baddest witch in Vegas," Isis said, from her knees behind Zack.

A blurred bubble formed under Zack's feet. Wherever Amelia planned to drop him, he knew it wouldn't be good. So he wouldn't give her the chance. Isis always chanted "lighter than air" which let her, or whoever she focused on, float. Could it be as simple as chanting? Now was as good of a time as any to find out.

"Um, lighter than air," Zack shouted, then concentrated on an image of himself floating off the ground. "Lighter than air!"

The chant saved him, but not in the way he expected. It was Amelia's feet which left the rooftop. Her body suddenly looked as if it was in a zero-gravity simulator. The surface beneath Zack's feet turned solid. The idea that he was working the energy, especially with zero training, went against all of his magician instincts. But that question could wait for later. At that point he had plenty of experts to turn to in his coven—

"Zack, she's trying to take off," Isis called to him.

Amelia reached out, unable to free herself from the sky. A portal formed in front of her. Zack gasped. Once through, Amelia would most likely pop out somewhere on the roof and then she'd be back on the attack. Zack had to do something, but what? Now with a Wiccan connection, he could manipulate reality in any way he wanted.

Wow, there were so many possibilities, so long as he didn't screw it up or lose control as had happened many times to Isis. He was, after all, a beginner, although the energy didn't strike him as being too hard to control. Maybe that was thanks to his imagination or his ingenuity? It could have also been his magic training which was focused on figuring things out. The portal moved toward Amelia, which meant he had to come up with something, and quickly.

A wind suddenly engulfed Amelia. It pulled her from the portal like a rip current yanking a swimmer away from shore. Zack didn't think of wind or try to will it into existence. But it worked. Maybe that was the key. The energy didn't work on wishes, but it somehow responded to the user's needs? In this case, he needed to get Amelia away from her portal, and that was exactly what happened.

"What…what are you doing?" Amelia shrieked.

Zack realized that Amelia had been dragged past the rooftop. She hovered above a thirty-story drop. He focused on pulling her back to the rooftop, but before he could, she dropped straight down. Her screams made Zack's heart jump. Somehow, the energy stopped. Both the wind and the lighter than air spells broke. Zack ran to the edge. Amelia's arms and legs flailed. She was clearly too panicked to react; otherwise she'd create another portal to fall through. Zack felt the same panic. He had no idea what to do.

"Isis," he called.

She did, after all, have a hell of a lot more experience than he did. "Yeah, allow me," she responded, now at Zack's side. Isis stared over the building's edge at Amelia. "Teleport!"

Amelia's body faded until it disappeared. She reappeared inches above the rooftop's paved surface. She hovered for a moment, then dropped face-first. The impact didn't injure Amelia, but it did knock the wind out of her.

She pushed up with her arms. Her head quivered

from the fall.

Isis dropped in front of her on one knee and wiggled her fingers near Amelia's face. "Sleep," she chanted.

Amelia's eyes drooped. "You got me," she mumbled. Then her upper body sagged against the pavement. Amelia fell into a slumber. For the first time, she looked at peace.

Isis peeked over her shoulder at Zack with a proud gleam in her eye. But Zack wasn't feeling the same joy or relief. A thought had crossed his mind, one that worried him far more than Amelia. For the first time in two sets of memories that spanned centuries, when he looked at Isis, his trust and faith in her wavered.

"What is it?" Isis asked.

"Did you know?" Zack backed away, putting distance between himself and Isis. "All this time, could you sense it?"

"Zack—"

"What about your family? Did they know?"

His hands trembled. In all those memories from that other reality, he couldn't recall a single sign that he was a witch. How could it never come up there, unless what he remembered wasn't real at all? Or were Isis and her family just that good at keeping secrets, even one that would have lasted two hundred years?

A pressure dug into Zack's chest as if someone reached in, clutched his heart, and squeezed. "Is that…is that why they invited me into the coven in the first place?"

"Zack, relax, listen to me—" Isis' eyes suddenly went wide in horror. "*Look out!*"

Zack spun around to see Erisa standing across the

rooftop. A blast of clear energy shot from her outstretched hand and smacked Zack in the chest. His legs wobbled, and his body collapsed against the cement. His vision blurred as he heard Isis scream.

Everything went dark.

Chapter Thirty-Three

The night before at the Felicity...

Zack entered the suite to see Isis in a chair at the end of the open kitchen's marble table. Sebastian and Selena were at the opposite end in seats facing her. Sacha leaned against the counter. Isis' face was red, her cheeks moist. "There's a problem," she said. "With Zack."

Selena answered, "What kind of—" She was cut off by Sacha loudly clearing her throat. Her gaze was on Zack.

"Come on in," Sebastian said. "Talk to us. Are you okay?"

"I...I need to speak to you all." Zack let out a deep breath and tiptoed closer. "It's important."

"You know we're here for you," Selena replied, "whatever it is."

Zack stopped in front of the table. He looked down at Isis who returned his glance. "I...I think you may be right about me."

"Right about what?" Sebastian asked through a hint of both concern and scrutiny. "What's going on here?"

Zack ran his left hand through his blond hair. "I...I can't stop thinking about Amelia. When I close my eyes, I see her face, and I can't stop...even when I want to. When I try to focus on you, or anyone else, my mind goes to her. It-it's exactly what happened to me with you on the day we met."

"The day we met," Isis sobbed, "Valeria had us both under a love spell."

Zack nodded. "Yeah, I know."

Sebastian stood from his seat. "Zack, are you saying you're under a love spell?"

"I don't know," he answered. "That's what Isis thinks. I feel so confused. But you're witches. You can tell for sure, right?"

"Sach." Selena eyed her sister. "Your senses are the strongest here."

"Right." Sacha strolled around the table and stopped in front of Zack. Her eyes dropped. "I can definitely sense the energy spinning around you. Zack, are you holding something in your pocket?"

He hadn't realized his right hand was in his jacket pocket. He slowly pulled it out. His fingers were wrapped around the heart-shaped object with five crystals forming a pentagon across the top.

"What is that?" Sebastian asked.

Zack held it in front of his face. "It's a memory box I bought Isis for her birthday. Amelia showed up while I was shopping and helped me pick it out. She told me to keep it on me and not let any of you see it."

"And that didn't make you suspicious?" Sacha threw him a scrutinizing eye.

"No, I never questioned her." Zack gasped. "Isis is right. I am under a spell, aren't I?"

"Objects are used as tokens for spells. They hold the remains of energy spiraling around them and the spell intact. But it takes a real strong witch to pull that off." Sacha seized the box from Zack. Her eyes closed tight. Her head tilted. "Whoa."

"Sacha!" Sebastian lunged to her side. "What is it?"

Sacha's eyes shot open. She closed and reopened them twice. "This girl, Amelia, does she have funky hair? Amazing yellow eyes?"

"Yes, she does," Zack replied. "How do you know?"

"Because I see her in my head." Sacha's mouth popped open. "She's a real beautiful girl. I need to meet her…"

"Those are enchanted crystals on that box. They're active! *Away from her!*" Selena swung her arm. The box flew out of Sacha's hand and landed in the center of the table. With a wave from Selena, the memory box ignited and burned. The flame then extinguished itself, leaving a charcoal mess in the middle of the table. The five crystals bounced across the table in various directions.

Sacha's eyes blinked rapidly. Her head spun in every direction. "Holy crap, the spell on that thing was powerful! I couldn't stop seeing her face."

"I knew it!" Isis snarled. "I knew that girl messed you up, Zack."

"But she couldn't have." Zack pointed a finger at what was left of the box, then at Sacha. "You just said only a powerful witch could hold their spell within the crystals after they leave its proximity. Amelia doesn't have that kind of connection."

"Erisa said Amelia doesn't." Isis bit her bottom lip. "She also claimed that she never lies, but we know that's not true."

"Amelia said the same thing, that her control is one

track. She just makes portals." Man, he hated having to defend this girl, especially now. "She was open about being a witch, yet I never saw her once attempt any other kind of spell. I don't believe she can make a love spell—" Zack's eyes opened wide. "But Erisa could. Oh man—"

"Hold on. Who is Erisa?" Sebastian asked.

"Amelia's mom," Isis answered. "She's also the leader of The Wiccan Circus. I knew something was off with that lady. But if the spell was hers, then they were working us together."

"Erisa, that makes sense." Zack grabbed his head. It was still spinning. "It's like an influence spell, right? I thought those are broken simply by knowing about it."

It was Isis who taught him that fact. Isis, his one true love. How could he let himself slip even for a moment? Damnit, he should have realized immediately that he was under a spell. He'd never betray his relationship with Isis, not if he was in his right mind. "The enchantment." Zack eyed everyone in the room. "It should be broken now. But how would I know?"

"How do you feel about Amelia right now?" Selena asked.

Zack closed his eyes and thought about Isis. The image was clear and uninterrupted. He then thought about Amelia's face and the way she'd look him directly in the eye while rubbing parts of his body in the most flirtatious manner. It made him feel uncomfortable, yet he couldn't tell her to stop. None of it was even real; it was all to sucker him into the trap, and he fell for it. Like a naïve idiot.

"Zack?" Sebastian patted him on the shoulder.

Zack opened his eyes and narrowed them. "I feel

angry. Manipulated. *Pissed off!*" He walked up to Isis, who stood from her chair. "I'm so sorry. I should have figured out immediately what she was doing to me. I'm such an *idiot!*"

Sacha threw a smirk at Selena and Sebastian. "I'd say the spell is broken."

"It's all right, Zack." Isis leaned in and gave him a hug. "In the end, you did see through it, and you're back. That's all that matters."

"Isis is right," Sebastian said. "Right now, that is what matters most."

"Oh, no, my friends," came a high-pitched voice from the suite's doorway. "I must wholeheartedly disagree with that belief. It is not what matters most."

All eyes turned to Simon who had joined them. Apparently, his television show had reached its commercial break. "If the detectives on TV have taught me anything, it is this!" Simon raised a finger in the air. "It is not enough to identify the suspect. You must also understand the motive. Why did this mother put a love spell on Zack? Was it simply to help her rather attractive teenage daughter get a mate? Did the daughter assault Isis in the desert just to stave off competition for Zack? I suspect a twist to this story, and I am sure it involves us all."

Sebastian eyed Isis. "Wait. What happened in the desert?"

"Simon is right," Selena said to the rest of the family. She peeked up at Sebastian. "There must be more to this. If it has anything to do with us, we need to find out what."

"Any ideas on how we go about that?" Sebastian asked the group.

Zack stepped forward and opened his eyes and mouth wide. It was his "I have an idea" expression. "We need someone on the inside. Someone they'll trust who can learn everything and let us know what to expect."

"Oh, is that all?" Sacha smirked. "How are we supposed to do that?"

"Why don't we put a spell on one of them?" Isis' question led to an awkward silence. Everyone glanced her way. She threw up her arms. "It's only right. They did it to Zack."

"It's not a terrible idea," Sacha mumbled.

"We're not going to lower ourselves to that level," Selena shot back.

"We don't have to." Zack waved his arms to get everyone's attention. "I can find out what they're up to."

"How?" Sebastian asked.

"All I have to do is show up. They'll trust me because they think I'm still under their spell." A wide grin formed across Zack's face. "Amelia invited me to The Sapphire tomorrow morning where she promised to share everything with me. I can fake the love symptoms and snoop around. They'll never know."

"Hmm." Sebastian nodded. "That could work."

"Whoa, Dad, wait up!" Isis stepped between the two most important men in her life. She grabbed hold of Zack's shirt. "You want to go over there and pretend you're still in love with Amelia so you can spy on them?"

"That's exactly what I want to do."

"Zack, are you crazy? If they catch you—"

"Amelia was talking about how they're going to

change the world," Zack replied. "I don't think she meant that figuratively. We have to know exactly what that does mean."

Isis sniffled. Her grip on his shirt tightened. "I feel like I just got you back. I can't lose you now."

"This has to be your choice, Zack," Sebastian said, after several quiet moments. "We won't think less of you if you don't want to take this tremendous risk."

Zack eyed Isis. Her expression left no doubt which way she leaned. But her concerns weren't necessary. Zack may not have been a witch like the rest of them, but he could still handle himself. "I'll be fine," he said, looking into Isis' eyes. "We've been together through two lifetimes. You're not getting rid of me so fast."

"I hope not," she whispered, in response.

"We can monitor you from here." Selena stood and joined her husband at his side. "If anything should go wrong, shout it in your head, and we'll be ready to teleport you out of there."

"Yes, you're one of us, Zack," Sebastian assured him. "We won't abandon you."

"I know you won't. I trust you all." Zack threw each member of the family a grin. He squeezed Isis' hand to reassure her. "Let's do this."

"Then if everything is settled..." Simon pointed a thumb over his shoulder. "I do believe my commercial break is over. May your adventure be even more intriguing than what the detectives on my program right now are handling."

Actually, Zack found the idea of being a spy kind of cool. Besides, what was the worst that could happen to him?

Chapter Thirty-Four

Now...

"Zack!" Isis cried. "Please, no!"

She hurried to his side and fell to her knees. Zack was on his back with his eyes shut. Isis laid a hand on his chest. There was no movement under his skin. Isis could barely feel a pulse. It was as if Erisa hit him with an EMP blast that shut down his entire system. Everything indicated that Zack was dying. But he wasn't dead yet. With the Wiccan energy, she had the power to speed up his heartbeat, get him breathing again—

Something grabbed Isis and yanked her back. It felt like a giant invisible hand wrapped around her waist and dragged her across the pavement. Isis jumped to her feet. She was now several steps from Zack. Across the rooftop, Erisa stared her down with glazed-over eyes and clenched lips. "You are not going to revive him," she said, through a dispassionate tone.

"Erisa, please, let me save him," Isis pleaded. "You made your point. Y-you don't have to kill him."

"This is penance for the actions you conspired in today," Erisa explained. "You tricked my congregation and destroyed everything my family worked for throughout the generations. With that comes consequences. Now, Zack must die for his part, and you will watch it happen."

Erisa held her hand above her head and pointed her palm upward. A fireball formed. It ran from her fingertips to her wrist. "If you try to save him, I will burn you where you stand."

"Then what?" Isis screeched. "You'll kill me, too?"

"I have not yet decided your fate. You will live with his death on your conscience, or I will grant you the mercy of joining him in the afterlife. Either way, I will resurrect my church, ready to resume the real Valeria's mission, and today will serve as a valuable lesson to those who dare try to dissuade me."

Isis stared at Zack's body. It was lifeless while Erisa's resolve stood firm. Isis had witnessed such cruelty from adults before, most notably from Erisa's heroine, Valeria. How proud she'd be of this new follower.

But Isis wasn't a typical fifteen-year-old. As a vampire, she had gone through experiences beyond her battles with Valeria. That included a world war and coming face-to-face with a distorted version of herself. She survived it all. Granted, those were the experiences of an earlier version of Isis who made sure they wouldn't happen this time around. But even if it wasn't her life, she still remembered those moments as if they were.

Isis stood up and straightened her back. She stared Erisa down through narrowed eyes. The fireball was bright and had Isis' name written all over it. But how many times had she stared down fire's deathly embrace? That wasn't the other Isis' experiences. Those were moments in her own life. Frankly, she was tired of being threatened with being roasted alive by every bully who loathed her. If ever she would stand up to that threat, the moment was now.

No one on this planet had a more powerful connection than Isis, and that included Erisa. Time to stop being scared and use that connection to its fullest. Isis had two dire crisis situations in front of her. The love of her life was dying, and a crazy witch was poised to attack. Both would require Isis' full concentration of the energy to overcome. But that was exactly what her folks had been training her to do. She would not lose Zack, nor would she let Erisa stop her.

"Restart his heart." Isis pointed her right palm over Zack and aimed the fingers on her left hand at Erisa. "Sever her connection."

"You still dare defy me," Erisa said. The fireball in her hand ballooned. "Very well."

Isis focused on both thoughts. She had to restart Zack's heart; she needed him to breathe again. She also needed to stop Erisa once and for all. Isis didn't want to compromise her principles by resorting to murder. But in this moment, she would not be denied. "Restart his heart, sever her connection." Isis chanted over and over, concentrating on both tasks.

"What ploy are you attempting?" Erisa roared. "No matter. Let that be your final moment of desperation."

Isis continued her chant. The energy crackled around both of her targets. The fireball in Erisa's hand grew until it engulfed her palm. The older and determined witch pulled back her arm. Then, like a pitcher aiming for the batter's head, she hurled the fireball Isis' way. Halfway across the rooftop, the ball of flame fizzled, then dissolved into a puff of smoke.

Erisa stared at her hand in disbelief. "The energy,"

she gasped in a moment of shock. "How can this be?"

Zack's chest lifted. Isis sensed a heartbeat, then another. It was slow, but at least it was beating. His pulse sped up. Isis focused her full concentration on her healing spell. She refused to be distracted by Erisa gesturing her hands in the air, or the shrieks that followed.

"You...you have severed my connection to Mother Earth," Erisa cried out. "That shouldn't be within your scope. My-my age, my experience, it is far beyond yours. My connection should be stronger...how?"

Isis threw Erisa a quick glance. She wanted to respond, maybe rub in the fact that despite all of the witch's presentation, she was outpowered by a mere teenager. But Isis wasn't about to risk Zack's life for a well-deserved quip. He was alive, but barely, which meant she had to work fast. She would not lose him. Not after all they'd been through together—

A loud explosion, like a firecracker, made Isis' head spin. Erisa's face went blank as if it had become an empty shell. Blood dripped down her shoulders from the back of the head. Her body fell over and smacked the rooftop. Isis looked past where Erisa had stood. She couldn't see anyone, especially with all the other rooftops being a few stories lower than The Sapphire's. Whatever just took her out could have come from anywhere.

Damn. Isis' spell broke, and right after she promised herself that she wouldn't get distracted. At least she healed Zack enough that his chest was now moving up and down on its own. A blur formed across the rooftop, then cleared. Selena and Sacha took its place with their hands clutched and Sebastian behind them. Hopefully their arrival wasn't too late.

"Oh my!" Selena screeched. She and Sebastian dropped to Zack's side. Selena quickly placed a finger against his neck, then an ear against his chest.

"Isis, what happened?" Sebastian asked her.

"Erisa…she hit him with some blast. I don't know what it was," she rambled through heavy breaths. "He stopped breathing. I restarted his heart, but he's not waking up—"

"Holy crap!" Sacha's scream grabbed their attention. She stood over Erisa's body, which lay on its side. Her head was soaked in blood. "She looks like she was shot in the back of the head. Isis, did you—"

"It wasn't me!" Isis refocused on her folks. "Can-can you save him?"

"Selena?" Sebastian placed a hand on her shoulder.

"I'm sure Sacha and I can heal him." She called to her sister, "Sach, we need you, quickly."

Sacha stood at the edge of the rooftop looking down. "Uh, there's a ton of police cars on the road, heading to The Sapphire." She about-faced. "Maybe we should get back to our place and then fix him up?"

"Can he be moved?" Sebastian asked his wife, the one with the most medical knowledge among them.

"I think so, but we have to heal him right away."

"I can teleport us back to the Felicity," Isis said. Her throat was dry from fret. "I can do it."

"Isis, listen to me." Sebastian stood and looked down into her eyes. "We know you have the ability, but not if you're distraught. Take a deep breath, clear your mind of worry, and concentrate on the location." The sound of police sirens reached the street in front of the building. "Let's not dawdle. We must go now."

Isis nodded, then did as Sebastian instructed. She put her emotions aside, content with the knowledge that Zack was in in good hands. Mom and Sacha could heal him. They were far better at it than Isis. She inhaled and focused on her bedroom in the Felicity. Once Sacha joined their huddle around Zack, the rooftop faded from view.

Chapter Thirty-Five

Sometime later…

Zack woke from what felt like the deepest sleep he had ever experienced. The brown ceiling above let him know that he was no longer on the rooftop of The Sapphire; it was one of the Felicity's suites. He had a pillow under his head and a soft cushion-like surface under his body. He was either on a bed or a couch. No, too roomy to be a couch. Was it his bedroom?

"Where am I?" Zack rubbed his eyes, trying to clear the fuzziness that filled his brain.

"You're back in the hotel, on Isis' bed," Selena's voice said. "You're going to be okay."

"I'm okay?" Zack remembered facing Isis on that rooftop. They stopped Amelia through witchcraft. His witchcraft. Zack had a connection to the energy after all, although it didn't feel at all like he was connected. Even more concerning was that Isis didn't seem surprised with this sudden revelation at all.

Then he remembered her warning. Zack spun around to see Erisa who pointed his way. Then his heart suddenly felt like it was about to explode out of his chest. The last thing he remembered was the thought that he was about to die.

Zack's hands on his bare chest revealed that he wasn't wearing a shirt. No jacket either, although he was glad to finally have that thing off. He reached down to feel his legs. At least he was still wearing pants.

His vision cleared enough to realize he was surrounded by a room full of onlookers. Isis watched him from a close distance while Sebastian had an arm around her shoulders. Selena and Sacha stood over Zack from opposite sides of the bed. "Welcome back to the living." Sacha squeezed his arm.

"Let's give him a moment," Selena called out. "Let him get his bearings."

"I thought I was dead." Zack pressed a hand against his chest. His heart thumped against his palm. "What happened to me? How am I still alive?"

"I wasn't going to lose you," Isis explained with a nervous relief in her voice. She walked up to the foot of the bed. "I restarted your heart."

Zack tried to lift his upper body. Selena placed a hand on his chest and pressed him against the mattress. "Take it slowly," she said. "You've been through a lot. The best thing you can do now is rest."

"Erisa!" Zack opened his eyes wide. He looked around the room. "We're all here, which means you beat her. What happened?"

"She's dead." Isis' response was barely a whisper.

"Did you..."

"No way!" Isis exclaimed. "Someone killed her, but I swear, it wasn't me. It wasn't any of us."

"That's a mystery we need to solve, but at a later time." Selena motioned toward the door. "For now, let's allow Zack to rest."

Sacha patted Zack's head then stepped away from the bed, following her sister across the room. Both sisters stopped and turned back when Sebastian said in a bold voice, "Hold on. I have something to say to all of you."

"What is it, Honey? Everything okay?" Selena asked.

"It is. Today we faced what could have been a serious threat both to us and possibly the entire world. Maybe this wasn't on the same scope as Valeria, but it was a threat nonetheless." Sebastian looked across the room at each member of the coven, his family. Including Zack. "And we won by working together. I want to take a moment to say to everyone in the room, great job."

"Thanks, Sebastian," Sacha answered with an eye roll.

With that, he followed the sisters into the living room. He threw a glance back, then shut the door on his way out. That left two. Zack shot his upper body into a sitting position.

"Are you...are you sure you're feeling okay, Zack?" Isis asked.

"Yeah, I think I am." Zack swung his feet onto the floor. Isis reached to help, but Zack waved her off. He stood from the bed on his own. His body wobbled for a moment, but he quickly regained his stance.

"You're supposed to be resting," Isis said.

"I know." Zack stared at Isis for what felt like an eternity. He knew this was inevitable—there were things between them that needed to be discussed. "Listen, Isis, I'm hoping things aren't going to be different or weird between us—"

"It won't be, not for me." She wrapped her arms around Zack's waist. Her eyes looked moist and puffy.

"You broke through a love spell from a powerful witch, and you did it for us. I don't think you have anything else to prove to me."

"We got lucky." Zack placed a hand against Isis' cheek. He looked deep into her eyes. "They couldn't have known we have two hundred years of memories together. It's probably why the spell never took full effect."

"Then you do believe all that really happened?" Isis' face filled with hope.

"We can't know for sure," Zack answered honestly. "But what I do know is that we both remember it. I spent most of the last few days confused. She had me, Isis, but my feelings for you, our connection, they kept trying to break through."

"Because our love is strong." Her mouth stretched into a grin. "And it's real. Things don't need to be different between us."

"I know, it is real. But that's not what I'm talking about." Zack stepped back and held out his hands. He willed them to glow, but nothing happened. "If I really am a witch now, I'm going to have to learn from you and your family. I mean, at the very least I need to learn how to control the energy so there's no accidents, right?"

"Um, Zack..." Isis bit down on her bottom lip. "About that..."

Isis' guilt-filled eyes said it all. Zack dropped his hands. "I'm not a witch, am I?"

"No." Isis shook her head. Her eyes widened, as if she expected an argument.

"So, it was all you?" Zack's looked up to the ceiling, and then he snorted. "I had a hunch that was the case. Each of you talk about how, as witches, you sense the energy around you. I couldn't. None of it was how you describe what it feels like."

"I'm sorry. I couldn't think of anything else to do." Isis wiped her eyes with the back of her hand. "Amelia was right. She was too fast for me. Everything I tried she saw coming. I had to think outside the box to fool her. I figured if she thought the energy was coming from you…"

"She'd get caught by surprise. So, you pulled a switch. That's brilliant!" Zack let out a loud laugh. "How do you like that? I thought I became a witch, but actually, *you* became a magician."

"Hey, I learned from the best." Isis' shoulders dropped. Her head shook from relief.

Zack wrapped his arms around Isis as they shared a much needed laugh. Then Isis' smile faded while she gazed into Zack's eyes. Her jaw trembled ever so slightly. Zack popped his head back. Something was wrong.

"Isis?" he asked. "Please talk to me."

"Zack, you…" She threw him a glance that said whatever she was thinking, she didn't want to say it out loud. But it was too late. She caught his curiosity. At this point, Isis had to say what was on her mind. Zack made a mental note to himself not to freak out, no matter what it was.

"Isis," he whispered. "Whatever it is…"

"She stopped your heart. You weren't breathing. I brought you back, but it was so close. I wasn't sure if I could."

"I know." Zack's face scrunched. "I was dead. I owe you my life."

Isis took Zack by the hands and leaned in. "Erisa tried to keep me from saving you. I was scared, but I did it. I took away her connection at the same time I got your heart to beat again."

"Two spells at once. I guess you finally mastered that." Zack pulled Isis' right hand against his chest. "Thanks."

"I'm just glad you're okay now."

"I am okay. Thank you."

Zack knew exactly what Isis wanted in the moment. She was saying it without using words. She wanted him to kiss her. Zack obliged, pressing his lips hard against hers. It didn't matter which reality they were in, and if it was two hundred years or just five months. Everything about this felt right. No wonder another witch couldn't keep him in a spell. Erisa's hold over him ended the moment Amelia kissed him, because it felt so wrong. His lips were only meant for one.

"I love you, Isis," Zack whispered. "I'm sorry I made you think otherwise."

"Again, not your fault." Isis ran her fingers through his hair. "I love you too, with all my heart, and I want us to be together for the rest of our lives. No matter how long or short that is."

Zack wrapped one arm around Isis' waist and led her to the window. They stared out at the Vegas skyline. It was a beautiful sight especially when the sun went down and all the lights lit up the city. It was one of the many things that made Vegas feel like the happiest place in the world, even when things felt dire. He felt Isis' eyes on him.

"You look lost in thought," she said. "I'll give you

a penny for them."

He wasn't sure his thoughts were even worth that. "I'm thinking how Las Vegas was my home for most of my life. It will always be a part of me."

"I know it is."

"Yet, when this set of shows are over, I'm ready to go back to New Salem. I think we can be happy and live a good life there."

"What about magic?" Isis asked. "It doesn't really excite anyone in New Salem, but they love it everywhere outside the village, especially here in Vegas."

"I think I'm okay giving it up, at least for a while." Zack threw Isis a grin. "Who knows, maybe without The Witches of Vegas, real magicians will return to the strip's theaters."

Isis' mouth opened. She leaned her head on his shoulder with an arm still wrapped around his waist. "I'm really glad to hear you say that, Zack, because I was thinking the exact same thing. I didn't want to say it because I was worried you'd want to stay."

"Nah, I think I'm ready to commit to that lifestyle." Zack slipped his hand against the back of Isis' neck. "It did work out for two centuries the first time around."

"So, we give up all of this for a quiet life where we know everyone better than they know us." Isis shrugged. "Maybe that wouldn't be so bad, plus my teleportation range has really improved. We can visit here anytime we'd like. Maybe someday in the future, we'll come back and do some reunion shows."

"That sounds great. People do love nostalgia." Zack returned his gaze to the Vegas skyline. "Now that we know we're on the same page, there's just one thing we need to do."

"Talk to Mom, Dad, and Sacha." Isis nodded. "I think they'll be okay with it."

"Yeah, I think so, too."

Zack and Isis held each other tight. He had no intention of ever letting her go again. They could have stared out that window together all day and night. At least until the ringing doorbell from the living room grabbed both their attention. It then rang again.

"Are we expecting someone?" Zack asked.

"I don't think so." The two raced for the bedroom door.

Chapter Thirty-Six

A million paranoid thoughts zipped through Isis' mind while Zack gripped the bedroom's doorknob. Who could be at the front door? Was it Amelia looking for revenge? Nah, if that was the case, she wouldn't bother ringing the doorbell. But what if it was the police? Did they know that Isis was on that rooftop when Erisa was shot? That would make her the number one suspect once they found the body up there.

Her family was in the living room, which meant they would be the first to deal with whoever entered the suite, friend or foe. The front door creaked open. A chill ran down Isis' spine. It warmed up once she heard Simon's jovial scream. "Ah, you're here, wonderful. Come in, come in, my friends."

Zack gave Isis a curious look, then pulled open the bedroom door. They dashed into the living room, relieved to find the last two people they expected to see walking into the hotel suite. "Paul! Natasha!" Isis said with glee.

Paul shook hands with Sebastian, who, based on his reluctance, was just as surprised to see them. Selena exchanged a hug with Natasha. "How did you two get here?" she asked. "I didn't think your teleportation range could reach Vegas from New Salem."

"It does not," Natasha replied. "I teleport us to Sweden. From there, we charter jet."

"What brings you into our neck of the woods?" Sacha asked, while being the recipient of another Natasha hug.

"You were in trouble." Paul removed his black leather jacket and tossed it on the couch. Isis couldn't remember ever seeing him so casual in a striped T-shirt and black carpenter pants. "We came to check in and make sure the problem was resolved."

Sebastian's head tipped. "And you knew about our situation, how, exactly?"

Paul motioned over his shoulder with a thumb pointed at Simon. "A call was placed to the president's office, and we were filled in."

"You called them?" Sacha glanced over at Simon.

"Of course I did!" The vampire stretched out his arms. "Did you think all I do here is sit around the hotel room and watch TV all day?"

"Pretty much, yeah," Zack whispered under his breath.

Paul faced Isis and Zack, looking them over from a distance. "How are the two of you?"

"We're okay," Isis answered.

"Yeah, we survived." Zack threw his arm over Isis' shoulders. "I became a witch, but it only lasted a few minutes."

"We saw." Paul returned his grin with one of his own. "It was a clever ploy, indeed."

Sacha's eyes squinted. "I think you need to fill us all in on that one."

"We would have stepped in and helped," Natasha said. "But we see, Isis, you have it all under control."

Isis' mouth popped open. The answer to the one lingering mystery just revealed itself. "It was *you*!" She pointed a finger at Paul. "You took out Erisa from a nearby roof."

"Actually, we were a wee bit higher than the rooftops, thanks to Natasha," Paul replied. "It was necessary, and I did have a clear shot, so I took it."

"Natasha helped you line up the shot?" Sacha asked in what sounded like a tease.

"Hardly," Paul scoffed. "I may not be a witch, but I was a special agent for my home country for many years before immigrating with my family to New Salem. I have never needed assistance hitting a target."

"Why was it necessary?" Isis walked up to Paul. Her forehead came to his chest. "I cut off her connection. She was no longer a threat."

"Untrue," Paul shot back. "From what I witnessed, she was a schemer and a manipulator. That made her a danger even without her Wiccan connection, which could eventually return. I did what I determined was necessary."

"What about Amelia?" Zack asked. "You didn't...um..." He rubbed a finger across his throat.

"Of course not." Paul lifted his shoulders, perhaps surprised by Zack's question. "We decided to give her a fresh start in New Salem. There, she will learn to use her connection responsibly. So long as she complies with our laws and acclimates to our lifestyle, she will have the opportunity to thrive."

Isis didn't want to ask what would happen if she didn't comply. Her folks exchanged a wide-eyed glance, showing definite concern over this plan. What about Zack who would have to see her once they returned to New Salem? Isis was...mostly sure the love spell had been broken entirely. But what lingering feelings would surface each time they passed one another? Amelia did try to kill them, after all.

"That would be the best thing for her, and we can certainly keep our distance." Zack rubbed Isis' back, giving her the unspoken reassurance she needed. "But be careful—she can be aggressive and rebellious. Not to mention dangerous."

"We have spoken with her," Natasha said. "Amelia says she is glad to leave this world and begin new life."

"Well, yay for her!" Simon clapped his hands over his head. "I believe we can redeem that young lady and turn her into a good witch that we can love and trust."

"I hope you're right," Isis muttered. She didn't have much confidence in Simon's assessment, especially since he barely met her. Isis wouldn't want to bet on Amelia's successful reform. But all the adults, including the vice president, seemed to think otherwise, so who was she to argue with them?

"Thank you for coming all this way to check on us." Sebastian waved a hand to the couch, offering Paul a seat. "It's much appreciated."

"Yes, thank you from all of us," Selena added.

"Of course. You are part of New Salem. That means you always have allies." Paul flashed a rare grin. It was as if he had just taken off his administrator's hat and set it on the coffee table.

"Paul." Natasha eyed her watch. "It is time I will go."

"So soon?" Sacha asked.

Paul dropped onto the couch. "Natasha will escort Amelia back to New Salem. I, however, have rented a room in this hotel for the night. I have also purchased three tickets to this evening's Witches of Vegas show. I anticipate an entertaining performance."

Zack's head tipped up. "Did you say three tickets?"

"Aye, Natasha and I did not come all this way alone." Paul's arms stretched across the top of the couch's backrest. "My two fellow travelers are hoping after the curtain closes, you could show them some of the attractions of this amazing city."

Zack peeked over at Isis. She didn't need to read his mind to know what he was asking. The glances her way from the rest of the family asked the same question. "Yes, I'd like that." Isis' answer was directed at Paul but it was meant for everyone else in the room, especially Zack. "I think I'd like that a lot."

Zack flashed her a huge smile. Having normal friendships was important to him. Isis was ready to try normal as well, for both their sakes.

"Not to worry," Zack said. "We'll show them a great time."

Chapter Thirty-Seven

Later that evening...

"So, are you enjoying what you've seen so far?" Sebastian shouted into the microphone to the sold-out crowd. They responded with howls and applause. "Great to hear! Now, prepare yourselves for something even more amazing!"

Isis waited behind the side curtain of the Felicity's stage, ready to make her first appearance of the night. Three chairs faced the audience. Zack sat in the center one with Sacha on his left and Simon on his right. The audience cheered when Zack came out, which meant they enjoyed his opening card act. It was, of course, nearly flawless. Amazing how much better he performs when not distracted by a love spell.

"Ladies and gentlemen," Sebastian announced. "Let me share two interesting facts about our youngest witch. The first is that tomorrow is her birthday..."

Isis inched forward. This was her cue to get ready to step onto the stage. She really hoped Dad wasn't set to lead the audience in singing "Happy Birthday." He did threaten to do exactly that earlier during their late afternoon training session. Please let this be one of those times where he was just teasing her. After everything she had been through today, the last thing she wanted was to end up dying from embarrassment.

"Hey," Selena whispered in Isis' ear with an arm over her shoulders. "This is it. Remember, we don't want anyone getting hurt, so they're each counting on you to keep them afloat."

"I know, focus on the energy around each individual chair," Isis replied. "Three separate spells all at once. I can do this."

"I know you can." Selena stroked Isis' cheek. "You proved your ability to cast multiple spells when it mattered most. Zack is alive because of it."

"Thanks, Mom." Isis took Selena's hand off her cheek and gave it a squeeze.

"And, the second fact, along with being an amazing performer," Sebastian explained to the audience, "she is also an accomplished juggler. Tonight, she combines both skills into one amazing routine. I ask now that we have complete silence in the theater so that she can concentrate on this seemingly impossible task. Ladies and gentlemen, please put your hands together for the future goddess of magic, *Isis*!"

Isis stepped out to a smattering of applause, then the audience went silent just as Sebastian asked of them. A light music played low from the speakers. Sebastian walked up to Isis, blocking her path. "Okay," he said with the microphone pointed downward. "This is something new for you. Just be careful—"

"Mom went over everything with me. She gave me all the warnings. I got this."

"Good," he snickered. "In that case, the stage is yours. Go wow them."

Sebastian patted Isis on the back as he passed. She moved to the center, positioning herself behind Zack's chair. With her hands on his shoulders, she looked out to the audience. Of course she couldn't make out anyone in the darkness behind the bright spotlight shining in her face. But even unseen she still liked to connect with them, just as she was taught to do.

The theater was eerily quiet. Suddenly one voice screamed, "Go, Isis!" It was Maya. She was somewhere in the crowd along with Jeb and her dad. The fact that they came all this way meant they were reaching out with a hand of friendship toward Zack and herself. It was time for Isis to drop her guard and let that happen. It would be different than how she remembered. Isis and Zack weren't ageless vampires this time around.

"Hey, quick question," Zack whispered, still facing the audience with a smile. "How did you figure out I was under a spell?"

Damn, he wanted to talk about this now? Isis placed a hand on top of Zack's head and leaned down. "Witch's intuition?" she whispered back. "Maybe because of our connection and how well I know you, or it was just a lucky guess."

"Oh." Zack's shoulders tensed. "Let's go with one of the first two, okay?"

"Yeah, sure, let's do that."

"Isis!" Sebastian's voice called from offstage.

Isis spun her head Dad's way. He stood with Selena at his side. His left hand twirled in a circular motion, a message to start, or in his words, not dawdle. She threw him a quick nod. The pride on both their faces did not escape her notice.

Okay, better get to work. Isis eyed each chair one at a time before stepping back. Sacha threw her a wink of confidence. Zack peeked over his shoulder. "Show them your stuff," he whispered. Only Simon gripped his seat tightly. She couldn't blame the vampire; she'd already dropped him once.

Isis focused on the chairs until she sensed the energy around each of them. She then raised her arms high over her head. The chairs responded by slowly levitating into the air. The audience "oohed." In this moment, Isis was able to control three objects all at once. Now she needed to put that control to the test.

It was time to juggle.

****

The blurriness around Amelia cleared up. She was suddenly surrounded by an environment that was different from Vegas, or any other place she had lived. The air smelled like leaves and wood after a rainstorm. There was no sound of traffic or even a vehicle to be seen. Four buildings surrounded the large circle of grass and dirt where she stood. Each had a massive number of cottages behind them. Beyond that were trees as far as her eyes could see in every direction.

"Wow, this is an actual place," Amelia blurted out.

"This area is known as the Quad," her escort, Natasha, explained in an accent Amelia's ears couldn't figure out. "It is center of village and busiest place at all times."

Busiest place? There were maybe ten people, half of whom were farmers, shuffling around. Others were exiting the four building doors and walking to the cottages. A few of the farmers paused in their work and looked her way. Apparently new people rarely came to this place. Amelia let out a loud yawn. She was more tired than she realized. She barely slept a wink on the plane ride to Sweden. Man, they could have saved a ton of time if Natasha would have just let her open a portal to…wherever here was.

"So, where am I staying?" she asked.

"You will find out soon," Natasha replied. "First, you are to meet village president."

"That right? When do I meet him?"

"Her, and you meet now."

Natasha waved a hand to the dark-skinned girl strolling their way. A boy who looked like a linebacker of the same complexion followed two steps behind. At first Amelia thought she was being ribbed. Neither of them could have been more than a few years older than herself. There was no way someone so young looking could be president, yet each farmer in the quad greeted the girl in a formal manner. Even Natasha stood at attention.

Once she approached, Amelia shoved out her hand. "Amelia Cross," she stated matter-of-factly.

"Greetings. I'm village President Tia. This is Jasper, a proud member of our task force. Welcome to New Salem." Tia shook Amelia's outstretched hand. "So you know, citizenship requires that last names are left behind. We are a close community, which will now include you."

Amelia leaned her head forward, studying Tia over. Her instincts had to be correct. "You're not a witch, are you, President Tia?" She still hadn't figured out the big guy, at least not yet.

"No, I am not."

"And you look around my age."

"I'm a few years older." Tia laughed. "I'm nineteen."

"Nineteen and you're the president?" Amelia smirked. "How did *that* happen?"

"You are flippant in your tone," Jasper growled. "Moving forward, you will need to learn to temper that, especially when speaking to authority."

Amelia's head snapped back. Such aggression and defensiveness from the giant. It couldn't just have been because Amelia spoke so nonchalantly toward his president. It had to be something more. She had a strong hunch. "Are you two an item?" A finger shot back and forth between Jasper and Tia.

From the corner of her eye, Amelia caught Natasha's glare. The Russian witch opened her mouth to speak—probably some nonsense about respect—but Tia waved a hand, cutting her off.

"Jasper is a witch just like you and many others in this village," the president replied. "His connection allows him to see into the future through his dreams."

"Really? You see the future? That is so cool." Amelia meant it, too. Her mom always claimed to have that ability, yet nothing she ever predicted happened. That included rescuing Valeria. What a disaster that turned out to be.

"It is why you are here now," Tia said. "In a recent dream, Jasper saw you in New Salem and how you will be able to acclimate into our culture with success." Tia flashed what Amelia took as a friendly, yet threatening smile. "Please prove him right."

Amelia threw her hand against her forehead and saluted. "Aye, aye, Miss President."

Tia's side glance pointed Natasha's way. It elicited a chuckle. She refocused on Amelia. "Here in New Salem, everyone has the opportunity to achieve any goal they wish so long as they have the fortitude and the willingness to put in the work. With that said, we

will be expecting great things here out of you, Amelia."
Tia moved back and shifted her body. It implied that
she had somewhere else to be. "Natasha will introduce
you to your new guardians. Meanwhile, I look forward
to getting to know you as a resident of our village."

Tia marched off. Jasper, after eyeing Amelia up
and down, followed.

Amelia had to admit—although not out loud—this
president was remarkable. She walked with a swagger
in her step, one that resonated importance, but without a
shred of arrogance to her. Damn, nineteen and in
charge. Maybe all that fortitude and hard work crap
wasn't just empty talk.

"So, guardians, huh?" Amelia's face squished.

"You stay with Milo and Hanna," Natasha
explained. "They are both witches and in charge of our
market. It is important place in New Salem since all
imports and exports go through them."

"What are they like?"

"From how I've seen them handle their workers,
very tough." Natasha waved Amelia to follow her. "But
so are you. It is good match. They will teach you how
to use your gifts in ways you never imagine. I am sure
what they teach will benefit both New Salem and
yourself."

"That works for me. Let's meet Milo and Hanna."
Amelia followed Natasha to the building she assumed
was the market. She stopped in place to watch Tia and
Jasper from across the quad. Tia conversed with two of
the farmers. Jasper looked on with his shoulders back
and arms at his sides.

A woman in blue scrubs stepped out of the building
with the glass doors. She waited patiently to speak with

Tia. Wow, to think this girl became the leader of the entire village by the age of nineteen. Amelia was sixteen. She was sure she could do better.

"Come," Natasha called to her. "They await your presence."

"On my way." Amelia took another glance around the quad, taking it all in. She nodded and mumbled, "Oh yeah, I'll be running this place in no time."

Epilogue

Later that night...

Zack's eyes popped open to the point he thought his pupils would explode out of his head. It was a reaction to the oversized bowl of ice cream placed in the middle of the table by the waiter. The bowl had eight scoops of four different flavors of ice cream covered in whipped cream and sprinkled with bits of cookies. There were also four bananas sticking out of the top like a spiked haircut.

Seated next to him, Isis' eyes were just as wide as Zack's. Her fingers were wrapped tightly around a spoon. Even wider were the eyes and mouths of the couple sitting across the table. Yes, this was definitely the best restaurant to bring their guests for a double date.

"Wow," Jeb exclaimed. "What is this thing called, again?"

"Banana-brownie-cookie sundae," Zack answered. "This is the only place that has it, and it serves up to four or five people."

"We totally need a place like this in New Salem." Maya waved a hand around the table, pointing it at every angle of the restaurant. "I've had enough of the dining hall. They don't make anything like this."

"What do you mean by serves up to four or five?"

Jeb stared at his spoon, then shoved it into a scoop of chocolate ice cream nearest him. "I'm pretty sure I could finish off one of these bad boys all by myself."

"That's called being a piggie, Babe," Maya sang.

All four at the table laughed. The biggest cackle came from Isis. It warmed Zack's heart to see her happy. After everything they'd been through, she needed it more than anyone else. In truth, he did, too. "We should dig in before it all melts," Zack said.

"Before we do, how about a quick toast?" Maya raised her glass, half-filled with red fruit juice. "First, to a fun show, although Jeb and I have some idea on how you did it all."

"I'm sure you do." Zack rolled his eyes.

"Second, to the birthday girl, Isis, who, as of tomorrow, is joining the rest of us in the big one-six club."

"To Isis." Jeb tipped his glass forward.

"And," Maya went on, "who is finally willing to hang out as friends and not just see us as walking future corpses."

They touched glasses and then drank. "I'm sorry about that." Isis' head dipped. "It's complicated, but I'm working on it."

"We both are," Zack added.

"How about for now we work on this huge cookie thingamabob sundae?" Jeb yanked out his spoon containing ice cream and chocolate chip cookie pieces. He shoved the end into his mouth and swallowed. "I want to see if there's really a brownie somewhere under all of this mess."

"There's actually more than one," Zack answered.

"Let's do it." Maya spooned a tiny scoop. "After

that, I'm anxious to see one of these dance clubs you told us about."

"They're a lot of fun," Isis said, through a smile.

All four ate away. Zack purposely avoided the banana near him in case Isis wanted more than just the one near her. He knew how much she enjoyed fruit. He couldn't relate, but he understood. Her free hand slipped under the table and cupped Zack's thigh. It was nice having a night out with another couple their age. In fact, it felt normal. At least for this one evening, it didn't feel like he was surrounded by witches. They were just teens having a fun and stress-free night. Zack appreciated it more than he could ever say.

Of course, something would interrupt the moment. Something always did. At least this time, it wasn't a world-altering crisis. It was simply his bladder. Zack wanted to ignore it and enjoy the sundae, not to mention the company. But it screamed for release.

"Hey, I'll be right back." Zack stood from the table.

"Everything okay?" Isis asked.

"Yeah, I just need to use the bathroom. Try to save a few bites for me, okay?"

"No promises," Jeb replied with a mouth full of ice cream and some of the brownie his spoon managed to find. Both girls giggled.

Zack scurried through the restaurant to the restrooms. Luckily there was no line. He pulled open the door to the men's room and bolted in. It was a large one-person bathroom with a long countertop that ran along the wall from the sink to the toilet. Once he stepped in and the door behind him swung shut, the pressure in his lower abdomen stopped.

No longer needing the toilet, Zack walked up to the sink and eyed himself in the mirror. "What just happened?" There was no doubt why he came in here, yet the intense sensation which demanded he find immediate relief disappeared as quickly as it started.

Zack was the only one here. His was the only reflection in the mirror, yet he suddenly felt a presence behind him. Someone was there. It could have just been paranoia, or was it? He couldn't see or hear anyone, but he also knew that witches were a thing. Living in a village filled with them taught Zack to trust his instincts more than his senses.

He spun around as fast as his body would allow. Sure enough, he wasn't alone. It was Isis, but her olive skin was faded by a few shades. Her spine was perfectly straight, and there was a look of experience across her face. Zack peeked over his shoulder at the mirror. Still no reflection, yet when he looked back, there she was in front of the door.

She held a round-headed mauve rose with a nine-inch stem against her plain light-blue shirt. There were three leaflets running down the stem. The petals on the rose's round head had random shades of pink mixed within the mauve. Zack was no botanist, but he was sure that rose didn't grow in the hot Vegas climate.

"Hey, there," she said, which forced Zack to back up until he pressed against the sink. It wasn't his imagination. She actually was in the bathroom with him.

"My God, you're…you're the Isis from before you changed time." Zack straightened himself, trying not to look like he was in the middle of a panic attack. "I thought you were, well, you know…"

"Yeah, I thought so, too," vampire Isis said. "Once I knew everything was set right, I closed my eyes and expected to no longer exist. I thought I was gone. But next thing I knew, I was surrounded and then recruited by...well, let's just call them a higher power."

"You mean like angels?"

"Definitely not angels." Isis stepped forward. Zack wanted to back up, but he was already against the sink. "But they do look after existence. They...we...were absorbed into the energy, but with independent thought. We make sure that no witch can use the energy to harm the natural course of reality. It's rare anyone is strong enough to do that, but if it does happen, we're ready to step in. We won't let a situation like Valeria changing history occur again."

Zack stepped forward. He was slow and hesitant. This was definitely Isis' face and body, yet she was so assured. He felt like a child around her. That was because she was two hundred years old and apparently survived the end of her existence. She was so familiar, yet also different, both from the girl he knew now and the one he remembered from the previous timeline. Isis, in every form, wore her emotions on her sleeve. This one seemed a little more detached.

"So, you are different people," Zack mumbled. "You're a whole other person from the Isis I know."

"That's not exactly the case," she responded. "I was her a long time ago, but now it's like I never was. My reality is no more, and history is back on course as it should be."

Zack raised his eyebrows as far as he could. "I'm trying to follow, I really am...this is really confusing."

"Try not to focus too hard on it." The wide-eyed

grin Zack knew well formed across her face. "It's complicated. All I can tell you is that my existence should have ended both times reality was changed. Now, your Isis and I are one in the same, but she has her own destiny to fulfill."

That did not clear up anything, but Zack was okay with it. To think there was a part of him, deep down, that still wasn't one hundred percent sure if any of that other reality actually happened. He wanted to believe, but deep down he questioned the validity of the memories Isis put in his head. Now he could never question it again. That was if he could trust his own sanity in this moment. Could this entire conversation be a hallucination?

As nervous and anxious as he felt, Zack's curiosity overran both emotions. He finally stepped forward. "These…whatever they are, whatever you are now, you exist because of what Valeria did?"

"That's also hard to answer." Isis shrugged. Then she nodded. "They—we existed long before Valeria went back in time. But, yes, we came about because of what she did."

"Wait…huh?"

Isis walked past Zack, placing the rose in his left hand. His fingers gripped the smooth stem. Isis pulled herself up on the sink's counter to the right of the mirror, letting her legs dangle. With her back inches from the mirror, she created no reflection.

Zack held the rose in front of his face and stared at it. Its strong scent was fresh, and the petals were fully opened. It struck a chord of déjà vu, but Zack was sure he had never seen it at any point in his life, at least not in this timeline.

"I miss that blank stare of yours when you're trying to figure stuff out," she said.

"This must be weird for you." Zack gulped, trying to swallow the saliva that filled his throat.

"It is. I know you're not my Zack, although up until this age, you were." Isis bit her bottom lip. At least that was familiar. "I'm happy the two of you pulled through this. I'm glad your love prevailed."

"It was our connection that helped me break that love spell, I think. Then we—" A thought smacked Zack's brain. "Wait, did you have something to do with that?"

"No." She shook her head. "It's the natural course of reality that we look after. Even then, we can't interfere, at least not directly, and not without good reason. We were sure Erisa couldn't open the portal to bring back Valeria, so we had no need to stop her attempt. No, this wasn't about her. I wanted to see that the two of you would overcome this challenge, and you did."

Zack's eyebrows rose. "You didn't interfere at all? You just sat back and watched?"

"Well…" Her lips stretched into a slight grin. "I may have influenced one of her dreams, but that was as far as I could go."

"Why watch us in the first place if that was all you could do?" Zack snapped. "Was it just out of sentiment?"

The smile faded. Isis' head popped up. At first Zack thought he offended her, but then it was clear from the nodding while staring at the ceiling that she was talking to someone else, someone who wasn't in the room with them, maybe not even on the planet.

After another nod, Isis refocused on Zack who clutched the flower against his chest.

"I don't want to freak you out, but there's another threat to reality on its way. In fact, it could affect all of history if it's not prevented."

"One involving us?"

"It'll involve our—your coven, and the people of New Salem. But Isis must be the one to face it." Her brown eyes connected with Zack's. "Believe me when I tell you she'll need you at her side to prevent it from happening, if she even can."

"Is it Amelia?"

"We don't know what the threat is, but we are sure it is something from outside this reality, and far worse than Amelia."

"Oh. Damn."

Zack's hands fell to his stomach. A pain filled his midsection as if he had been punched in the gut. Great, just when he thought his days of stressing over his new life with the witches was over. So much for that. His concern suddenly turned to the rose between his fingers. The last thing he wanted to do was crush this fragile but beautiful blossom. Zack loosened his grip and pulled it away from his stomach.

"Sorry," he heard the older Isis say. "I didn't mean to dump this on you."

"This threat." Zack looked up at her. His head tipped. "This is going to be another Valeria, isn't it?"

Isis nodded. "It may be as bad, or it could be a whole lot worse. We don't really know. What we sense is that the world's only hope will be the two of you together. If you didn't beat Erisa's love spell, the world as you know it would have been doomed."

"Whoa!" Zack found himself breathing heavily. A million thoughts passed through his brain, but one pushed through to the front. "Don't *you* have the power to stop this? You *are* Isis, but with a hell of a lot more experience. At this point your connection must be through the sky, right?"

"I'm not a witch or a vampire anymore, Zack," she responded. "In fact, I'm not even a physical being. I'm part of the energy now, as are they. I guess you can say we're all one, in mind and soul."

Zack noticed she didn't use the word "body" in that familiar phrase. He reached out with his right hand and tried to tap his palm against her arm. His hand went straight through as if he were swatting at air. "You're not really here, are you?"

"I'm here," she replied. "And I'm also everywhere else."

"Like the energy."

Isis pointed at Zack, her acknowledgment of his statement.

"When is this big threat coming?" he asked, staring down at the petals on the rose in his left hand. "What can we do to prepare?"

"There's nothing you can do to prepare, Zack." She jumped off the counter and landed on her feet. "But right now, your double date is out there waiting on you. So go have some fun, okay?"

"After two hundred years, that's your answer?" Zack flung his right arm in the air. "Just go have some fun?"

Isis shrugged. "There's not too much else you can do, at least not at this point in time. I don't know exactly when this is all supposed to happen, or what it's going to look like, but I do know it's not happening tonight. You have time."

"Great, something new to look forward to—"

A tapping sound from behind made Zack's heart jump. It was a knock on the door followed by a voice from the other side. "Zack, are you okay in there?" It was Isis. His Isis.

"Should I—" Zack twisted his wrist as if to simulate turning the doorknob. The former two-hundred-year-old Wiccan vampire waved a hand to the door.

Zack spun around, grabbed the knob, and pulled. Isis' face was filled with concern. "Zack, what's up with you?" she asked. "You've been in here for over ten minutes, I was worried."

"Isis, you have to come in here."

Her head snapped back. "Into the boy's room?"

"Yeah, and quick, you have to see who's in here!"

Zack spun back to the bathroom. It was completely empty. Damn, maybe he was having some sort of nervous breakdown and he did just imagine the whole thing. He was sure he saw and heard her. It seemed so real, and yet…

He looked down. The purple-and-pink-headed rose was still in his left hand, exactly where the other Isis placed it. It couldn't have been his imagination, not when he was holding the tangible proof. Zack tried to speak but couldn't. Instead, he held out the rose for Isis to see.

"Ooh, is that for me?" Her mouth opened wide. "It's beautiful."

"Yeah, I think it's for you."

"You think? What does that mean?" Isis took the

274

rose from his fingers and sniffed. Her raised eyebrows and nod meant she liked the fresh aroma, but it also sparked her curiosity. "Where did you get it? Was it on you all this time?"

"Um…" Zack focused on the entire conversation. He didn't want to lose any of the details, vague as they may have been, as it affected their future.

"Zack?" Isis took his hand. "Is everything all right? Did something happen?"

Zack thought about it for a moment, then smiled. "It's a hell of a story, and I'll tell you all about it later." He wrapped his arm around her shoulders. "For now, let's enjoy our night out."

Isis took another sniff of the rose, then leaned her head against Zack's shoulder as he led her back to the table. No need to worry about the future, at least not tonight.

Isis, Zack, and The Witches of Vegas
will face the impending threat in

Wiccan Mirror

Coming soon...

Follow the author for updates
on Twitter – @MarkRosendorf
Or on Facebook – Mark Rosendorf's
The Witches of Vegas

A word about the author...

Mark Rosendorf is the proud author of The Witches of Vegas series, an award-winning series which includes *The Witches of Vegas, Journey To New Salem* and *Witch's Gamble*. The first of the series, *The Witches of Vegas*, earned the 2021 RONE award in young adult fiction.

When he's not writing, Mark is a high school guidance counselor for students with special needs. He holds a Master of Science in Education from Long Island University and is a former professional magician. He is happily married and lives in Queens, New York.

Mark is currently working on a script for a live action version of The Witches of Vegas.

His books are published through The Wild Rose Press.

For more information on Mark and The Witches of Vegas, check out his website:

www.markrosendorf.com

Thank you for purchasing
this publication of The Wild Rose Press, Inc.

For questions or more information
contact us at
info@thewildrosepress.com.

The Wild Rose Press, Inc.
www.thewildrosepress.com